Isabella Mumphre

Secrets of a Ma

Secrets of an Az

Secrets of a Hopi Blue Star

Secrets of a Christmas Box

Secrets of a Mayan Moon

An Isabella Mumphrey Adventure

Book 1

By

Paty Jager

Windtree Press
Hillsboro, Oregon

This is a work of fiction, Names, characters, places, and incidents either are the product of the author's imagination or are used fictitiously, and any resemblance to actual persons living or dead, business establishments, events, or locales, is entirely coincidental.

SECRETS OF A MAYAN MOON

Contact Information: info@windtreepress.com

Windtree Press
Hillsboro, Oregon
Visit us at http://windtreepress.com

Cover Art by Christina Keerins
CoveredbyCLKeerins

PUBLISHING HISTORY

First Edition by Windtree Press 2012

Published in the United States of America

ISBN 978-1-952447-54-9

Special Thanks:

To Cynthia Rothwell, http://blog.guatemalangenes.com/ for her help with Guatemalan life and the area.

And to a fellow writer, Sharon Prado, who educated me on Venezuelan history and men.

Chapter One

Dr. Isabella Mumphrey shoved her glasses tighter on the bridge of her nose and pursed her lips. She'd yet to fail at anything she'd set out to do. Grad school at seventeen, doctorate in anthropology at twenty-two. There had to be a way to get more funding. Grant forms, statistical data, and the letter from the dean, stating the funding for her department was going to be cut in half, sprawled across the coffee table.

"Hello! Hello!" her cockatoo caterwauled as her cell phone emitted the thundering beat of Native American drums.

Stretching to relieve the tight muscles in her shoulders, Isabella didn't hurry to snatch up the phone. The only people who called were from the university or her father. She wasn't in the mood to speak to her illusive father, and the university would have only one reason to call—to tell her to start making cuts.

"Quiet, Alabaster, I'm getting there." She glanced at the number and frowned. It wasn't her father or the university.

"Hello?"

"Isabella, it's Virgil Martin."

The excited voice of her family friend and mentor shoved all worries to the side, and she clutched the phone to hear him better.

"Where are you? I didn't recognize the number."

"I'm at the *Ch'ujuña* dig in Guatemala. Get your shots, pack, and get down here. I've found something truly remarkable, and I need your knowledge of Cholan to help me decipher a stone tablet." If his excited tone hadn't overrode the order, she would have wondered if this was the same man who took such care to show her the world she'd come to love.

"You know I'd come help you if I could. Right now isn't a good time for me to go anywhere. They're pulling my funding. I can't fly off to Guatemala now." In all her twenty-six years she'd never told Dr. Virgil Martin 'no'. He was the father her own flesh and blood refused to be. He'd listened and held her when she cried over the treatment she'd received at boarding school. It was hard for a seven-year-old to fit in with thirteen and fourteen-year-olds. When she wanted to throw intellectual tests, he'd talked her out of it. And he was there cheering when she received her doctorate of anthropology.

"This tablet could help you get funding. The information on it could make the anthropology world stand up and take notice of your work. And I have a wealthy man who is willing to pay us half a million to decipher the tablet."

Isabella clutched the phone tighter to her ear. "Did you say half a million dollars?"

"Yes. He wants to be the benefactor to give the information to the Maya people and is willing to pay us to decipher the tablet. I'll split the fee with you." His voice became muffled.

"What were you saying, Virgil?" She strained to hear as her mind spun. Two hundred fifty thousand would buy enough time to finish her research.

"Nothing. A local wanted to use the phone. I need your answer. I can't do this alone. But we can do it together."

Virgil had never steered her wrong. If he thought between the two of them they could decipher this tablet, garner more prestige, and make half a million, she had no alternative than to fly to Guatemala.

"Call me back tomorrow night, and I'll let you know when I arrive."

~*~

Hot humid air choked Isabella as she stepped through the glass doors of the Mundo Maya airport and into the shaded portico.

After asking for a sabbatical and suffering through the vaccinations, she'd bought a ticket to Guatemala, and following the university's recommendations regarding packing for the jungle, she'd boarded the plane. Twenty-four hours later, she wanted a shower and a soft bed, knowing after tonight she'd be sleeping on a cot until she and Virgil deciphered the tablet.

Isabella pushed her light-weight glasses higher on her nose and scanned the empty portico. With her box of survival equipment clutched under one arm, she plucked at her clinging cotton tank. The arid Arizona heat back home was more tolerable than gagging on this humidity.

The shaded portico spared her eyes from the bright sunlight beyond the cover. A small man stepped from the shadows of a concrete pillar, blocking her path. His facial features were classic Mesoamerican.

The man barely stood as tall as her shoulder. Her lips started to curve into a welcome smile when sunlight glinted off a large, wide-blade knife he pointed her direction.

The knife grew to the size of a machete in her mind as the man stalked toward her, his face scrunched in an evil sneer. Fear gave way to anger.

She was bigger. She knew martial arts. She could…what? Inhaling deep, she focused on her center and waited. Shamutz! All those years of Taekwondo and in a crisis all I can think to do is scream and run. But her throat constricted and her legs remained rooted to the ground.

Her gaze flicked to the knife point growing closer. Panic tried to squeeze up her dry throat. She would be stabbed and robbed and there wasn't a thing she could do, if her frozen limbs were any indication to her bravery.

The travel agent and Virgil had warned against traveling alone in rural areas, but she'd assumed the airport would be safe. Swallowing the fear building in her throat, she breathed slowly. Someone had to see what was happening. She craned her neck, stared at the terminal doors, and willed someone to step from the building and frighten the man away. Inside, there'd been guards. Where were they now?

The man and his dark beady eyes stopped within knife striking distance.

"Get me the package."

"What?" His thickly accented English confused her, however,

9

even in her panic she couldn't help but notice his eyes peering holes in her cardboard box.

She clutched the box containing her "survival" vest, a vest of many pockets filled with everything needed to get out of any situation, and shook her head. "You can't have my vest." She'd die before giving up her security armament. She'd had in her possession a facsimile of this vest since she was ten. The contents had helped her out of several mishaps. With shaking fingers, she dug into the side pocket of her broomstick skirt for the centavos she had at the ready for the taxi. "I'll give you this." She held out her hand, palm up, showing him the coins.

Yellow teeth, pointed as a spider monkey's, punctuated the malice in his smile. "No money. I want package."

Indignation stirred her blood. The items in the box could mean the difference between life and death in the jungle. She stared at the man and the knife. *Are the contents of the box worth losing my life right now?* Not finishing her genealogy project would be the same as death. She had to help Virgil and get the money to fund her project.

She weighed the options. *Maybe if I show him there's nothing of value in the box, he'll take the centavos and leave.*

She tipped her package toward the man. "See, 'Doctor Isabella Mumphrey'. That's me and this is my box. There's nothing in it you could possibly want."

His dark beady eyes peered at the box and back to her. The stare down was getting them nowhere. Twenty-four hours of travel and the rush to get ready beforehand had netted her little sleep and an anxious demeanor. *All I want is a hot bath and a bed before I step into the jungle tomorrow.* She shifted into her most obstinate glare, allowing irritation to pulse from her eyeballs.

The man's face darkened with exasperation, and he jerked the knife toward the package. "Get it to me."

Annoyance overrode exhaustion and fear. "Fine, I'll show you there's nothing in here you'd want." She jerked her free arm out of the backpack strap.

The weight of the pack dropping off her shoulder spun her body and swung the bag. The pack hit her assailant's hand with force, knocking the knife to the ground and flinging her box to the concrete six feet away.

The tape popped loose, spilling a dozen small blue books across the gray concrete. The word 'Passport' caught her eye before the man scrambled about gathering the books into the box.

Passports? How did those get into my box and what happened to my vest and survival items?

"What? How…" By the time she'd raced through all the possible scenarios of how a switch might have occurred along the route, the man ran down the street with her box under his arm.

"Hey! Wait!" With mixed disbelief and horror, she watched the man dive into a four-by-four truck and speed off.

How did my things get switched for passports? Reporting her items missing would throw suspicion on her. And she didn't have a clue at which layover—Phoenix, Miami, or Guatemala City—the switch took place. Frustration buffeted her temples. "I need my gear if I'm going into the jungle." Insecurity inched up her backbone. Without her vest, she couldn't set foot in the jungle. Couldn't get to Virgil and secure her funding.

Two security guards strode out the airport doors, snapping her attention to the deadly weapon at her feet.

In one quick motion she snatched the assailant's knife off the ground and slipped her backpack up onto her shoulder. She gripped the knife handle and held the weapon hidden in the folds of her flowing skirt. Being tossed in a Guatemalan jail would hinder her chance to get the tablet deciphered and back to the states in time to save her department. And it darn sure wouldn't be good for her health.

The guards stopped a respectful distance back.

With herculean effort, she plastered a cordial smile on her face as her whole body shook. She pressed the knife deeper into the folds of her skirt. Her latest encounter proved the knife might come in handy.

"Could you help me get a taxi?" she asked, surprised by her casual tone when urgency pounded at her temples.

The thinner guard raised a hand and like a hallucination in an old B western, a compact car emerged, pulling up to the curb. The faded paint and noticeable dents were a worry. The word "Taxi" painted boldly on the side and the fact security deemed the conveyance trustworthy, eased the coiled tension in her gut.

"*Gracias,*" Isabella mumbled, when the other guard held the door open for her. If they'd known what she'd brought to their country in her box, they'd escort her to jail. A chill of apprehension sent shivers through her limbs. How had she ended up with passports? She'd had her assistant at the college box up the vest and supplies, marking it with the university's exempt status. Had Crystal put the passports in? She didn't believe the girl would have had the time or the knowledge to put together a package of false passports. They had to be false to be worth smuggling. If they caught her with the passports or caught wind she'd smuggled them, it was a good probability she'd be in a Guatemalan jail for a long time.

Forcing her lips into a friendly smile, she worked to cover her nervousness. She slid into the back seat, keeping the knife hidden in her skirt the best she could. Her bottom dropped into an indention in the cushion. The blade of the knife pressed against her thigh. The urge to pull it away from her leg was squelched by the unwavering watchful gaze of the guards.

"Enjoy your stay, *seño*." The guard tipped his hat, and the taxi jerked away from the curb.

"Where are you going?" the taxi driver asked. His dark brown eyes stared at her from his rearview mirror aimed at an awkward angle to accommodate his slouched position.

"Hotel Casa Amelia, *por favor*."

"That will be ten centavos," said the driver, reaching a hand over the seat.

She dropped the coins into his upturned hand and allowed her body to wilt against the back seat. Sighing, she leaned her head back and wasn't surprised at the solid feel of wood rather than upholstery. Weariness seeped into her arms and legs. Terror couldn't take hold until she was locked in her hotel room. She now believed the warnings she'd read to visitors of this country. Her elation at being able to keep her department fully functional had outshined the warnings.

She'd endure *Xib'alb'a*, the world beneath the earth ruled by One Death and Seven Death, to keep her department and project alive. She'd worked too long and hard charting the DNA of the Central, North, and South American natives to have things shut down now.

Fear and her nerves subsided. In a few weeks, perhaps even days, she and Virgil would crack the tablet's code, and she could spend all her time on research instead of chasing down funding.

The excitement in Virgil's voice when he'd called had sparked her excitement. Not only would this trip help her department, it was her first dig outside the U.S. All her internships had been at North American native digs. Finally, she would add an international dig to her resume.

A stretch of open road gave way to dirt streets winding between houses made of crumbling stone, cardboard, and tin. The buildings were more impoverished than any she'd witnessed on reservations or slums of cities. Growing up, she wasn't allowed anywhere near this type of living conditions. As an anthropologist she had a need to discover if these people were happier than ones in fancy buildings with running water and mortgages they couldn't pay.

Even as she wished to learn, her sense of survival drew her away from the window as the occupants sitting in front of the small buildings stared forlornly at the vehicle. *I have so much.* Isabella dug into her backpack as the taxi rolled to a stop at an intersection. Two young boys pounded on her window.

She reached for the handle.

"Do not lower the window," the driver cautioned and inched the car away from the sullen faces of the boys.

"I could have spared them a centavo or two." She craned her neck to peer at the small group of children forming in the street behind them. Not one of them had shoes and their clothing hung like rags on their bodies. Her heart went out to the children. She'd been fortunate to always have everything she needed and to never feel hungry. Never know desperation. Only loneliness.

"If you had offered, they would have surrounded the vehicle." He glanced at her in the mirror. "You must learn not to show your wealth here or to give. Those who have less will take advantage."

Those were the same words her travel agent and Virgil had told her. Virgil's exact words had been, *"Don't let that tender heart of yours get you in trouble before the guide I'm sending shows up."*

"We are here, *seño*, Hotel Casa Amelia."

The car stopped in front of a three-story white stucco building with fresh green trim. The inviting open door and lush plants in pots on either side welcomed. This part of town held none of the poverty they'd just traveled through.

The driver draped an arm over the front seat. His good-natured smile was the first sign of welcome she'd witnessed since setting foot in Guatemala.

"*Gracias*. Since you speak English so well, could I ask you a couple questions?" She raised the hand with the knife, and his eyes widened. "If I keep this will I get in trouble?"

"Where did you get a knife such as this, *seño*?" His gaze remained riveted on the long, wide blade as she held it up for him to see.

"A man outside the airport."

"They do not sell those as souvenirs."

A nervous giggle tickled her throat. "No, they don't." She shoved her glasses back up to the bridge of her nose and wiped at the dampness clinging to her neck and chest. "A man wanted my box. I tried to tell him it was mine. My name was clearly written on it, but when it popped opened, my belongings weren't inside."

His eyes narrowed. "What was inside? Did you tell this to the security?"

"I was afraid if they saw the knife and then I told them…" She held her tongue. She'd said too much to a stranger already.

Isabella shook her head. "All that matters is my vest and supplies are gone. I have to get more before I continue on to the archeological dig at *Ch'ujuña*."

The man stared at her then waved at the knife. "Would you know this man if you saw him again?"

"Yes. Even though at first the only thing I saw was this knife, I'll not forget his nasty teeth or his dark eyes." A shudder rippled her skin.

"How did you get the knife?" His dark eyes studied her face.

Her face heated under his scrutiny and her mortification, realizing how close she'd been to possibly losing her life. "I knocked the knife and the box to the ground when my pack slipped and swung." She hadn't done anything as daring as her movie idol Indiana Jones. No, clumsiness saved me, not bravery. Her heart hammered realizing what the consequences could have been if her backpack hadn't become off balance. She had no doubt the man would have hurt her to gain the package.

"You are very lucky." He exited the car and came to her door.

Lucky? She wrung her shaking hands as he opened the door. She'd never believed in luck, but this was the first time her clumsiness worked for good.

Isabella slid out and stood next to the driver who was a bit shorter than her five-eight height. Her sandals were a small barrier to the heat of the cobblestone street. She dug in the outside pocket of her backpack where she kept a small amount of money for tips and necessities. "If I give you the same amount as the ride here and extra money to wait ten minutes while I write up a list of items for you to get, would you be interested?" She counted out ten coins and what she deemed would pay for the items she'd need.

The driver smiled. "I would be happy to help you, *seño*."

"Good, give me about ten minutes to get registered and make a list."

He nodded and Isabella entered the welcoming doors of the Casa Amelia.

Chapter Two

Augustino Konstantine waited in the lobby of the Hotel Casa Amelia for a frumpy old anthropologist to arrive. Her plane had landed two hours ago. What kept her? He didn't wait well. Never had. He liked to be in motion. When in motion he was harder to catch.

He lowered his newspaper to view the young woman striding into the hotel. Thin, average height, and even without curves, she was far more interesting than the paper he'd reread the past hour. A flowing, wrinkled, colorful skirt swirled around her long legs, and a cotton sleeveless top clung to the dampness between her breasts, accenting two pert nipples. The weight of her backpack, pulling her shoulders back, amplified the fact she didn't wear a bra.

Attention piqued by her lack of certain clothing, he studied her closer. A long, reddish-brown braid stopped at the middle of her back. Her narrow face hosted thick eyebrows that couldn't be hidden by the skimpy glasses she pushed up the bridge of her small nose sprinkled with just enough freckles to give her a youthful appearance. She had full sensual lips. Staring at them brought to mind many ways they could pleasure.

This could be a good form of entertainment this evening.

She approached the registration desk.

"*Seño*, how may I help you?" the clerk asked with more

enthusiasm than he had when Tino registered.

She deposited her backpack on the floor at her feet. The horn handle of a twelve-inch Guatemalan blade protruded from the side pocket. Tino's curiosity spiked another notch.

"I have a reservation. Dr. Isabella Mumphrey."

Tino snapped the paper down and stared even harder at the woman. This was the frumpy, old anthropologist he was to guide? His gaze scanned the length of her one more time while tuning in the conversation.

"Ahh, Dr. Mumphrey, Dr. Martin said you were to get the finest room, no?" The clerk acted like a simpering fool giving the doctor her key and expounding on all the wonders of the hotel.

"*Gracias*. May I borrow a paper and pencil? I need to make a list for the taxi driver."

The clerk handed her the items. She stepped to the side of the counter and began writing.

Why would she make a list for a taxi driver? Curious, Tino folded the paper and strolled to a spot beside her. So intent on her list, she didn't even acknowledge his presence as he leaned, reading the items. Army knife, candle, braided fishing line, hooks, swivels, 24 gauge snare wire…

"You are planning a trip into the jungle, no?"

She started at his voice. Deep green eyes rimmed in gold stared at him from behind wire-rimmed lenses. She blinked, focused on him, and narrowed her eyes.

"Didn't your mother teach you manners? You don't look over people's shoulders to see what they're doing." She picked up her list and held it to her damp shirt.

"*Mi mamá* did teach me manners, no? I am Tino Kosta, your guide to the dig at *Ch'ujuña*." He held out his hand, waiting for her to shake.

Her gaze traveled from his extended hand up his arm to his face. She squinted her eyes and glared at him.

"You're not of Mesoamerican descent, so you can't possibly be my guide. Are you in cahoots with the disgusting little man who stole my property?" She bent toward her backpack, giving him a good view down the front of her blouse.

Sí, she didn't wear a bra. The nipples peaking through her clingy shirt sat atop palm-sized mounds. Now, being a man who liked his hands filled to overflowing when it came to handling a woman—

"¡Carajo!" The pointed end of the large knife that had been tucked in the doctor's backpack waved inches from his nose. "What is this about?" A woman who ran around without undergarments shouldn't be offended by a man viewing her body.

"You tell me what this is about? I was naïve once today. I won't make that mistake a second time with you *banditos*."

He had to give her credit. The knife didn't shake, and her words dripped with the right amount of bravado and control.

"Dr. Mumphrey, Ezzabella…"

She frowned at the use of her given name.

Tino shrugged, sent her a smile he reserved only for his grandmother, *abuela* Juanita, and resumed, "I am not a *bandito*, and Dr. Virgil Martin did hire me to bring you to the dig."

Her gaze slid from his face to the knife and back. "Show me proof you are who you say you are."

He slipped a hand in his pocket and drew out his guide credentials and driver's license provided by the Drug Enforcement Agency. "I cannot give you Dr. Martin's request. He contacted me by phone." Okay, he lied on that one. He hadn't spoken to Dr. Martin. The guide Martin hired was probably celebrating with his family. It wasn't often he was paid triple to let someone else do his work.

Isabella lowered the knife and scrutinized his credentials and driver's license.

"*Seño*, is your list ready?" A man, Tino recognized as an undercover *policia* walked into the hotel.

"I'm sorry, I was distracted and haven't finished." Isabella set the knife on the counter and returned to her list.

"What is the list for?" Only disreputable people or fools made friends with the *policia*. More than half in the rural areas were corrupt and involved with the very people he was out to destroy.

"My vest and survival gear were stolen en route. I need to replace them before I go into the jungle." She continued writing, her eyes remained fixed on her growing list.

"I have everything we will need for the trip."

"There are items I prefer to have with me." She leveled a determined gaze on him and pushed her glasses up. For a slip of a woman she exuded authority and snobbery.

"¿*Seño?*" The man he knew to be a *policia* studied Tino.

"You can go." Tino waved the man away.

"I need my things." The panic in her eyes would have been laughable if her hand hadn't gripped the knife handle. "I can't go into digs without my gear."

"We will drive to Sayaxche tomorrow. It is better outfitted for the jungle traveler than this town. You can write your list in your room with air conditioning."

Her eyes widened at the words "air conditioning".

She turned to the *policia*. "*Gracias* for waiting. I'll get my things myself tomorrow." She held out a slender hand. "It was a pleasure meeting you. And thank you for your advice."

The man smiled warmly and clasped her hand. "*Que Dios la acompañe en sus viajes.* Luck be with you on your travels."

The warm smile and genuine warmth in Dr. Mumphrey's eyes surprised Tino. She'd come across as a hard-edged, snobby scholar until now.

"*Gracias.*" She released the *policia's* hand and retrieved her knife and backpack. She turned to him. "What time do we set out in the morning?"

Tino wasn't willing to give away anything with the *policia* stalling by engaging the clerk in a conversation. He snatched her backpack and placed a hand on her elbow, escorting her toward the terrace in the back.

"I'll take my pack, and why are you hauling me out here?" She struggled against his hold on her and reached for her bag.

"I wanted to show you this." He motioned to the sun setting over Lake Petén Itza to distract her. He didn't need the *policia* or clerk butting into the conversation.

"Oh my!" The whispered words held reverence. Dr. Mumphrey unzipped a pocket on her backpack and pulled out a small camera.

Tino watched her adjust dials and snap photos. She immersed herself in the scene, changing angles and muttering. The glass-like lake with the mountains looming behind never failed to invoke this reaction from visitors. Gazing beyond the woman to the setting sun over the water, he wondered how long it had been since he'd really appreciated the beauty around him. Too long. He rolled his head and shook out the tense muscles in his shoulders. Not since he vowed to avenge his family's deaths.

Dr. Mumphrey drew in two long, deep breaths and slowly exhaled. He shifted his view to encompass the woman. Her body relaxed, the simplicity of innocence softened her features. He'd believed from the woman's name, occupation, and status, he would guide an old British woman who was a hardened traveler. This woman should still be in grad school if his deduction of her age wasn't as misplaced as his impression of her name.

She faced him. "Why did you drag me onto this terrace?" A slender finger pushed her glasses back in place.

"How did you come to know the man who brought you here?" He doubted she knew him to be the *policia*. He wasn't in uniform, and she hadn't treated him like he held any authority.

"He was my taxi driver from the airport. Why?" She leaned closer, a quizzical expression on her face. "You weren't very nice to him." Her tone reminded him of his *mamá's* scolding. His heart squeezed with regrets and the empty pain memories of his family evoked.

Tino motioned to two chairs on the edge of the terrace. Dr. Mumphrey sat but held her hand out for her bag. He handed it to her. "How did you acquire such a fine example of a Guatemalan knife? You just arrived, no?"

Her face paled. "A man at the airport…" Rather than the hard-edged tone she'd used on him so far, her voice wavered.

"The *bandito* you accused me of friending?"

"Yes. I barely stepped outside the airport and this man, with this knife," she tapped the handle, "accused me of having his package." She peered into his eyes. "It was my box. Security didn't allow me to bring some of my survival items on the plane in my backpack, so I packed them and my vest in a box and sent it through baggage using the university's exempt status for packages. You know, to avoid the delay of an inspection." Isabella shrugged. Her whole body slumped into the chair as if deflated.

Tino resisted the urge to rub a hand up and down her arm. Instead, he curled his fingers around the chair arm. He couldn't become attached or feel anything for anyone. This assignment required he get into the jungle around the *Ch'ujuña* dig. DEA had received word a new drug route into Mexico was being set up. Nothing gave him as much pleasure as apprehending and putting behind bars the men under the man responsible for his family's death. One by one he would take away Garza's underlings, and then his family, until he felt the same loss Tino lived with.

Tino pulled his thoughts back to the terrace and the means to get him near the dig. Moonlight glistened on the blade of the knife hanging from the doctor's bag.

"How did you get the knife?" He hated to bring up something that obviously upset the woman, but he needed to know everything about the mishap. Anything illegal usually was connected to the drug trade, making it his business.

"My clumsiness helped for a change." She shook her head slowly as if not believing her own words. "I was-am—exhausted. The man insisted the box was his. I planned to take off my backpack and prove the box had nothing he wanted. Only the weight of the pack and my irritation caused the bag to slide down my arm, swing, and whack the knife out of his hand and throw my box to the concrete. It popped open. But my vest wasn't inside, it was—" Her wide almond-shaped eyes continued to seek answers. "He grabbed the contents and ran away. Leaving the knife behind."

Do I look sincere? Will she believe I'm one of the good guys? He needed to know what was in her box. Tino laced his voice with sincerity, "I will not pass on anything you say to the authorities."

Her head tilted as she continued to peer at him. "How do I know Virgil-Dr. Martin hired you? You could be a part of any of the illegal activities I read about in this country."

"True. But do you think I would have stated who I was in front of the others if I had plans to kill you? I sat in the chair in the lobby long enough the clerk can identify me should something happen to you. And the taxi driver…that is not his profession. He's *policia*."

Dr. Mumphrey's eyes widened, and her full lips opened, giving rise to thoughts he shouldn't harbor about the woman. She was his ticket into the jungle around the dig and nothing more. If he let their relationship wander into anything other than guide and ticket, they could both end up jungle casualties.

"You knew he was the police? How? And why didn't he tell me?" Her hand clutched her throat. "Shamutz! I showed him the knife! And told him about the missing contents."

Tino straightened in his chair. He couldn't cross examine her without reawakening her suspicions. "Not all the *policia* are bad. I do not know which side of the law he is on, but if he withheld from you that he was *policia*, it is good you did not tell him too much." Had she mentioned the wrong contents in her box?

She nodded and sighed. "I don't know what to do. My package was used to smuggle—" Her shoulders rose and fell as she ran a finger around the lens of the camera on her lap. Indecision wrinkled her brow and she pursed her lips.

He didn't want to press and appear too interested, but at the same time he wanted to help. And the only way to help was to know what they were dealing with. "What was supposed to be in the package?"

"My survival vest. Instead there were passports. At least a dozen." She glanced up, her green-gold eyes beseeched him. "Why did they use my box to smuggle in passports?"

"I do not know."

He shook his head. There could be more going on at the dig than perhaps even DEA knew.

Chapter Three

After the day she'd had, Isabella accepted the guide's offer to walk her up to her room. She sneaked furtive sideways glances as they climbed the stairs side-by-side. He was handsome in a roguish way.

"Be in the lobby at eight."

His deep, soft voice with an unmistakable Latin accent fluttered her stomach.

She nodded and stopped at the door of her room. Before she could slip the key into the lock, his fingers closed around her hand.

"Allow me to unlock the door and take a look."

His hand holding hers and the intensity of his eyes stole her words. She didn't like the implication but nodded and relinquished the key.

"Stay here." He grasped her shoulders and set her to the side of the doorway. The lock clicked, and he disappeared into the room.

Gathering her wits, Isabella stepped into the room behind him. Moonlight filtered through the thin curtain, highlighting his silhouette as he searched the closet, the balcony outside the window, and under the bed. Cool air from the air conditioner met her at the same time as its droning hum.

"What are you looking for?"

He snapped to attention and stalked toward her, stopping when his toes nearly touched hers. "I told you to wait outside."

"And I asked you what you're doing." She wouldn't back down. If someone was out to get her, she had a right to know who and why.

"Looking for unwanted creatures." He grasped her hand turned it palm up and dropped the key.

Her arm tingled. One-by-one he closed her fingers around the key, his gaze locked on hers. Heat vapors like the Arizona blacktop slithered up her neck and scorched her cheeks.

"Eight."

The husky timbre vibrated her stomach. He released her hand and disappeared out the door.

The curtain rustled. Isabella spun and stared at the closed door, clutching the key in her fist. The man did things to her body with just his voice. She shouldn't trust him, but there was something about him that gave her comfort. Deep down her gut told her that was dangerous and she'd end up hurt.

She tossed the key on the table and stripped. Washing with a cloth and basin of water her thoughts turned to her guide. Tino Kosta. He was definitely not of Mesoamerican descent. He didn't have the classic flat facial features or dark coloring. His features were more European in appearance—less native. A Ladino. Someone of European descendants that traveled to Central America to make their fortune in coffee or some other export, married a local, and stayed. His dark blue eyes, while showing mirth at times, remained blank. As though he feared his secrets could be read in his gaze. His full black brows, shaggy black hair, and stubble shouted he didn't use his looks to get what he wanted. No, his demeanor didn't reflect a man who made a living escorting people about the jungle. He came across as a man on a mission. His name had Latin and Greek origins. How had he become a guide in Guatemala?

His accent affected her like no other male voice. The timbre, softness, and lyrical qualities…she pressed a hand to her quivering belly. But he'd conversed in front of the taxi driver with a definite emphasis on appearing not as well spoken, while alone with her, his English had been flawless and heady with that sultry accent. So many questions.

She slipped into a clean tank and panties and under the lightweight bedding. The raucous noise from a bar or party reminded her of trying to fall asleep during college parties in the dorm. But the long day and monotone of the air conditioner's drone took hold, and she drifted to sleep within minutes.

~*~

Street noises and the soft glow of sunshine awakened Isabella. Stretching, she glanced at her wristwatch. Seven-thirty. Her stomach rumbled. Tino hadn't mentioned whether they'd grab a bite to eat. She didn't linger in bed or in her thoughts. Today, she would experience her first jungle excursion. Her rumbling stomach fluttered with anticipation. The only other digs she'd worked were in Arizona. This was her first big trek into another country and another biosphere. Excitement bubbled out in a gleeful laugh.

Isabella stepped into khaki pants, tucked the cotton ribbed tank she slept in into the waistband, and cinched her belt. She grimaced at the small cut in her skirt before she rolled it up and stuffed the garment into the bottom of her bag. She shoved a pair of wool socks in her boots, and then situated the footwear and a long-sleeved shirt on top of the other items in her backpack. The extra apparel would be handy when they hopped in the boat to head down river. Before that, riding in a car, there would be no need for the extra clothing to ward off mosquitoes. She slipped into her sturdy walking sandals.

With the knife tucked into the side of her bag for easy access, she slung the backpack over her shoulders and headed out the door.

In the lobby, she found Tino lounging in a chair.

"You are ready early." He reached out to take her backpack.

She shook her head. He may have sounded convincing last night, but she'd hidden her passport, identification, and traveler's checks in her bag until she bought a new vest.

He dropped his hands and motioned for her to exit the building.

"I'm starving. Can we get something to eat before we head out?" She stepped out the door and spotted a dirty truck parked in front of the hotel.

"I packed food and beverage."

Isabella raised an eyebrow. She wasn't going to fall victim to Montezuma's revenge. "Purified?"

"*Sí*. I do not tolerate the water around here any better than *gringos*." He opened the passenger door on the truck.

Isabella climbed in. A duffel bag sat in the middle of the seat. She placed her bag on the floorboards and squeezed her feet in beside it. Tino climbed in behind the steering wheel. She studied him. If he cleaned up, his sultry eyes, sun-bronzed complexion, and Anglo features could grace the cover of any men's magazine. She pictured him on GQ dressed in a white linen shirt, sleeves rolled up to his elbows, and white slacks with loafers and no socks. The image sent a warm wave of desire rippling across her skin.

She'd better get her romantic thoughts turned. They'd only bring her hurt just like before. "I've already determined you aren't from around here. How did you become a guide in Guatemala?"

He revved the motor and shot away from the curb. "I have been a drifter and just landed here."

His off-handed remark sparked even more interest.

"Where all have you drifted?" Her stomach growled louder than her voice.

"The duffel on the seat has food." Tino's attention remained on the road as they wove their way through shacks made of anything the occupants could get their hands on to keep out the heat and rain.

Isabella focused her attention on the food in the bag rather than the hungry-looking children. Her heart ached to roll down the window and dole out the food to the unhappy faces. Her father always found fault with her generous—though he called it tender—heart.

Her fingers wrapped around a warm foil package. She pulled out the foil, then bananas, mangoes, and avocadoes she found nestled together in the duffel.

"Keep digging. There should be *queso fresco* wrapped in a banana leaf." Tino's gaze strayed from the road to the pile of food she'd placed on the seat beside her.

"There's enough food in this bag for the town." She found the leaf bundle. Her fingertips grazed something cold and hard. Curious, she ran her fingers over the object.

A hand gun.

Shivers slithered up her arm and centered in her chest. If Tino was part of the group who used her to transport passports, he wouldn't have allowed her access to the bag with his weapon, would he? She shot a glance his direction as her heart raced. He was relaxed, unconcerned about her rummaging in his bag and finding the gun. In the jungle, it made sense a guide would have a gun. Her racing heart slowed, and she chastised herself for thinking he was anything other than the guide Virgil hired.

His voice registered as he reached toward the bag.

Isabella jerked the bag back, but not before he plucked a banana. Air squeezed out of her lungs. She didn't know which would have been worse, him reaching for the gun or finding her clutching the weapon.

"W-what?" She worked to focus her mind on what he said and not the unhealthy direction her thoughts had spiraled.

"We need enough food to get us from here to the dig. It could take two to three days depending on the rains." He stared at her, one dark brow raised in question.

Could he tell she'd found his weapon? Should I just come out and ask him about it? Bravery had never been her strong suit, but directness—she had that by the boat load. She slipped her hand back into the bag and withdrew the gun.

"What is this for?"

He glanced her direction. Annoyance flashed in his eyes, but his body didn't tense. Tino shrugged. "There are creatures in the jungle that only respect modern weapons."

"Do you plan on using this to force me to give up my valuables, or worse, my organs?" In her experience, bluntness always shocked the truth from people.

He rolled his eyes. "¡Carajo! You are one paranoid señorita."

"I'm usually more trusting, but after my encounter yesterday, I'm not sure who to trust. I'd think you could understand. You have all the right answers about the dig and about Dr. Martin, but I've also read all the warnings about this country."

His lips formed a straight line, and his gaze drilled into the highway ahead. "Put the gun away and eat. I am not here to harm you. I use the gun to tranquilize jaguars. Traveling about as a guide, I also tag the cats for the government."

Isabella settled the revolver back under the clothing. His lack of agitation over her discovering the weapon and his nonchalant comment about her paranoia led her to believe he was the guide sent by Virgil. The bit on the end about tagging jaguars… Everyone knew they used rifles for tranquilizing. Her guide had secrets.

She opened the foil and found a stack of tortillas. The scent of the warm corn rumbled her stomach even louder. "Do you want a tortilla?"

A muscle on the side of his jaw moved under the scruff of dark whiskers as he chewed his banana. Again, her mind took up the puzzle of her guide. His demeanor and speech spoke of education, yet he dressed low class.

Tino's seductive dialect cut into her musings.

She hadn't heard a single word he said. "What?"

"After I finish this, I will take a tortilla."

The evening before he'd lapsed back and forth from refined language skills to more native sounding words. This morning, he was all refined. This guide Virgil sent piqued her interest in many ways. She didn't back down from a challenge, and dissecting Tino's background the next two days would be a good distraction from the anticipation of what she would find at the dig.

Isabella unwrapped the banana leaf and found a mildly aromatic white cheese. She crumbled some on the top tortilla, rolled it up, and took a bite. The tangy cheese and sweet tortilla made her mouth water and satisfied her stomach.

"Have you been to this dig before?" Tino asked, tossing his peel out the window as they sped down the highway.

"No. Virgil—Dr. Martin—called me ten days ago and requested I come down. He needs my help to decipher a tablet." She already owed Virgil so much. He'd encouraged her curiosity about her Native American roots, and then helped her enter the graduate program at a young age.

"Decipher a tablet?" Tino glanced at her, his eyebrows arched in question.

When asked about her life's passion, even if he held a gun to her head, she'd talk.

"He discovered a Mayan tablet that he believes holds great worth and knowledge for the Mayas. But he needs my help. My thesis was on Mayan symbols." Electric jolts of excitement zipped up her spine. She shoved the last bite of the tortilla in her mouth and dug through the side pocket of her backpack for her journal. Every scrap of information she'd discovered in a Hopi dig that resembled the Mayan culture was written in this notebook. As well as all her notes on Mayan symbolism.

"I've written four papers on Mayan symbols and language using what others have uncovered." She stared at her notes and drawings.

"This is your first trip into the jungle?" His condescending tone suggested he considered her a tourist.

"I've read everything ever written about this area and the Mayas." She glared and challenged him to test her.

"Books cannot prepare you for the first time a caiman snaps at you, a howler monkey makes the hair on the back of your neck tingle, or the constant buzz of the mosquitoes hoping to snack on you." He sent her a lopsided smile that slipped her irritation down only a micron.

"I'm sure I'll be startled the first time I see or hear these, but I assure you I am not some scaredy-cat." She wouldn't tell him about her aversion to bats. From her research on the area, they were her greatest fear. The flying mammals filled her with unfathomable terror.

"Speaking of cats, you ever come face to face with a jaguar? Now there is a beautiful creature." His voice dropped an octave and made her wish he spoke of her in such an ardent fashion.

"No, I've only seen photographs."

Tino rolled up his right sleeve. Two long raised red marks ran from his elbow to his wrist. "I did not get one big female knocked out completely when I tagged her."

"I didn't think they attacked humans?" She stared at the red raised slashes on his muscular arm.

"They usually do not. But she did not care for me straddling her and injecting something under her skin." His eyes lit with excitement. "We rolled around for some time before she ran away."

"Were you scared?" Her admiration for Virgil's choice of escort escalated.

"At first, but her breath reeked, and there was still hair in her teeth and blood on her lips. I struck her on the nose hard, and since she had a full belly, she left me alone." He glanced at the food beside her. "I will take a tortilla."

Isabella studied him. The wrinkles at the corners of his eyes and merriment in their dark blue depths gave rise to the assumption he made the story up. Was he a good con-artist or was he playing with her gullibility? Virgil always said her naïveté would get her in trouble.

"¿Tortilla, por favor?"

She dropped her gaze to the food, dug a corn wrap from the foil, and crumbled cheese on it. She rolled the tortilla and handed it to him. Their fingers touched and her gaze jerked to his face. Was that a smirk on his lips? His touch and nearness jostled her insides like a fast ride on a teeter totter.

Isabella peeled a banana and took a bite. The flavor outranked any banana she'd eaten in her life. Eating fresh picked fruit would be a treat on this expedition. She stared out the window and noticed a large plume of dark gray smoke beyond the dry lowlands.

"Where is that smoke coming from?"

"The edge of the rainforest. The climate has been slowly growing hotter and drier even here where it rains nearly seventy inches a year. Careless agriculture, industry, and drug trafficking cause fires that spread into the rainforest." He glanced her direction. "We will go through a burned section along the Pasion River."

She couldn't fathom a fire in the rainforest. Wasn't everything wet and therefore more likely to snuff out a fire than feed it? Mixed varieties of deciduous trees dotted the landscape of rolling hills covered in yellow grass. The road gradually climbed a steep rock and coniferous forested grade before easing down into a lowland valley once more. The trip was as diverse in scenery as the many native languages of the country.

They passed through a small town of adobe huts with palm thatched roofs. Women attending chores wore the traditional bright colored skirts and blouses of the region, and the men wore jeans, no shirts or shoes. Children, barefoot and curious, lined the street.

"Is there a chance to stop and visit?" Her interest in people of other nationalities could never be sated. Peering at their audience she wished to learn more about the Mayas of today.

Tino shook his head as the vehicle sped away from the village. "I want to get a good distance downriver before the afternoon rain hits."

"With the shorter trees and open areas, I forget we're in a rainforest." She took in the lowlands with patches of mahogany trees and rolling grass-covered hills around them. Twisting in the seat, she peered back at the town they left behind. "This isn't the picture you normally see on a documentary about the rainforest."

"They do not get as much rain here. We are headed closer to the rainforest and once we get on the river we will be heading into the denser forest."

Isabella dug in the duffle bag. "Where's the drinking water?"

"Drinks are in the back."

Tino pulled the truck over and stepped out. He'd have to be more careful around the doctor. For all her gullibility, she had a mind that deducted and researched. Keeping his true identity a secret from her would be a challenge. He retrieved a can of Gallo and a canteen. He slid under the steering wheel, handed her the canteen, and popped the top on the beer.

She frowned. "You aren't going to drink and drive? It isn't even noon."

Her attitude reminded him of his initial perspective of her, when he only knew her name. Sour and bossy. "Yes, this is my beverage of choice since the water around here is unsuitable to drink." It wasn't his drink of choice. He only used it as a prop to reinforce his cover of a bum who could only get a job as a guide.

"But beer? You could purchase juice or soda." She narrowed her eyes. "What happens if you get drunk and can't find your way to the dig? We'll end up stranded in the jungle."

"I have never become drunk. I drink only when I am thirsty." The gall of her to imply he didn't know his way around the jungle. He sneaked a peek at the Government Issue watch with GPS strapped to his left wrist.

"I still think you could make a better choice. Alcohol has a drying effect on the body."

Tino stabbed her with a you've-got-to-be-kidding stare. "What is sticking your clothes to you?" A sheen of perspiration glistened her skin, adding more definition to her collarbone and high cheek bones. His blood heated at the sight. He tamped the sensation down. Doctor Mumphrey wasn't his type, she was out of his league, and he didn't make attachments. In his line of work all he could enjoy were one nighters, and she wasn't the one-night type.

Isabella didn't blush, but the indignant set to her jaw slackened. Her slender fingers unscrewed the lid on the canteen. Closing her eyes, she tipped her head back, and raised the vessel to her lips. Contentment transformed her features to the childlike innocence he'd noticed the night before. She slowly drank, savoring each mouthful and swallowing in slow motion. The effect more erotic than anything he'd seen before.

¡Coño! Tino stared out the window. The sooner he got her to the dig the better. His protective instincts had kicked in. Not good. Once he dropped her off it was *adios* intriguing *señorita*.

He put the truck in gear and pressed down on the throttle. The truck lurched forward.

"Hey!"

Tino glanced over. Her shirt front clung to her chest, emphasizing her nipples and small bumps of breast. He couldn't pull his gaze from the sight. The small mounds, while not his usual choice, were damn tempting.

"Why'd you—"

She shrieked and pointed to the road.

Tino glanced at the road and swerved the truck in time to avoid hitting a tour bus.

The truck wobbled then settled as his fingers gripped the steering wheel. He stared straight ahead at the road. His heart hammered at the near collision and his uncontrolled infatuation with the woman's breasts astounded him. Every woman he'd ever dated had curves and full bodies. This stick-shaped woman shouldn't cause his brain to mush every time he looked at her.

"Sheesh, where did you learn how to drive?" Isabella pulled the garment away from her skin, fanning the material.

He watched from the corner of his eye. She ran a hand up inside her shirt and fluttered the cloth.

"You'd think in this heat it wouldn't take long to dry."

He nearly groaned as her actions enlarged the sleeve hole, giving him a view of her chest. Tino forced his gaze back to the road and thoughts to the agent in Sayaxche who had a boat waiting for him. Better to set his thoughts on the mission than the distracting woman.

He'd meet Roberto where the informant rented boats to the tourists and the cartels running up and down the river setting up drug drops and shuffles. Roberto was the DEA's best informant of activity in the region, and the only person in the region who knew Tino's true identity and purpose.

Tino didn't like having anyone in the area know who he was and why he was there, but he needed the man's help to get in the area of the new drug shipments.

He shot a glance at Isabella. The woman's gullibility could prove troublesome, which meant he should stay with Isabella while she shopped for her items, but he needed time alone with Roberto.

She'd stopped fanning her shirt. Her attention centered on peeling an avocado with the large knife she took from a *pirata*. How had she been selected to carry the contraband passports? Did her travel agent set it up? Or was Dr. Martin using his young colleague's infatuation for him to get passports smuggled into the country and perhaps Mayan artifacts out?

The thought of her mooning over some old archeologist soured his disposition. She was a good-looking woman, a bit on the thin side, but he knew plenty of men who liked their woman less rounded. She had brains. Too many. Her mind worked fast and conjured up more fiction than a spy novel. He found her wariness of him insulting, but thought it would do her well to use that fear on anyone else she encountered while in Guatemala. He'd found though most of the locals were honest, you never knew when you'd come across someone working in black market organs, adoptions, or drugs. That included the *policia*.

"Wow! These are even better down here than in the states." Green clung to her fingertips as she took another bite of the avocado. "They're so fresh! People in the states would go bananas to taste this." She finished the fruit and started to peel another one.

"Eat that one faster than the last. We have only ten minutes until we reach Sayaxche." He would have liked to question her about her life. She was a walking contradiction—innocent, brilliant, gullible, and tough. But getting close to her or anyone was a bad idea. His revenge could easily spill over onto anyone he called a friend.

Chapter Four

Isabella studied the rustic settlement of Sayaxche. The highway merged with less sophisticated pavement and dirt streets at the edge of town. Adobe, cane, cardboard, and metal formed the sides and roofs of small houses. The town center hosted colorful stucco buildings ranging from pristine condition to crumbling walls and faded paint. A web of utility wires hovered over and between the structures. Their truck emerged from the narrow street onto a dirt river bank edged with colorful boats of various sizes. The wide murky river sloshed around the boats and slithered onto the bank.

Tino stopped the truck near a small wooden dock with a handful of less decorative boats.

Isabella stepped out of the vehicle and stretched. Cars and tour buses were parked to the sides. A wooden ferry carried freight trucks across the water to a road on the opposite shore beginning at the river's edge and disappearing into the forest.

"There are few businesses, but I think between the *farmacia* and the *mercado* you will find most of what you need." Tino locked the truck and waited for her to join him at the front of the vehicle. "I will show you the stores then come back and load our supplies into the boat."

Isabella nodded and fell into step, taking in all the sights and people as Tino strode along the dirt path. Mostly groups of tourists hovered along the river bank, but as they walked the streets, she noted the locals and their curious gazes. If Tino left her alone, she could spend some time conversing with the locals. The thought hurried her feet along. The faster she got rid of him, the sooner she could nourish her passion of learning about different cultures.

"Here is the *farmacia* and just over there," Tino pointed down the street, "is the *mercado*." He put a hand on her arm, drawing her attention to him. The heat of his hard palm and his solemn gaze captured her attention. "This town is usually safe, but be careful. You are a *gringo* woman and alone."

She waved off his concern. "I won't attract trouble. You're starting to sound like Virgil."

Tino's eyebrows rose. "Then trouble follows you?"

Heat hotter than the climate rose up her neck and scalded her cheeks. "No."

He continued to stare at her. His dark blue probing gaze caused her feet to shuffle, her heart to race, and her gaze to drop to her dusty toes.

"Do your best to not find trouble. I would like to head downstream in an hour." He squeezed her arm and spun on his heel, striding away from her.

The words flowed over her as a caress rather than a reprimand. She rubbed her upper arm and watched his long, graceful, confident strides. A few spots and a long tail and he'd fit right alongside a jaguar in the jungle. She shook off those thoughts and stepped to the door of the pharmacy.

She pulled out her list and walked to the counter. "*¿Hola, Me podría ayudar encuentre estos artículos?*"

The man behind the counter grinned. He couldn't read her list written in English. She tried to explain the items if she didn't know the exact words. Her Spanish reflected the dialect of the many Mesoamerican languages she studied, making it hard at times for the clerk to understand exactly what she said. She, however, left the pharmacy smiling. There were only a few items left to find at the mercantile.

She'd managed to learn a little about the people of Sayaxche while they searched the store for her items. Most of the population were Maya descendants from the Petén region. The store clerk was

35

proud of his heritage. She agreed with him that he had every right to be proud. His predecessors were highly intelligent people.

Isabella stepped into the street, her purchases tucked into her backpack.

The hum of an engine purred along the street behind her. She moved to the side, but the vehicle didn't pass. The *mercado* was half a block away. The sides painted in colorful advertisements beckoned to her like a butterfly to a vibrant flower. The hair on her arms tingled as the vehicle continued to follow. Isabella glanced over her shoulder at the mud-brown car. Two men sat in the front seat, both dressed better than the locals. They smiled and nodded, but something about them sent a shiver of apprehension slithering up her back.

She ducked into the store and immediately captured the attention of the clerk. "*Hola, necesito éstos.*"

The man smiled. "I have anything you could need, no?"

"Oh, thank goodness, you speak English. I had a hard time explaining my needs to the other store owner." She forgot her unease in the street and followed the man to the back of the store and a pile of fishing vests. She tried on the ones with the most pockets. After she found one that fit well, she made sure it also had two inside pockets with snaps.

Following the store owner up and down the aisles, she picked up the remainder of her items. An army knife, water-proof matches, foil, braided fishing line, hooks, snare wire, knife blades, magnetized sewing needles, and safety pins. She paid for the items. "Do you have a room where I can change?"

The man showed her a small, simple room in the back of the store. It would do. She only needed room to spread out her newly purchased items and secure them in her vest along with her valuables.

"*Gracias.*" She smiled at the man and closed the door. There wasn't a lock. Fearful someone might barge in, she shoved the small table up against the door. She dumped all her purchased items on the table. Items allowed on the plane, like her micro LED flashlight, nutrition bars, and water purification pills she pulled out of her backpack pockets. Emptying the last half of a tin of mints into a small vest pocket, she popped one in her mouth and filled the container with the necessities for survival.

On the bottom of the tin, she placed a small signal mirror, two xacto blades, several yards of nylon string, two magnetized sewing needles, a Fresnel magnifier, safety pins, and two feet of aluminum foil folded into a small square. She rolled mini magnesium fire starter and tinder tabs in a sealed bag and taped it. Using the knife, she chopped off an inch of a candle and tucked it into a corner of the tin, placing the remainder of the candle in her backpack. Two quart-sized zip-lock bags were folded into a small square along with a glass vial of twenty water purification tablets. She wound fifty feet of braided fishing line on a sewing bobbin and nestled it in the tin along with a plastic tube of hooks and swivels. Ten feet of twenty-four gauge snare wire looped around the inside of the tin.

Snapping the lid shut, she placed it in a pocket of the vest and smiled with satisfaction. She was now prepared for anything. These items would ensure her survival if she became separated from Tino or later, God forbid, she ended up lost in the jungle or in the ruin.

She pulled a roll of zip-lock plastic bags from her backpack and filled one with her first-aid items, stuffing it in one of the pockets on the vest. Another plastic bag was filled with nutrition bars and added to a pocket. Last, she pulled her driver's license, passport, travelers checks, and health record from her backpack, placing them in a water proof bag and storing the information in one of the inside pockets of the vest. In the other inside pocket, she placed her journal and a pencil.

After she'd stored the extra items in her pack, she slipped her arms into her long-sleeved shirt, pulled on wool socks, and laced up her boots. The heat in the room beaded perspiration on her forehead. She donned the vest, buttoning it up the front, and slung her backpack over her shoulder.

Isabella shoved the table away from the door. The hot stifling air of the small area proved more sultry than the humidity outdoors. Sweat trickled down the sides of her face. She stepped out of the room, light-headed and groggy.

"*Seño*, you need something for your head if you are traveling on the river, no?" The clerk held a wide-brimmed palm-leaf hat out.

"*Gracias*." She handed him five quetzals from an outside pocket of her backpack.

"*Por favor, seño!*" He dropped the coins in his pocket. "You are always welcome to my store."

She nodded and stepped out into the hot sun, thankful the man had suggested the wide-brimmed hat. It provided more sun protection and breathability than her canvas hat.

"*Señorita viene, Mi abuelo dijo que usted quiso ver nuestra herencia.*" A boy of about six grasped her hand and tugged.

"Your grandfather has something to show me?" Isabella followed the child's small finger as he pointed back to the first store she'd entered. The clerk's enthusiasm about his people had been infectious. What could this child and his grandfather wish to show her about the history of the Mayas? She glanced around and then down at the boy's excited face. Her curiosity won out over any mistrust. She allowed the child to lead her down the alley.

~*~

Tino glanced at his watch.

She was late.

Fifteen minutes late.

"Roberto, watch my things." He stomped up the street. What could possibly take that long to purchase? Granted, she had a long list, but she had a list. It wasn't like she had to make up her mind about the items.

He stalked into the *mercado* and peered up and down the aisles.

"May I help you, *señor*?" A small man, most likely the owner, scurried up to him.

"Has a *gringa señorita* with reddish-brown hair been in here?"

"*Sí.* She was charming, no?"

¡Coño! Where did she go? "How long since she left?"

"Ten, maybe fifteen minutes." His earlier cheerful smile faded. "Is she missing?"

"Did you see which direction she went?" Tino couldn't squelch the unease tightening his chest. He didn't want something to happen to the doctor for professional reasons and personal. It wouldn't look good on his report that he lost a civilian he was using to infiltrate the drug traffic, and he didn't want to think what could happen to sweet Isabella should she get caught up in his job.

"Pedro's grandson was talking to her." The man stepped out the door and pointed to the *farmacia*.

"*Gracias.*" He jogged up the road to the other store. Tino burst through the door. "Pedro!"

A man old enough to be his *abuelo* stepped from behind the

counter. "*¿Si?*"

"*¿Dónde tomó su nieto a la mujer de gringa?*" He questioned Isabella's whereabouts.

The old man shook his head. "*No sé.*"

Tino glared down at the man. "*Debemos encontrarla. Ella es importante.*"

"I saw where Juan took her." A boy of about ten or so stepped from the backroom.

"Show me. Quickly." Tino didn't like the thoughts bouncing in his head. Had the man who accosted her at the airport followed to make sure she didn't tell anyone about the passports? Or had the *policia* followed to cover up the passports? He jogged behind the boy down alleys and into the square in front of an old church on the outskirts of the buildings.

"*Gracias.*" He motioned the boy to return to the store and pulled his gun from his shoulder holster. A mud-crusted car stood to the side of the church. Tino approached the vehicle slowly. No one inside.

He stepped toward the side door of the building, but voices in back drew his attention.

"Those are the only clothes I have while I'm here."

Isabella's disgruntled tone made him smile. She didn't sound like they had hurt anything other than her pride.

"Do you mind? I don't know what you're looking for, but I guarantee it isn't in my panties." Her tone grew more aggressive.

Tino poked his head around the side of the building. His gut twisted with fear. One man had the carved, bone-handle knife pointed at Isabella and another man tossed her clothing out of her backpack.

Tino stepped into the open, pointed his gun at the man with the knife. "*Señors*, I believe the lady would like you to leave her belongings alone."

Isabella threw a round kick, sending the knife through the air. Tino ignored the assailant running away and sprinted toward Isabella and the man scrambling after the weapon. His heart lodged in his throat when the man knocked her in the side of the head with his elbow, sending her glasses into the air. She fought back with spunk, agility, and well-landed hits. He grabbed the man's shirt, yanking him off Isabella as she kicked, landing a solid blow to the assailant's crotch. The man cursed and doubled over.

Isabella sprang to her feet, shoved loose strands of straight hair behind her ears, and glared at the man writhing on the ground at his feet. "Don't ever hold a knife on me again. I don't like being the victim." She stomped over to her glasses, shoved them on her face, and snatched up her strewn belongings, cramming them into her bag.

She may have dismissed her assailant, but Tino wasn't that generous. His fear for the woman angered him. He channeled the anger on the assailant, shoving and prodding the man to the back of the building, where he propped him up against the stone structure.

"What were you looking for?" he asked, holding the man's head up by his hair.

The assailant's pain-dulled eyes didn't reveal a thing.

Tino shook him. "Why are you bothering the *señorita*? Who sent you?"

The man's face became a replica of a bulldog, saggy and unintelligent. The assailant's confusion squelched Tino's worst fears. He hadn't been sent by anyone. This was a random mugging.

"I suggest you find a safer way to make money than attacking people." He shoved away from the man.

Isabella stalked over to them. She slashed her attacker with a glare. "I can't believe you drew that innocent child into this. You should be ashamed of yourself." She wielded the knife under the man's nose. "If you try something like this again, I'll find you and cut off your fingers. I do believe that is one of the Mayan punishments for stealing."

The man's eyes widened.

Tino grasped Isabella's arm and pulled her away before the laughter bubbling in his throat erupted.

"We need to turn him over to the police." She yanked her arm out of his grasp.

"We do not have the time to sit while they find someone to take your statement." Tino directed her back to the river.

"You can't just let him get away with that." She stopped, crossing her arms and glaring at him.

"It would be futile to try and get him arrested. The law here, especially in remote places such as this, is slow and does not always work for the innocent." He gripped her upper arm, making her continue walking. "We need to get down the river. Trying to get him arrested will only make us have to wait until tomorrow or possibly the day after to leave."

She double-timed her steps at his last comment. Tino smiled. Now he knew her weakness—she wanted to get to the dig as quickly as possible. Was it to work or to see the archeologist? The latter burned in his gut like rancid food.

At the boat, he nodded to Roberto and helped Isabella into the native conveyance. He chose a boat like the locals used to deter *banditos* along the water route. He knew the more remote places to pull over should the rain prove too much later in the afternoon and where to camp for the night at the confluence of the Usumacinta.

Isabella took a seat in the middle facing forward, and he sat in the back by the small outboard motor.

Tino tugged on the rope and started the motor. He eased away from the dock.

She shot him a narrow-eyed stare. "For someone who only drinks when thirsty, that's a lot of beer."

He sent her a wicked grin. "I get real thirsty out here on the water."

"I've never ridden with a drunk in a boat. How easy does this capsize?" She swayed her body back and forth, making the water slosh against the sides and splash over the edge.

"Keep that up and you will make a tasty dinner for a caiman."

Her body went stone still and she stared straight ahead.

This could be a fun trip after all. Nothing like keeping a woman in line with threats she could be eaten by the local predators.

Chapter Five

The farther downriver the boat chugged the thicker the cloud of mosquitoes grew. Isabella sprayed repellent on her hat and clothes. Scrunching her eyes tightly shut and drawing her lips inward, she applied the disgusting spray to her face and neck. The astringent smell gagged her and she coughed. Having rid herself of that constant nuisance, she pulled out her camera and took photos of the feathery green Castilian cane hanging from the trees like curtains. Huge mahogany trees reached toward the gray clouds filling the sky.

"To your right." Tino's whisper was as heavy and sultry as the humid atmosphere.

She turned her head. The bright reds of macaws, vibrant yellows of the toucans, and vivid blues and greens of smaller birds splashed brilliant colors among the somber green canopy of the mahogany trees.

"It's beautiful!" She clicked the camera to the beat of the chattering birds. She wanted to stay mad at Tino for the way he'd brushed off her attack. After contemplating the incident and remembering stories of the slow judicial process in foreign countries, she realized her own stupidity didn't merit stalling their trip.

"Why do you think they picked me to steal from?" She'd thought she carried herself in a manner that didn't shout "victim".

"Female. *Gringo*. Spending money. Walking by yourself." Tino shrugged. "They were not local. I think they were traveling through, saw an opportunity, and took it."

"But how did they know to get the grandson of the man I'd discussed local history with? I would never have gone if the boy hadn't said his grandfather had something to show me." It still burned she'd been so naïve to follow that boy to the church. But he'd said his grandfather asked him to show her a stone with markings.

"One of them might have been in the store when you were talking to the old man." He passed her the canteen. "Where did you learn to kick like that?"

"Five years of taekwondo. I'm glad I didn't quit the classes." If only that training had kicked in at the airport. She put it off to her jet-lagged metabolism then, but today, she'd determined she wasn't going to be a victim.

She read the respect in his eyes before he trained his gaze on the trees looming far above the riverbank.

"What are you doing after you drop me off at the dig? Is there someone there you have to bring out?" She'd wondered about him traveling the distance only to return empty-handed. That seemed like a waste of his time.

His gaze remained riveted to the jungle as he answered. "I was not told of anyone returning. I plan to look around for jaguars and tag a few of the adults and a couple kits."

Her scalp tingled. Was he being honest with her? There were moments, like after the attack, when she observed honesty, but when she asked certain questions, he slammed a door shut.

"Have you always had an interest in animal husbandry?" Large drops splat on her hat and her legs. She glanced up and nearly drowned as rain gushed out of the sky like God pouring a bucket. The water washed across her lips. She stuck out her tongue and cringed. DEET, mingled with rain, tainted her tongue. Her eyes burned as the chemical ran into them.

Tino headed the boat toward the riverbank and pulled the gun from his shoulder holster. Isabella peered through stinging eyes to see if danger lurked on the riverbank. The blur of green plants, dotted with colorful blobs, no doubt flowers, didn't appear the least bit threatening.

The boat stopped abruptly. She fell forward onto her backpack. Tino leaped over her agile as a cat, traversed the length of the boat, and hopped onto shore. The boat surged a couple times as he pulled it higher aground. Isabella shoved her glasses firmly on her nose, picked up her pack, and scrambled the length of the vessel the best she could with pouring rain and blurred vision.

Tino held out a hand to help her over the bow. She accepted since her drenched pants clung to her legs making it hard to move.

He pulled the boat all the way out of the water and tipped it on its side.

"Why did you do that?" The thunder of the rain pelting through the vegetation drowned her words. When he didn't respond, she slipped through the mud to his side. She leaned toward him and said loudly, "Why did you pull the boat out and turn it on its side?"

He started at her voice, then leaned closer. His gaze dipped to her wet clothing then back to her eyes. "I stopped and pulled the boat out of the river because it could rain enough to weigh the boat down. I flipped the boat to keep the supplies dry." He motioned toward a large-leafed plant.

At the plant, he dropped to the ground and sat under a large frond. Isabella sat with her back to the plant's stalk and arranged herself and her backpack under an ample leaf.

"How long will this last?" Water washed down around their raised seat on the plant's roots.

Tino shrugged. "A few minutes, several hours. Hard to say."

She pulled off her hat and ran a hand over her wet head. "We just sit here?"

"Sí." Tino tugged his brimmed hat over his eyes and leaned against the plant like he planned to take a nap.

Isabella humphed, unbuttoned her vest, and dug out her waterproof journal. If the rain forced her to stay here, she might as well reread her symbols and be ready to work as soon as she arrived at the dig. With only sixty days until the department was dismantled, she and Virgil would have to work long hours if the tablet he found proved to be tricky to decipher.

Tino smiled as the professor tucked her nose into a small journal. Under the brim of his hat, he watched her peer into the book, narrow her eyes, then widen them as if an idea dawned. She drew out a pencil and scribbled in the book.

She'd shown spirit and handled herself well in both her attacks.

44

Her determination to get to the dig was admirable. He hoped she carried out her mission and returned to her college without any more mishaps. Her beauty and innocence had grown on him. He'd hate to see something bad happen to her. His blood surged as she licked the end of the pencil.

His thoughts couldn't go that direction. Revenge burned hotter than his desire for this or any woman. It had to. It was all he'd dreamed and lived since his family was taken from him.

He glanced at Isabella. Even in contemplation she made a seductive picture. As ridiculous as it was to feel protective of a woman he'd never see again once he delivered her to the dig; the temptation hovered. He could remain in the area and pop in now and then to see how she was doing, or even watch her from a distance.

No. I cannot.

Tino slammed his eyes closed and banged his head against the plant, raining water down on himself and Isabella.

"Hey!" She shook her journal and glared at him.

"Sorry."

"How is it you speak English so well?" She opened her vest and the journal disappeared.

"I watch lots of American movies." Tino slumped more against the plant and pulled the hat down lower on his face. The last thing he wanted to do was talk about himself.

"Have you seen Indiana Jones?" The awe in her voice drew his gaze to her face.

Her eyes sparkled, her cheeks tinted a deeper pink, and her lips tipped in a wistful smile.

"*Sí.*" Where was this leading? She wasn't really an artifact hunter, was she?

"Isn't he wonderful how he gets out of all those dangerous situations and remains so loyal to the artifacts he finds? And that whip..." She pulled her glasses off and rubbed them with her soaked shirttail. Placing them back on her nose, she frowned and tugged them off. "I tried to work a whip once."

The thought of her with a whip and black leather unzipped to her belly button, fitting snug over her hips, and displaying her long legs flashed in his mind and brought his body to attention.

"It was a disaster. I really should have tried it outside, but I was embarrassed and ended up breaking a table lamp, hooking the whip on a table leg, scuffing the floor, and scaring the daylights out of Alabaster, my cockatoo."

"They are not easy to handle, I hear." He held back the chuckle tickling his throat.

The roar of the rain lessened. Less than an hour. A light rain today. He stood.

"Where are you going? It's still raining." She started to stand as well.

"Stay. The rain is letting up. I am getting food. As soon as the rain stops, we will head on downriver. There is still a good distance to travel to the spot I plan to spend the night."

She nodded.

Tino dug through the supplies in the netting and found the already prepared lunches he'd purchased at the café in Sayaxche. He snatched a Gallo for himself and juice for Isabella.

Her eyes narrowed when her gaze landed on his beer. He smiled and handed her the juice and her portion of the food. For a skinny woman she ate like a soccer player. She'd downed all her food before he ate half of his. Her lingering stare at his fruit had him handing it over to her.

"You eat a lot for being skinny."

"I have a high metabolism. No matter how much or what I eat I can't gain weight. It's as much a curse as people who can't lose weight. People think I have an eating disorder because I'm thin and they see me eat a lot. Believe me—it's not something I embrace. As a teenager, when my hair was cut short, women would tell me I was in the wrong restroom." She glanced down at her chest.

Her dull eyes and grimace tugged at his sympathy. Tino reached out, touching her cheek.

"I did not think you were a boy, even before I saw the long braid down your back."

A weak smile tipped the corners of her mouth. "Thanks. But I know my body isn't appealing." She sighed, drawing in a deep breath and letting it out slowly.

Her skin was soft and slicked with rain. Drops clung to her wide, full mouth. He couldn't draw his gaze from her lips. Knew he shouldn't let the lure of her unhappiness and pheromones get to him, but he lapsed.

And leaned in.

Brushed his lips across hers.

Her eyes opened wide, and she stared into his. Curiosity replaced the surprise.

He pulled back, but kept his hand cradling her jaw. He smiled. It had been a long time since he'd locked lips with someone so innocent. Her emotions swam in her eyes. Uncertainty, curiosity, longing. Her lips remained partially open accommodating her rapid breathing.

Tino drew her face to his. "Do you wish another kiss?" He stared into her eyes, felt the racing of her pulse where his hand rested under her jawline and the puffs of her warm breath on his lips.

"Yes..." Her eyes fluttered closed and she leaned closer.

He chuckled, marveling at how easily she could be seduced. The thought also soured his disposition. Would she be this easy for someone else? Say Dr. Martin? Or a drug lord?

Groaning, he released her and sprang to his feet. She nearly fell face first in the mud, but he didn't move to help her up. If he touched her again so soon, he would kiss her, again. Neither one of them could afford an emotional entanglement. Especially him.

She rose to her knees, sputtering. "Why you hypocrite!" Her cheeks flamed a deep red like the scarlet macaw. "I can't believe you...you..." Her features twisted. Anger filled her tear glistened eyes.

Pendejo. Jackass, that's what he was. The rain no longer poured. The gentle trickle refreshed after the innocent yet scorching kiss. He righted the boat and slid it into the river.

"Come on. We can travel in this." He offered his hand to help her in.

She declined, climbing into the boat by herself and squeezing her body against the side when he moved past her to the motor.

At least he didn't have to worry about answering any more of her questions. She rode the rest of the afternoon in silence, pointing her camera at colorful birds and aquatic life along the river. She staunchly kept her eyes to the front of the boat in an almost humorous way. But he still felt like a heel. He could tell by the slight droop of her shoulders his rejection had shattered her already fragile ego. Yet, he knew if he had kissed her again, he wouldn't have been able to leave her at the dig and walk away.

Her vulnerability seduced his protective nature.

He hadn't been able to protect his family, but he could avenge their deaths. That was his focus. Not protecting a tempting professor. His goal since becoming a DEA agent was to seek revenge on the man who murdered his family. Even if it took the rest of his life.

Chapter Six

Isabella climbed out of the boat, keeping as much distance between her and Tino as possible. He'd humiliated her, and she couldn't get away from him. They were stuck together tonight and all of tomorrow until he delivered her to the dig. His taunting her with a kiss and then drawing away as if she were some vile creature hurt as deeply as the things Darrell Rutley had said to her face in grad school.

She walked into the forest, hunting for a place to have a few moments to herself.

"Do not go far," Tino called in his seductive Latin accent.

She cursed her reaction to his voice, raised a hand acknowledging his order, and tromped deeper into the trees. The murmur of the river faded away in the steady drone of mosquitoes. She slapped at the leaves on the plants and wandered deeper. Rustling in the underbrush shot her heart into her throat. Jaguars were nocturnal, weren't they? A small, furry, pig-like animal trotted across her path, followed by five smaller versions.

She giggled at her jumpy nerves and the animals' comical parade as she watched the last one disappear through the greenery. The waning light enlarged the shadows. Reluctance played war with her logical self. She should return to the boat before darkness descended and she couldn't find her way back. But her pride, something she usually didn't consider, wouldn't let her face Tino.

Not yet.

It was stupid to believe he wanted to kiss her. Tino was handsome, virile, and so unlike any of the men she'd met during her college days or professionally. Exactly the type who toy with women like me. His chivalry and her attraction to him made her feel attractive, something she rarely experienced. But the way he brushed her off after he'd initiated the kiss... He'd only proved he could kiss her and not that he wanted her. She mentally slapped herself at her stupidity and virginal cravings.

The walk hadn't settled her anger. Reliving the event only escalated her rage.

How could one be a genius yet stupid about life lessons?

She pulled out what she now considered her knife and hacked at the plants along the way. With each swing she lopped off something of Tino's. Blue penetrating eyes. Devastating smile. A hand, so good at soothing her. The other hand. Her smile grew, and her frustration turned to the healthy exhaustion of an extensive taekwondo class.

Isabella wiped a sleeve across her sweaty brow and heaved a sigh of contentment. The vigorous exercise worked wonders on her disposition.

A fierce roar vibrated through the trees.

Her heart stopped and air screeched from her lungs. The sound echoed all around her. Ducking, she covered her head with her arms. Her hands shook as she lowered her arms and peeked through the foliage. A second roar, closer and fiercer than the first, filled the air and shivered her skin. Was she surrounded by jaguars?

The crashing sound of an animal charging through the forest jerked Isabella into motion. She scurried for a tree, wrapped her arms around the smooth trunk, and climbed it like a flag pole. Adrenaline worked her feet faster than her arms, and she lost more distance than she gained.

Her heart pounded in her chest as the thrashing grew louder, closer.

The sting of bile rose up her throat. She spit and clung to the tree. "Ezzabella! Ezzabella!"

Through the pounding in her ears, Tino's muffled call registered at the same moment he charged into her sight. His gaze found her up the tree, and he immediately scanned the underbrush, his pistol mimicking the action of his eyes.

"What are you doing up there?" he asked, pushing the gun back into its holster. The growing darkness hid the details on his face.

"A jaguar roared. I was getting away from him." She used her best indignant tone, but the snicker coming from Tino reminded her she was mad at him. Savior or not.

"Jaguars do not hunt for another couple of hours. What you heard was a howler monkey." He stepped to the tree and reached up to help her down. "And a jaguar could climb this tree faster than you."

She kicked at his hands and worked her way down the trunk of the tree. The bark dug into her palms and tugged at her clothing. Funny, she hadn't noticed those things when climbing.

"How do you know it was a howler monkey? I thought they made…monkey noises?" She kept her gaze averted as she straightened her pack. Rarely did she find something she didn't know about.

"This is the time of night they start calling, telling others to stay out of their territory. They call at sunrise, too." He grasped her hand, leading her through the forest. "I thought you knew all about this area."

His joking tone only fueled her mortification. Jerking her hand from his, she swallowed her pride. She had boasted she knew everything about this country. "It seems evident that reading about a place and actually visiting or living there are two different things."

He peered at her over his shoulder. "You are a quick learner."

Another roar rolled through the canopy. The fierce, deep, guttural growl trembled her insides and she flinched.

Tino slowed, touching her arm as if to comfort but not fully committing. "That is the howler monkey. He stays high in the trees and is harmless."

She nodded, still unable to peer into his eyes. He was being darn nice to her considering she'd fallen apart at a monkey's call.

They walked into a cozy camp. A tarp draped across a rope in tent fashion, the corners tied to tree roots. Their supplies were stacked at the far end, and a small gas burner hissed under a pot of water simmering over the blue flame.

"You've been busy." She eased the backpack off her tired shoulders.

"It does not take long to set up camp." He dug into a box and pulled out two packages of dehydrated dinners. He held them up and grinned. "In the jungle we serve only the finest cuisine."

She couldn't stop her quivering face muscles from smiling. His attempt at levity proved more comical than his actual words. His misguided attempt at calming her almost allowed her guard to waver. But not quite. She had to prove to herself she could be civil and not fall victim to his seductive voice. "So, you're a five-star chef?"

His deep blue eyes bore into hers. "I am five star at everything I do."

Staring into his eyes and knowing he'd charged to her rescue, she believed he was. Her gaze dipped to his lips. His kisses proved more than five star. Squeezing her eyes shut, she willed every ounce of her being to shed the memory of his lips. It was a onetime happening. Nothing more and the sooner she let the whole thing go the better.

Tino swallowed the groan of desire bubbling in his throat when Isabella stared at his lips then closed her eyes. Was she hiding regret? He knew pulling away from her earlier had wounded her pride. But he couldn't let his body overrule his head. Once he touched her intimately, she would be his responsibility. Once he gave a piece of himself to someone, they became family. And he'd been raised to protect family. He couldn't worry about her at the dig while chasing drug dealers in the jungle. It was a good way to get himself killed.

He sliced the meals open and dumped them into the pot of boiling water, glancing at the tent. Two tents would be more appropriate, but he hadn't expected his client to be a charming, enticing *sirena*. From the name and occupation he'd been given, he'd expected an old, grumpy woman who would fall asleep way before him and snore.

Isabella moved away from the fire, untangling her hair. The rain and her trek in the trees had loosened half the strands. Her long, thin fingers worked the braid loose and then combed through the straight auburn tresses. Shimmers of copper reflected the faint glow of the waning light.

Tino shifted his attention back to the food. Watching her carved her image into his mind and made him want things. Things like running his fingers through the strands to see if it was as silky and tantalizing as it appeared in her hands. He stirred the stew and inhaled the aroma. It wasn't nearly as fragrant as his mother's stews.

A pang of regret pierced his chest. Eight years and he still missed his mother's cooking, her soft body hugging him, his father's hearty slaps on the back and praise for his athletic abilities and brains, and his younger brother's adoration. Grief gripped him, twisting his gut and holding him hostage just as it had the night his *abuela* called.

He stood abruptly and paced into the darkness as tears stung his eyes. He missed his family. They had been close. Loved one another without fail.

He still remembered the night he received the call at the university. "*Augustino, tu mamá, tu papá, y los pequeños, todos son muertos.*" His *abuela* Juanita's voice had shaken as she told him his family's small jet had been gunned down by drug runners while flying to South America to visit relatives. She asked him not to take revenge. He had respected her request until four years ago. At his grandmother's death, he entered the training program for the DEA. He would seek revenge for his family and for his *compadre's* son—his godson who had died of an overdose. And for all the other families who lost loved ones to the parasites who traffic drugs.

"Tino, I think our dinner is ready." Isabella's soft voice floated to him on the warm evening breeze.

He swiped a hand over his eyes wiping away any trace of tears, took a deep breath, and sauntered back to the fire. Isabella had dug two tin plates out of the supply box along with utensils and a beer for him. She'd arranged the items neatly on the covered box.

"This looks nice," he commented and sat cross-legged on the ground across the crate from her. She looked warm in her long-sleeved shirt and vest. "You should take your vest off. You look warm."

She shook her head. "This is my survival vest. It has everything I would ever need should I become lost."

"Does that happen often?" He raised an eyebrow, wondering if he should have let her wander alone earlier.

"No. In my profession I go to remote areas. I like being ready for any circumstance." She patted one pocket. "I have first aid items here." She patted another pocket. "Food." Another pocket. "Survival equipment. Every pocket has a function." Her eyes shimmered with confidence, and her sensual mouth tipped into a smug smile.

53

"Do you wear that to bed?" He hadn't meant the words to slip out so intimately. But they did.

Her eyes widened and she inhaled. "I-I attach it to my backpack, which I use as a pillow."

"In other words, you are ready to run at a moment's notice." He nodded and picked up the stew, dishing it onto their plates. "I like that. It is a good practice, especially here, when you never know when a drug trafficker or artifact thief could come upon you."

She stared at him. "I know there are problems with these undesirable people in this country. Reading the travel advisories is enough to make one think twice before coming. But the Guatemalan government is behind all the efforts to dig up information surrounding their Maya ancestors. The archeological digs are safe."

Tino shook his head. "Do not go to the dig with the attitude you are safe there. As with all countries, there are corrupt people in government. Not all of them have their people's interest. They only wish to fill their pockets with money." He cleaned up his plate.

"I'm sure Virgil has taken precautions to make sure everyone at the dig is there for the right reasons."

The faith she put in this man frustrated Tino.

"The crooked are sly and can cover their tracks. Do not depend on your faith in another to keep you safe. The only person who is looking out for you, is you."

She stared down into her plate, scooting the uneaten food around.

"Eat. Just be vigilant when you are at the dig."

Tino picked up a mango. He sliced off one cheek with his knife and scored the orange flesh while Isabella finished her portion of stew. He inverted the skin and fruit handing her half the prepared mango. "Eat this and I will clean up the dishes."

"I can help. You don't have to wait on me." She started to rise.

"It is what I get paid for." His statement, though not true at all, caused a frown to wrinkle her forehead.

He gathered the dishes and the pot and went to the river to wash them. Crouched by the river, deep in thoughts of how to get through the night knowing Isabella would sleep only inches away, he rocked back on his heels. A branch cracked to his right. His senses sprang alert as he drew his gun.

His breathing resumed to normal as dark objects dropped from the branches and glided over his head. Fruit bats on the move. Though ugly, they were harmless. He stared across the dark water glittering like diamonds from the reflection of the moon shimmering on the surface.

A light on the distant shore caught his attention. The only boats on the water as they traveled downstream belonged to locals. He knew for a fact no one lived on the other side at this bend. He'd picked this spot knowing it was a safe place to spend the night from traffickers and locals looking to help themselves to supplies.

Who camped over there and why? He'd tuck the doctor in for the night and then slip across the river and investigate.

Tino picked up the clean dishes and headed toward the soft yellow glow of the gas lantern he'd hung from the end of the tent. Isabella must have lit the lamp. It shone like a beacon. If he could see the light across the river, whoever was over there could see this one.

¡Coño! Now he would have to stay on this side to protect the doctor in case someone came nosing over here.

He dropped the dishes. They clattered into the box. Isabella jumped and faced him, her toothbrush protruded from her mouth and light gleamed off her scrubbed clean face. A mosquito cloud hovered above her head. The whole scene should have knocked sense into him. But instead, he felt sucker punched by her purity and tranquil beauty.

"What?" she asked around the toothbrush in her mouth.

"Do not take too much longer. I want the light out soon." He stomped past her and was rewarded with a fragrant whiff other than DEET. A spicy, earthy scent that reminded him of sex. He ran a hand over his face and knelt at one end of the tent. This space was much too small for the two of them. He grabbed his sleeping bag and mosquito net.

"Why are you taking your bedding out?" Her voice drifted above him.

Her accusing tone did little to squelch the need flaming his groin.

"Are you done?" He grabbed the lamp and doused the flame. With luck, whoever the light belonged to across the water hadn't noticed their lantern yet, or if they had, didn't have time to judge where to find this camp.

"Yes. But you didn't answer my question." She stood beside him. Her spicy scent twined around his head, arousing his senses even more.

"Look across the water." The other light still twinkled like a grounded star.

"Who is that?" her voice dropped to a sexy whisper.

Tino swallowed a groan and shook his head. "I do not know, but I would rather they did not know we are here. Go to bed."

"Are you sleeping out here to keep guard?" She knelt beside him. Her shoulder touched his and her exotic scent pulsed his blood.

"Yes. Do not worry. I am a light sleeper and no harm will come to you tonight." He told himself not to look at her. But his head didn't listen. His neck twisted, and he stared into her eyes.

Enough moonlight reflected off the river to sparkle in her eyes and accentuate silver highlights on her high cheekbones. He'd never stared at such kissable lips before. They were his downfall. He leaned, bumping shoulders. His gaze locked on her tongue darting out and wetting lips that called to him like a hummingbird to nectar.

He raised a hand and smoothed a stray strand of hair from her face. Her head tilted, pressing her cheek into his palm. The heat and softness of her skin, her alluring scent, and full wet lips beckoned.

He leaned in to taste.

"Eeeee!" she squealed and shoved him away as she scampered into the tent. "Get it away! Get it away!" Her arms and legs flailed as she flopped around inside the tent.

"What? Get what away?"

Tino dove into the tent, ready to do battle. He found nothing other than Isabella and their supplies. He grasped her wrists and flattened her on her back, his body pressing hers into the foam pad.

"What are you afraid of?" he asked, wondering if he'd been about to kiss a woman with a sanity issue.

"The bat. It was-was hideous! I h-hate bats!"

Her tense body vibrated. He welcomed the sensation, sliding his hands up her arms and experiencing the satin caress of her hair.

"The bats here are fruit bats," he calmly explained. "Now if that spicy scent I smell were fruity, you might have a problem."

Even in the darkness, he felt the weight of her gaze on him.

"I don't care if they only eat fruit. I-don't-like-bats. They're ugly, nasty creatures that should never have been placed upon this earth."

"They have a right to be here, too." He softened his voice and inhaled her scent. The pressure of her hips against his, her warm breath fluttering against his damp skin, and the realization that her body had grown limp, set off warning signals in his head. This was one time when his body overruled his head. His hands continued to explore her long neck and dainty ears. He hadn't touched a woman so intimately in a year. That had to be the reason he found it hard to keep his hands to himself.

She rolled her head slowly from side to side. "No bats."

He heard her swallow. Lowering his mouth, his lips hovered above hers. "There is no room for bats in here with the two of us."

"N-no room." Her breathing quickened.

He wasn't a saint. Never claimed to be. Fighting his conscience was useless. He ran the tip of his tongue across the seam of her lips. She gasped and he captured her mouth. Her full lips were soft, pliable, and so succulent.

He drew back to change the angle of the kiss, and she followed him. Her eagerness, heat, and clumsiness affirmed his assumption. She was an un-plucked flower. The knowledge hardened his *miembro*. He pressed against her.

She gasped, wedged her hands between them, and shoved back, gulping for air.

Yes, she was a virgin, and he wouldn't be the one to take her gift even though every nerve in his body was about to explode with need.

He pushed up to his knees. She remained on her back, one wrist resting on her mouth. If a splash of moonlight could penetrate the small quarters, he was sure he would see recrimination darkening her eyes.

"I will not apologize for kissing you. You, Ezzabella, are made for kissing. But, as a gentleman, I will be sure that does not happen again." He backed out of the tent, grabbed his bedding and mosquito net, and walked a short distance away.

Tino stared at the light still winking at him from across the water. He would find it easier to swim the caiman infested river and walk unarmed into a drug deal, than to sit in the boat with Isabella tomorrow. He went into the kiss with the plan to make her forget the bats and enjoy the honor of his kisses. Now drugged by her enticing mouth, he was filled with even more need to protect her.

Disgust writhed in his mind. He'd just crossed a line he hadn't crossed since losing his family. He now had someone other than himself to look out for. That knowledge made him vulnerable and scared the hell out of him. He'd done a lousy job protecting his family.

Chapter Seven

Isabella spent most of the night reliving the blood-heating, body-shocking kiss she'd experienced with Tino and chastising herself for allowing it to happen. But her inquisitive nature had to dissect and look at the data from all perspectives. This was, after all, her first real lip-locking with a man. Her father and Virgil had brushed quick kisses across her lips over the years. When Virgil's lips had touched hers, she'd tingled with excitement, but those sensations were nothing compared to the explosion Tino erupted in her. His bold kiss had been full of passion. She'd expected nothing less of a Latin man but, my…she fanned her face with a hand. Reliving the kiss heated her like the jungle sun.

She had to remember the kiss meant nothing to Tino. Even though it was a mind-blowing experience for her, it was only an experiment and something that shouldn't happen again. The only one to get hurt from allowing this to continue would be her and she never wanted to feel the anguish of one-sided love again.

Sunlight shone into the tent. She'd heard Tino during the night, pacing, groaning, and even, she was sure, cursing. She touched her lips with her fingers. He said she was made for kissing. Happiness bubbled in her chest. No male had ever thought of her other than a skinny bookworm. The idea of being a woman who was kissable, desirable, lifted her emotional self-esteem. She plucked at her top clinging to her sweaty body. Her thoughts drifted to last night and Tino's arousal pressed against her. Her skin became infused with a different heat. He'd thought her good for more than kissing. The evidence of his hard shaft rubbing against her thigh was proof. Heat flashed through her body; both embarrassment and excitement. Could she shake the thrill of being desired as a woman and still act normal around Tino?

He was from a culture noted for the males being lovers. She most assuredly was not his first conquest, and he would probably treat her as he had before, with ambivalence, tolerance, and a bit of amusement.

Isabella shook her head. She couldn't let his kiss make her react as if he were her first crush. He had found her a good distraction, nothing more, and she would view the encounter as data for further research.

The tarp whisked away, revealing the green canopy of the forest beyond the white gauze of her mosquito net. Isabella craned her neck and spotted Tino diligently folding the canvas.

"We leave in five minutes." His surly tone caught Isabella's attention.

His tense jawline and dull eyes suggested lack of sleep. His tone and lack of eye contact spoke of an awkwardness they hadn't encountered before the kiss.

Why didn't he display the macho haughtiness she'd expected? She wadded up the mosquito net and stood, placing a hand on his arm to stall his movements. His muscles bunched under her fingers, and his gaze moved from her hand to her eyes. The apprehension and apology she witnessed in his gaze quirked the sides of her mouth.

"Do not apologize for kissing me."

He started to open his mouth. She placed a finger on his warm, exciting lips.

"I know it went farther than either one of us anticipated, but you don't have to worry about my mooning over you like a lovesick teenager. While it was wonderful and I understand it meant nothing to you. I'll use the data in other encounters." Her stomach fluttered as his eyes widened then became hooded by his eyelids.

Her intelligence told her she was just a distraction and to not let any of their encounters become emotional.

A smug smile curved Tino's lips, and the glint of machismo she'd witnessed so often in his eyes, flared. He leaned in and tapped a finger on her nose.

"I may be the guide, but you could help out," he quipped, rising to his feet and gathering their equipment.

Relief swept through her tightly strung body. They could return to normal.

Isabella slipped into her vest, picked up her backpack, and helped him carry their supplies to the boat.

"Did you see anyone?" Isabella nodded toward the other side of the river.

"No. They are either camped or traveling inland." His tone sounded skeptical.

"Are they hunters or locals?"

"Either would be better than *narcos*—drug runners…they could be trouble."

The worry in his voice twisted her insides. She didn't want to be killed or kidnapped in the jungle when she had so much more to discover.

"Get in." Tino held out a hand to assist her into the boat.

Isabella grasped his fingers. The contact tingled all the way up her arm. She sat down and rubbed her hand on a pant leg. The murky river swirling around the boat presented a good distraction from the thoughts banging around in her head. Tino put a hand on her shoulder for balance as he slipped by her to the back of the boat. Heated impressions of his fingers lingered on her shoulder long after they pulled away from the bank and chugged down river.

Shaking his charismatic hold on her would be hard, but she must. Once he dropped her off at the dig, they would most likely never meet again. Sadness pressed on her chest like a vice. He was the first male, besides Virgil, to see her as something other than a threat or a freak. Obviously, the two had hit it off or Virgil wouldn't have asked Tino to pick her up. The idea of the two men she liked being friends settled her nerves over kissing Tino. If Virgil trusted the man, it said a lot about Tino's character. His behavior this morning, feeling he'd overstepped his bounds with their kiss, also said a lot about her guide.

"How did you and Virgil meet?" she asked, peering over her shoulder at Tino.

He continued to scan the shoreline. "We have never met."

After all they'd been through so far, she didn't believe Tino would cause her any harm, but the fact that Virgil had been so carefree in hiring just anyone to bring her to the dig stung a little.

"Then how did he know you are an honest guide?"

"He actually hired my friend who could not make the trip." Tino studied her. "Do you still believe I might cause you harm?"

Her ears burned at the hurt shining in his eyes. "No, I just thought since Virgil asked you, I mean your friend, oh, you know what I mean. I assumed you two had met." Socially inept, she blundered just as she had as a teenager in the masters program at the university.

"You and Dr. Martin have a unique relationship." His face remained stony and bland, but his eyes flashed with—contempt? Why this emotion toward a man he'd never met?

"Virgil is a good friend of my family, my godfather and mentor. I excelled at academics and entered the graduate program at the University of Arizona at seventeen." She shuddered remembering the cruel comments made by some of the other students. "It isn't easy being so young and tossed into that kind of academic atmosphere. Virgil was on staff at the time and helped me whenever I had problems with the other professors and students."

"Why would they bother you?"

The wrinkles on his golden-brown brow brought a smile to her lips. He clearly had never been in an academic situation.

"They'd spent more years than I had getting into the graduate program. They were jealous and felt threatened." Isabella wiped at the sweat trickling down her neck as Tino edged the boat along the shoreline to their right. Caimans lazed in the sun along the bank. The knobby bone plates on their back resembled dinosaurs. One opened its long snout showing many pointed teeth. The animals looked as if they slept, but she knew, just like her colleagues, they waited for her to make a wrong move so they could gobble her up.

She shuddered.

"Do you still fear your colleagues?"

Tino's concerned voice filtered through her thoughts as he maneuvered the boat into a larger body of water. The river must have converged with the Usumacinta.

She squared her shoulders and stared into his eyes. "There is only so much money for research and expeditions. A bad word here or rumor you aren't conducting by university rules can get your funding pulled. I'm always scrutinized by the older members."

But even all the scrutiny couldn't dampen her desire to learn more. "Researching my family tree in grade school I discovered I'm one eighth Hopi. That triggered my interest in Native American people and my curiosity about the Aztec, Inca, and Mayan cultures. During a dig in Arizona, I discovered a hieroglyphic much like those found in Central and South America. That discovery and research led me to my thesis. Peoples, tribes, from North America traveled south to Central America and traded. To carry my thesis further, I'm currently writing grants for funding to do DNA testing. Virgil said I'd get paid well to help him decipher a tablet he found at *Ch'ujuña'*. This trip is to keep my department open." She waved at a family shoving a boat off from the shore. A ramshackle house peeked out between the foliage behind them.

"We are nearing a community. See the increased activity on the water." Tino navigated the boat out to the middle of the wide river to avoid collisions with the locals along the shore. Isabella had given him a better glimpse into her life. She idolized the doctor and felt she was a victim of her colleagues. Grad school at seventeen. He was still trying to decide what to do with his life at that age. She said very little about her family. This puzzled him. He missed his loving family every single day. He had his *compadres*, god-parents, his aunts, uncles, cousins, and school friends in Venezuela, but they knew nothing about his secret life as an agent. They only knew he wandered about looking for adventure by tagging wild cats. If they knew of his secret life, they could talk to the wrong people and it would put them all in danger.

The river made a large sweeping curve to the west revealing a small village landing. Hot, mid-day sun bore down on the un-shaded river. He glanced at Isabella in her palm hat. It was good protection here on the river, but once they set foot on the jungle trails, the hat could be stashed in her pack. The high green canopy of the forest trees would filter the scorching rays of the tropical sun.

He checked the GPS on his watch. They still had several more hours on the river, once they passed this settlement, and before they would trek through the jungle.

Tino maneuvered the vessel to the shore and stood when the hull scraped the riverbank. He stepped around Isabella and over the bow of the boat. The water came mid-calf as he tugged the vessel onto shore.

Isabella rose.

"We will grab something to eat then continue up river. The dig site is a couple more hours by river and then a good two hours on foot." He helped her over the bow and onto the shore. His fingers clung to her hand longer than necessary. At the end of this day he would hand her over to Dr. Martin and never see her again. He shouldn't feel a loss. He'd only known her for two days. But in those two days he'd come to know her better than any other person who had crossed his path since his family's demise. His hardened heart was slowly cracking and allowing this remarkable woman to seep in.

She stood beside him as he negotiated by hand signs with a young man to hold his main supplies until he returned and to watch the boat until they were ready to continue on down the river. Satisfied that the boy wouldn't sell his goods, Tino slung his backpack over his shoulders and motioned for Isabella to follow him. He'd barely ventured into this part of Petén before, mainly due to the communication problem. Mayas deep in the rainforest spoke the language of their ancestors and few knew Spanish. With little knowledge of their language, he had trouble making inquiries about drug shipments. That was why, until now, his assignments had been down on the southern border of Guatemala, sabotaging shipments of drugs flown into remote airstrips. The DEA had recently heard of a new route down the Usumacinta River, and he'd been ordered to see what he could find out.

Tino found a shady spot and two wood crates to sit on at the edge of the small gathering of adobe huts roofed with palm fronds. He placed a Gallo in front of himself and a can of soda water in front of Isabella. Digging into a side pocket of his bag, he pulled out fruit, rolls, and cheese. "It is not much, but it will sustain us for the trip."

He handed the food to Isabella. Her gaze traveled over every inch of the community. Her desire to speak to the locals and gather more information was evident in her eyes. The few locals, watching them with curious stares, appeared harmless. If she could glean useful information without knowing their language, he wouldn't stop her.

"After we eat, if you wish to try and visit with the locals, I do not mind waiting."

She rewarded him with a wide, full smile and glittering eyes.

"*Gracias*. I would love to visit with them about their ancestors and way of life." She ate with her usual vigor. A grin tugged his lips

64

when she pulled out the large knife she carried and cut more cheese, placing it inside another roll.

Isabella eased her backpack onto her shoulders and stood. He took that as a signal she was ready to visit with the locals. Tino put the remaining food into his pack and shouldered it.

"Let's try the old man over there. He seems as curious about us as you are about them." Tino headed toward the man, a friendly smile on his lips.

The man watched their approach, but his gaze remained on Isabella.

"May we speak with you?" Tino asked in Spanish, doubting the man would understand their request.

The man shook his head and chattered in a language unfamiliar to Tino.

Isabella stepped forward, her face glowed with excitement. She haltingly spoke back to the man.

Tino touched her arm, drawing her attention to him. "What is he speaking?"

"Cholan." Her grin grew.

"You know this language?" Her intelligence surprised him once again.

"I know bits of it. Not enough to learn what I'd like to know, but enough to impress him to let me in his home."

Tremors rippled up Tino's arm when she grasped his sleeve and followed the old man through the small door of a hut.

Entering a structure with only one exit attacked his nerves like being in a pit full of army ants. He scanned the dark interior, expecting an ambush. The light across the river last night and the report from his friend at Sayaxche about the increased traffic on the Pasion River and in this forest in the last three months had him suspicious of everyone. For all he knew, this man received compensation to keep strangers away.

The house proved empty of other occupants, but cluttered with stone engravings of various sizes. Isabella dropped to her knees in front of a flat gray stone three feet tall and covered with carved figures. She opened her vest and drew out her small journal.

She spoke to the man and motioned as if drawing in her journal. He nodded and smiled.

"I'm going to be a while. I want to copy these markings and take photos. The man says when his grandfather was a small boy he found this along the river. It looks like a story about a ceremony." Her eyes shone brightly as she returned her attention to the markings on the stone and her journal.

Tino glanced at the man. He watched each precise mark Isabella made, oblivious to Tino's presence. The small dark building worked on his nerves, creating anxiety.

"I will be outside when you are done."

Isabella waved her hand absently.

Tino exited the house and found a spot in the shade at the corner of the next shack. He slipped his pack off and sat with his back against the adobe wall, drinking soda water. Two men, younger than himself, sauntered between the houses. Though their gait was unrushed, the set of their shoulders and the way they scanned the area ignited his interest. These two were the right age to be pulled into drug running. Money and adventure tempted many young men.

The men stared at him, their hands edging toward their lower backs. *Guns.*

He'd just arrived and wasn't about to blow his cover this soon. He smiled and pulled out a Gallo. He popped the top and turned his attention to several children carrying on a frog-hopping contest in front of a house across the way.

The two kept walking. The guns they'd started to reach for stuck out of the back of their waistbands. They were in town either to move goods or to check the area before bringing some in. Would his presence stall their actions? Or would they get rid of him and Isabella if they became suspicious? He didn't like the latter idea. She was innocent. The quicker he got her to the dig and away from his business the better.

His shade slowly diminished, exposing more and more of him to the hot sun and accelerating the twitching of his nerves with every minute Isabella spent in the building. He lost control of his patience and poured the beer on the ground. Tino stood, swung his pack on, and stepped around the corner.

At the far end of the line of huts, the two men stood deep in discussion with an Anglo male in his fifties. Dirt on the man's knees gave the impression he'd been kneeling or crawling. But he didn't strike Tino as a victim or the groveling type. His facial expression and verbal delivery showed a man used to giving orders.

Tino glanced at the dark interior where Isabella sought her answers, then back to the men in deep discussion. He slipped between the neighboring houses and made his way around to where he could better hear the three men. His first priority centered on stopping drug runners. Isabella was safe as long as she remained in the house with the old man.

Chapter Eight

Isabella thanked the old man again and tucked her journal into her vest pocket. Once she settled in at the dig, she'd study the drawings and do a more thorough reading. This broken corner of a larger stone tablet told of a ceremony for the moon god. Her skin tingled with excitement. If the ease in which she deciphered this stone was any indication, she'd have Virgil's tablet decoded and be back in the states with her funding in plenty of time.

Sweet joy warmed her insides unlike the tropical heat steaming her skin. She was anxious to share her newfound information with Tino.

She stepped outside the small home and blinked at the bright sunlight. How long had she sat meticulously replicating the drawings into her journal? Isabella patted her camera. She had photos too, but the poor lighting and the flash hadn't combined well to capture every detail of the stone engravings. The small nuances of an artist's portrayal of a character told as much as the character itself. Twisting her wrist, she glanced at the watch her father had given her on her twenty-first birthday. He told her all anthropologists and archeologists wore this style. Each year on her birthday he arrived, kissed her forehead, and took the watch to be cleaned and a fresh battery installed. When he returned, he replaced the watch on her wrist, kissed her forehead, and disappeared for another year. At first, she thought his actions corny, but now she realized it was her father's way of making sure the watch always worked and she always had a piece of him with her.

Two o'clock. She scanned the area around the house. Where was Tino?

Isabella settled the backpack on her shoulders and meandered between the buildings and back toward the boat. A five-minute walk covered the small settlement. She'd expected to bump into Tino. At the boat, the boy and the supplies all remained at the edge of the wide river. But no Tino.

She asked the boy in Cholan if he knew where Tino went.

His thin shoulders rose and fell.

She scanned the area again. Where could Tino be? She didn't know the word for tavern but with hand motions and her limited vocabulary she managed to get a response from the boy.

"No."

No tavern, no anything that she could see to occupy Tino. He wouldn't leave her stranded. Her instincts told her that much.

Not one to sit around and wait, she stared at the river and the boat. Could she navigate the river by herself? Dock and find the location where the trail led to the dig? Her mind said she could figure it all out, but her gut clenched in uncertainty.

So, she sat and waited until the heat and her curiosity drove her away from the river and back through the village. Sunlight filtering between the trunks of the trees intrigued her. Any sunlight in the jungle came from above. The high foliage of the mahogany and palm trees didn't allow for strong light under the canopy but rather a soft natural light with muted shadows.

Isabella stepped out of the trees. The intense sunlight, the heat, and the ravaged vision in front of her struck like a well-placed taekwondo kick to the midsection. Tears welled in her eyes at the stark landscape. Ash covered the once-green forest floor. Black stumps, shriveled blackened plants, and dead trees sporadically poked out of the ash. This devastation didn't go on for miles, it had been contained and men worked on the far side turning the soil.

But what of the fires that did get out of control? The chatter of birds in the trees to her left reminded her of the creatures that lost their homes. Deep in her thoughts, she leaned against a tree and watched the men prepare the earth for planting. How did one determine the loss of a forest against the production of food for the locals?

A hand rested on her shoulder. The heat and weight told her it was Tino. Her inner debate over the ethical use of the forest came to a halt.

"It's sad."

"They are lucky their clearing did not burn out of control." Tino squeezed her shoulder.

"I agree. I can imagine the devastation a runaway fire could cause. One would think in a rain forest the vegetation would be too wet to burn." She ran a hand over the cool, damp bark of the tree she leaned against.

"The forest is not as saturated as in years past. Each year less rain falls and the pattern of the weather alters. These changes have caused the rain forest to become drier and more susceptible to fires." He slid his palm down her arm and captured her hand. "Come. We must hurry if we are to arrive at the dig before dark."

Isabella nodded. She should extract her hand from his but the strength of his wide calloused hand holding her was new. The comfort and warmth it instilled in her, took her by surprise.

She slipped her hand from his. "Where were you? I looked all over the village."

Tino regretted taking her hand. It was plain she didn't appreciate his touch after last night. But touching her felt right. Shoving aside his ego, he smiled at her. He'd known if she wasn't in the old man's shack she would be looking for him. Her inquisitive mind wouldn't let his disappearance pass unnoticed. The worst part…he hadn't yet come up with a convincing alibi.

"I went for a walk and lost track of the time." He stopped beside the boat and helped her climb in.

She spun around and stared at him with accusing eyes. "I don't believe you."

Her bluntness kept him on his toes. He curved his lips in the kind of smile he'd reserved for his *abuela* Juanita and said, "I heard the locals spotted a jaguar recently. I went in search of the animal to see if I could tag it."

Her eyes narrowed as she watched him. "I thought you said they didn't come out until dark?"

Tino shrugged. "I said that yesterday so you would not become more frightened." He leaned down, untied the boat, and pushed it into the river.

Isabella squeaked and plopped her bottom onto the seat.

He jumped in and moved past her to start the motor and navigate into the center of the river. Keeping his DEA business from her was proving difficult. Her intellect dissected everything, another good reason to rid himself of the enticing doctor.

"Did you find signs of the jaguar?"

"Yes, I will return after I drop you off." The motor sputtered and caught. He spun the boat and steered it along the river bank about thirty feet from the shoreline. The river was wide and, in the middle, flowed a strong current that would carry them faster but also would hinder his steering of the small craft.

"Is there another settlement where the trail to the dig starts?" Isabella batted at the pesky cloud of mosquitoes and pulled out her can of DEET.

"No, but there should be boats at the landing. It is the only way to get supplies in and out of the dig." He wondered about the men he'd followed from the settlement. The two younger men had climbed into a boat and headed up river, while the older man settled into a small boat with a powerful engine and gunned himself down river, in the same direction he and Isabella traveled.

"Are you considered a game warden since you tag cats?"

He looked over at Isabella. Her inquisitive mind never rested. "You must be exhausted every night when you go to bed."

Her brow furrowed and she stared at him. "What do you mean?"

"You are always thinking up questions and working your mind. It must be exhausting." Smugness squeezed his chest. He had directed her attention on something other than himself.

"Stimulating. I enjoy solving puzzles and piecing together history. Don't you enjoy using your wits to outsmart the animals you tag?"

"*Sí.*" *¡Coño!* She put the conversation back on him. "I do not run into a jaguar every day. That means I get to rest. Like now, when I work as a guide I sit back, steer the boat, and enjoy the scenery." He let his gaze drift from Isabella's head down her body to her sturdy hiking boots and back up to her cheeks which took on a red hue to rival the macaw.

"Do you always watch the scenery inside the boat and not around you?"

The hint of insecurity ringing in her voice injected him with a need to make her see her worth. "No. There has never been another in my boat who rivaled the scenery."

Her cheeks deepened in color and she directed her attention to the forest pressing into and over the edges of the river.

Tino focused on the shoreline. The trail head should be in the next thousand meters of river.

"I see the boats!" Isabella pointed at the shoreline at the same moment he spotted the small boat with the large motor.

So the man he'd watched at the settlement was part of the dig. Why would he go all that distance to talk to those young men and not bring back any supplies?

Tino navigated the boat up to the shore, hopped out, and pulled it aground. He helped Isabella out of the boat and gathered his gear. He walked over to the small boat and touched the engine. Still piping hot.

"Here's a snack to eat along the way. I want to get you to the dig before the sun goes down." He handed Isabella an energy bar and shouldered his pack. Setting out at a brisk pace, he headed up the trail.

"Are you scared of the dark?" she snickered.

"Always the smart remark. No, trying to find your way around in the jungle at night is next to impossible."

"But there's a clear trail."

"When it gets dark it will not be so clear." He continued up the path at a good clip. They might catch up to the man who had docked right before they arrived. Fifteen minutes up the trail, he detected the low rumble of the man's voice from the settlement.

Tino pivoted and placed a finger on Isabella's lips. He leaned close and whispered, "I hear a cat. I am going to try and sneak up on him. You continue up the trail. I will catch up when I have either tagged the cat or lost him."

She started to open her mouth. He had to find out what the man was doing. Tino pressed a brief kiss to her lips, nudged her up the trail, and left the well-traveled path to move quickly and quietly through the trees toward the voices.

Isabella stared at Tino's back until he disappeared among the tree trunks and ferns. The man was full of contradictions. First, he says hurry we have to get to the dig before dark then he goes chasing off after a cat and leaves her to fend for herself.

And he kissed me again. It was reminiscent of the type her father and Virgil buzzed her lips with. Only warmer more intimate. I like collecting kiss data. As long as she remembered all this kissing meant nothing to Tino. Either that or he'd been in the jungle way too long.

Sighing in resignation, she squared the pack on her back and set off on the path to *Ch'ujuña*.

The first thirty minutes of the path proved easy walking. The well-cleared trail had smaller, less discernible paths jutting off on either side now and then. Were they animal trails? If so, would a jaguar come bounding out in front of her with Tino in pursuit? As the path started a gradual climb, vegetation crept onto the trail narrowing the passageway.

This didn't make sense. How were supplies delivered to the dig site with such a poorly maintained path? She pulled out her knife and hacked at vines hanging across the trail from the shorter copal and cedar trees. Sweat mixed with the humid air and mosquito spray trickled down her neck and back. The handle of the knife became slick, slipping and throwing off her aim as she hacked at the vines.

She stepped forward and something crunched under her foot. Raising her boot, she stared at a four-inch-long squashed beetle. Shudders rippled across her shoulder blades. Insects and snakes, while not a favorite, usually didn't make her squeamish. But the size of this creature gave rise to what other huge invertebrates she might encounter.

Silence cloaked the forest as smothering and unnerving as a blanket thrown over her head. The eerie quiet injected Isabella with fear. No one but Tino knew where she'd gone. What if something happened to her? To Tino?

Rain poured from the sky breaking the silence. The rhythmic sound and refreshing coolness lifted her spirits. Her hat did little to protect her from the rush of water over her head. She took it off, unbraided her hair, and let the water pour through, cooling her scalp.

Within minutes, water gushed down the path.

Isabella stepped out of the way of the stream and tucked her body against a tree trunk, perching on exposed roots. She'd have to wait out the storm. Alone. Where was Tino? How much farther to the dig? If the rain hadn't been using the path as a stream bed, she could continue.

She dug in one vest pocket, pulling out a nutrition bar. In another pocket, she found a plastic bag. Opening the bag, she caught rainwater, sealed the bag, and slid it into a pocket while she ate the bar. The whole grains and natural sweeteners of the bar dried her mouth. She drank the pure rain water, savoring the sweet taste, and refilled the bag, placing it in an outside pocket on her pack. The cool, refreshing liquid might come in handy later and it didn't need to be purified.

The rain stopped as abruptly as it started but water continued to gush down the path. A glance at her watch helped little. Patience was needed traveling in this forest. Fortunately, her studies of ancient people and cultures gave her a Zen-like ability to perceive patience as a virtue. With slow, steady digging and research, she would learn all there was to know about the people who first inhabited the Americas.

A mist crept in, settling over the forest. The ethereal feel and quiet seeped around her like the relaxing warmth of a steam bath. Savoring the moment, she closed her eyes and inhaled. The moist air, laced with exotic floral scents and decaying plants, perfumed the air. Nothing could be better than standing in a rainforest enjoying the wildness and peace. Birds moved about the canopy above. Their raucous squawks reminded her of Alabaster, her cockatoo. He no doubt was thriving in the care of Mrs. Sullivan, her next-door neighbor. He molted and became defiant when she was home, but loved her neighbor.

"¡Carajo! What are you doing here?" Tino's loud whisper and accusing tone jarred her pondering.

Isabella's heart hammered against her breastbone. Her eyes shot open and she spun toward Tino's voice. He stood on the path where she'd cut the vines.

She willed the adrenaline his appearance produced to lessen and pointed the knife at him. "You told me to continue to the dig."

His arms crossed. A sardonic smile raised one side of his mouth. "You are headed the wrong direction."

"But...the path..." The wrong way? The arm holding the knife dropped to her side. If Tino hadn't found her...

Tino's arms encircled her as she swayed.

"I could've...jaguars...narcos...I could..." She stared into his eyes. The knowledge that spun in her head was revealed in his dull gaze.

"Mi pichón, what were you thinking? You are lucky I found you."

74

His voice caressed her frazzled nerves.

He called her his little dove. Her heart pattered in her chest.

Then the macho tone of the rest of his comment sunk in and raised her feminist antennae. "I wouldn't have been on the wrong trail if you hadn't charged off after some wild animal." She pushed out of his arms and willed her backbone to snap straight and her fear to dissolve. Anger was always better than giving into fear. "Did you find the jaguar?"

"*Sí.*" His gaze drifted over her left shoulder.

He was hiding something. His posture and avoidance screamed deception.

Narrowing her eyes, she stared at him. "I don't believe you."

He shrugged. "Believe what you wish. The trail to the dig is back down this path." He brushed past her, heading down the trail.

"Errr," Isabella growled, throwing up her hands, and stomping behind him. She hated he lied to her, she had to rely on him, and the elation that had coursed through her body when he'd stepped out of the forest.

Tino couldn't believe Isabella took the wrong path almost ending up in the small contingent of narcos he'd followed. The group he tailed converged for a reason. Unfortunately, he'd left before finding out what. A niggling sensation warned him to get back to Isabella. Now he knew why. She'd been about to burst into something deadly.

He glanced over his shoulder to make sure the noise she made meant she followed and not headed off in another direction. She'd looked completely at peace when he came upon her. From the condition of her wet clothes and stringy hair, she hadn't taken cover from the rain. Her acceptance of what nature tossed out, and the way she struck out alone brought a smile to his lips. She was unlike any other woman he'd ever met. There were a few tough females he had come across in his line of work, but none of them would have put up with what Isabella had so far without complaining. He was sure of it.

He found the path to the dig and turned.

"How do you know this is the path to *Ch'ujuña?*" Isabella's voice held a hint of awe.

He would die before he told her he'd put the coordinates in his watch. Her believing he was a great guide bumped his ego up a notch.

"This is a kilometer from the river."

"How do you know that when we came from the other direction?" She stopped and placed her hands on her hips.

"When I came this way, I noted the distance and the path markings." *Coño, she is hard to impress.*

"Then you're positive this is the path?" She straightened her pack and took a step forward.

"*Sí*, this is the path. Another half hour and we should be at the dig." He trudged along the narrow path, keeping an eye out for the narcos. He had no clue which direction they would go once their meeting was over.

"That stone the old man had…" A grunt trailed her words.

The zing of metal hacking at a thick vine rang in his ears. Isabella had a fondness for using the knife she confiscated.

She grunted, again, and the blade thunked, again. "It has markings that tell of a ceremony. But it's only a small piece of a much larger stone."

"Is it information that is useful?" He swung around to find out why she hacked at a vine when they should be moving forward.

"I think so. I mean, for the Mayas to have written the story down, it had to have been a significant ceremony."

Before he was aware of her movements, the blade sliced in his direction. He ducked to the side of the trail. The shiny metal sliced through a vine very close to where he'd been standing.

"Stop!" Tino grasped her hand clutching the knife. "Why are you hacking up the vines? They are not in your way."

She rotated her thin shoulders. "Guess I just felt a need to take out frustrations." She opened her fingers.

Tino grabbed the knife handle and placed an arm around her. Her body shook from exertion.

"I have never seen someone of your stature so strong and determined." She must have braided her hair as they walked before she started slashing at the jungle. Her shiny brown braid draped over his arm. The reddish-brown color reminded him of his favorite horse as a child. Maybe that was what drew him to her—the fond memories of his childhood full of love and hope. Something he believed he could never capture again. Not without his family.

"I learned early that strength and determination weren't given to you, you had to develop them and then hang on to them when others

76

tried to knock you down." The steel in her words drew his gaze to her face.

"You sound as though you went through life alone, but you mentioned parents." Sadness filled her eyes. He drew her closer, but his gaze remained fixed on her face.

"I have parents. Busy parents who gave me money and things, but they never gave themselves. It was up to me to learn to fight my battles and to depend on myself. If not for the food, clothing, and a place to live, I could've been an orphan for all the time I spent with my mother and father."

"That makes you even stronger." He leaned down to look under the brim of her hat. "You are a special person, Ezzabella. Do not let anyone ever tell you any different." He couldn't stop the path of his lips even if a wild animal or drug trafficker came upon them.

Once he delved past her lips, tasting of nasty DEET and salty sweat, he plunged into her sweet mouth. She opened to him willingly as her arms wrapped around his neck. Their tongues met, explored, and tangled. For all her innocence, her passionate body was ripe for the picking. She trembled in his arms and pushed tighter against him. Her hips moved against his growing desire in the age-old dance of passion.

If they weren't in a jungle and he wasn't the wrong man for her, he would have fulfilled her needs. Tino ran his fingers through her hair and held her head in his hands. Gently, he drew back, holding her head away from him when she leaned forward.

"No, *pichón*, this cannot go any farther. We have different paths to take. I want you to have no regrets. If we were to carry on as we both wish, you would one day look back and be unhappy." His own desire burned hard and rigid in his pants.

Her fingers played with the hair at the nape of his neck. The delicious feeling of her finger pads skimming across his skin and her body pressed to his ratcheted his desire.

He groaned and drew his body away. "Do you even know what you do to me?"

"I believe you're giving it away." She glanced down at the bulge in his pants.

"*Mi pichón*, how can one so innocent be so wicked?" He liked her playfulness and her directness.

"I am a scientist. I report the facts as I see them." She smiled and shifted away from him. "And I know for a fact your body likes my body." She let out a light-hearted joyous laugh. "It has been proven, Darrell Rutley, that I am desirable."

Jealousy, an emotion he had never experienced before over anything, ignited his gut and tightened his muscles. "Who is Darrell Rutley?" The question popped out before he could stop it. He did not want to learn any more about this woman. He did not want to care about her, her past, or her future.

"A man in grad school I liked. I was too young, too naïve. It was my first puppy-love crush."

Her eyes lost the light of good humor and dulled. "He said no one would ever love me because I'm too bony and too smart."

"He was intimidated by you and used words he knew would hurt." Against his better judgment, Tino raised her face to his. "You, Ezzabella, are very desirable and your body and intelligence has everything to do with it." He lowered his lips to hers and kissed her not with desire but with the honesty of his words. She had grown on him, in him, around him. In the two short days he'd known her, she had wheedled her way into his senses and it was going to be damn hard to walk away from her once he handed her over to Dr. Martin at the dig.

He withdrew slowly, kissed the tip of her nose, and smiled. "You are going to be hard to forget." Tino pulled the knife out of the tree he'd sunk the blade in to hold it, took hold of her hand, and led her down the trail. His words echoed in his head as he moved closer and closer to their parting. Common sense told him to let go of her hand, work to get her to the dig, and then disappear from her life. Forever. His lonely self wanted to find a way to stay around the dig to keep an eye on her and spend more time with her. His need to achieve his life goal battled with his desire to experience what Isabella had to offer. His bitter self told him to dump her at the dig and continue to exact his revenge. He could always look her up when it was all over.

Isabella tugged her hand from his. He stopped. The small act of separation gave him a moment of what leaving her would be like. At the news of his family's deaths, he'd been devastated. He'd clung to his *abuela* Juanita. Then his grandmother left him, too. In a short time, Isabella had filled the gap his family's deaths had notched in his soul.

78

"I need a drink." Isabella pulled a bag of water from her pack and guzzled. Her eyes met his through the clear plastic. She lowered the water. "Would you like a drink?"

"Where did you get this?" he asked, taking the offering.

"I collected rainwater."

Her actions didn't surprise him. Darrell what's-his-name was right. She was one clever individual. The man had been an idiot to let her intelligence scare him. Though he himself was Venezuelan and preferred his women to think of him as the person who could take care of all their problems, he'd spent enough years in the United States to know a woman was sexy when she could take care of herself.

"That was quick thinking. With the afternoon rains this time of year, you should be able to keep a clean supply of water." He handed the bag back to her and continued along the trail.

"Are you hungry?" she asked.

"I am fine." He had learned to go without food for many hours when on a mission.

"I have nutrition bars."

The words came out as a plea rather than an offering. Was she also grasping at ways to extend their time together? His growing infatuation for her was untimely, and he doubted she felt anything more for him than extracting data. When she had matter-of-factly said that this morning, he had wanted to pull her into his arms and show her data. But he also saw the vulnerability in her eyes. She was using the data ploy to keep her distance. She had more or less said he was the first person since being shunned to kiss her. He didn't want to be used as a way for her to explore her new found passion. Though it could be fun to teach her the ways of seduction… No, he must stay focused on the real reason he was in this part of Guatemala. Garza.

His mission was to find out where and what Paolo Garza's new route to Mexico was along the Usumacinta River.

"I am fine. The trail is widening, we must be getting closer." The din of voices and movement in front of them stopped his forward motion. If this wasn't the trail to the dig, he didn't want to put Isabella in danger. Cautiously, he parted the plants and peered through. The man he'd followed from the settlement stood beside another taller, more distinguished man, a compound of tents behind them. Their conversation registered in his ears as Isabella shoved past him.

"We made it!" She grasped his hand and led him toward the two men.

Chapter Nine

"Isabella, I'm so happy you made it." Virgil smiled like a doting parent. The realization that this man showed her more affection than her own parents struck her with the same knee-buckling impact as Tino's kisses. How she'd dreamed of a day when her own father would look at her this way.

After all she'd been through to get here; she wanted to feel the comfort of a parental embrace. She dropped Tino's hand and hugged the one person who had always believed in her and championed her. His long, lean body was so like hers, she'd often dreamed he was her father instead of Theodore Mumphrey. Theodore was tall, broad shouldered, and muscular. He'd played rugby in college and after.

"I can't believe I'm here and helping you." She leaned back and stared up into Virgil's familiar face. His hair, as always, needed a clipping, but he was meticulously shaved, unlike Tino, with scratchy stubble on his face.

"The minute I saw this stone, I knew it was something special, and you were the person to help me unwrap its mystery." Virgil's gaze traveled from her face past her shoulder. His brow furrowed and his eyes narrowed. "Who is this man? Where is Juan?"

Isabella shot a glance at Tino. His face remained blank, but sparks of anger darkened his narrowed eyes. If she didn't know better, she'd believe he was jealous. The thought brought a pleasant warmth to her chest even as she berated herself for forming such a strong attachment in so short a time.

She held out her hand, but Tino didn't take it. Why was he acting so aloof? "Tino Kosta, Dr. Virgil Martin, my mentor and family friend." Isabella shifted to keep both men in view. "Virgil, Tino Kosta, my guide."

"What did you do with Juan?" Virgil approached Tino like a lion stalking his prey.

Isabella moved to step between the men, but Tino placed a hand on her arm, drawing her behind him protectively.

"Juan, he had a family emergency, no? He ask me to guide the *señorita*."

He responded in a semblance of illiterate native phraseology. Why did he do that around everyone but her? The way he peered at Virgil and didn't back down contradicted the aloofness of his words.

Tino continued to stare. Virgil motioned for her to come to him. She was torn. Her loyalty to Virgil won out even as her heart cried out to Tino. She didn't want him to think she took Virgil's side over his. But Virgil was family, sort of, and Tino a mysterious stranger.

"Why didn't Juan contact me about the change?" Virgil again motioned for her to join him.

"He did not have time." Tino's gaze didn't leave Virgil's face.

Isabella stepped toward Virgil. Tino glanced toward her and his jaw muscle twitched.

"As long as Isabella made it safe, that's all that matters." Virgil placed an arm around her shoulders. "Doctor Isabella Mumphrey, this is Professor Rupert Walsh, a colleague from Britain who has been instrumental in acquiring permission from the Guatemalan government to allow us to dig."

She extended her hand to the other man who had witnessed the chest pounding between Virgil and Tino. He was of average build, perhaps in his mid-to-late fifties, judging by the small paunch hanging over his belt and the bald spot she noticed when he removed his hat.

"A pleasure, Dr. Mumphrey. Virgil hasn't stopped spouting about your knowledge of Mesoamerican history and symbolism." His soft, flabby hand didn't grip hers in a firm handshake. His narrow set eyes above a large nose gave him a piggish quality.

"I'm sure he exaggerated. He's a long-time family friend." Isabella couldn't shake the unease this man's touch roused. She dropped her hand and caught Tino studying the man. Why was he so interested in Professor Walsh?

She spun toward Virgil. "I discovered a piece of a stone in a house in the settlement. I'm wondering if it is part of what you found." She pulled out her journal and flipped to the last pages where she'd meticulously copied the carvings.

Virgil stared at the renderings. His brow furrowed in thought as his finger traced one of the markings. His eyes sparkled when he looked up at her.

"The symbols do have a certain similarity and could well have been done by the same artist." His voice cracked. "I told you when you were small you would solve any riddle if given the right information. I think we may have found your pieces."

Her love and adoration for this man filled her heart.

"Do you really think so?"

Virgil took her by the elbow and led her toward the cluster of large and small tents setup in an open area to the side of a small hill. She noticed an opening or doorway into the hill, which had to be the "tell" or mound of dirt covering the Mayan structure being excavated. The largest tent proved to be the artifact tent housing all the extracted treasures of the past. Two medium-sized tents stood end to end with a stove pipe sticking out of one: the cook tent and mess tent. Smaller tents dotted the perimeter of the camp and one with a barrel above it stood off to the side.

"*Señor* Martin."

Tino's voice sent embarrassment scorching through her. She'd become so caught up in her examination of the camp she'd forgotten about him.

"Yes?" Virgil pivoted toward Tino, turning her as well.

"It is getting late, no?" Tino again phrased his words like a local.

"And?"

She heard and felt Virgil's irritation. Isabella peered into the face of the man she'd admired her whole life. Yes, there it was, a slight tick in his temple. Why did Tino irritate him?

"You would give me permission to spend the night at the camp, *sí?*" Tino's gaze didn't waver from Virgil. His words were soft but his intent stare declared he would take nothing less than an invitation.

Virgil waved his hand. "You may spend the night. Find an empty tent."

"I will pitch my own, *gracias*."

Virgil dismissed Tino, but Isabella continued to watch him. Tino glanced at Walsh's retreating back, then shot her a wink and a nod.

Why did this man act like two completely different people? It thrilled her he would spend the night at the camp. She wasn't ready to part ways. He was a puzzle. One she wanted to piece together.

"Isabella." Virgil's command yanked her from her thoughts and she followed him.

At the opening of the artifact tent, three young women cautiously used small brushes on pieces of stone sitting on a makeshift table. Their hushed voices reminded her of the university library. More pottery, stones, and bones were layered in a box at the end of the work area.

Virgil stopped. "Annie, Jaycee, and Paula, this is Dr. Mumphrey. She's here to decipher the markings on the large stone we found and possibly connect some of these pieces." The women all looked up at Virgil with adoring eyes.

Isabella extended her hand to each of the women. "I'm pleased to meet you and honored Dr. Martin called me in."

Annie and Paula returned the handshake and bathed her in genuine smiles. Jaycee returned the handshake with a hard squeeze and didn't keep the glint of jealousy from sparking in her brown eyes. This one was out to claim Virgil. Isabella had witnessed it before at digs. There always seemed to be one undergraduate at a dig who was looking to score with the head archeologist. She'd have to warn Virgil. No doubt he hadn't a clue.

"We're all sharing a tent, but there's enough room if you want to bunk with us," Annie offered.

"Dr. Mumphrey will be staying in the tent next to mine." Virgil's comment brought titters from Annie and Paula and a glare from Jaycee.

"Thank you for the offer. It looks like Dr. Martin has my whereabouts settled." Isabella wasn't sure if she liked her tent next to Virgil. Why did he act as if they were an item in front of these

84

women? The thought of anything physical beyond a fatherly peck and embrace curdled her stomach, which growled again from hunger.

"Ahh, it sounds like you still have a voracious appetite. Excuse us, ladies, while I find Isabella something to eat." Virgil once again took her by the arm, signifying he dominated her. She didn't like it. But out of respect she wouldn't confront him until they were alone.

"Are those the only woman here?" she asked as she gently extricated her arm from his grasp.

"No. Eunice Isakson is here also."

"I've worked with Eunice before. She's a fantastic lab technician." Isabella was glad to hear she knew at least one of the other crew members. The woman was close to Virgil's age, but she and Eunice had formed a bond on another dig.

"We are on a low budget. She's also our artifact analyst, photographer, and cataloger."

"I'll be lucky to get a chat with her if she's doing all of that. But I can help when I need a break from decoding."

Virgil stopped and regarded her. A charismatic smile lit his face. "I was hoping you'd stick around and help out."

"I can only stay a month. I have to return to the university with my share of the money." She peered into Virgil's frowning face. "I can't let my department close."

"What about your parents? Are they okay with your being in the jungle?" He placed a hand on her arm.

"You know them; they don't really know or care where I am as long as they can do what they want." She hadn't meant for the words to come out so harsh. But she hadn't told them about this trip or her need for the funding. Her whole life she'd fought her own battles and found her own answers.

"Isabella, they care for you in their own way. Neither one of them was cut out to be a parent. They've given you all they know how to give."

"I know. I just…" She smiled up at him and couldn't keep from lacing her arms around his waist. "Your kindness and affection have been my salvation."

He kissed the top of her head. "I know. You're the daughter I never stopped long enough to make."

"Excuse me." A female voice squeaked behind them.

Virgil eased out of her embrace and they swung around to face Jaycee. Laser beams of hatred pierced Isabella.

"What did you need, Jaycee?" Virgil asked, spinning Isabella toward the mess tent entrance.

The subtle hint propelled her feet into the tent. She didn't want to be anywhere near Jaycee. The woman obviously took their embrace to mean something other than it did. Heat inside the tent, twice as stifling as the outside jungle air, took her breath away. The space needed cross ventilation.

The tantalizing aroma of roasting meat rumbled her stomach even louder. A native stood beside a cook stove. He stepped forward, extending his hand.

"*Seño*, please sit, I will bring you a cold drink and fruit. Dinner is not served until eight." His English wasn't perfect, but he was easy to understand.

"*Gracias*. Please call me Isabella, and you are?" She took the offered juice.

"Pedro. I cook for the wonderful people teaching us more about our people." He smiled and returned with a large platter of bananas, cheese, and tortillas.

"This looks good and the meat you're cooking smells wonderful." She sipped the drink and savored its cool sweetness.

He puffed out his chest. "I learn to cook in United States. Doctor Martin, he like my cooking and ask me to help in my own country."

"You were learning to cook in California near UC Berkeley?" She knew Virgil ate out rather than hiring a cook.

"*Sí*. Dr. Martin, he stay late one night. I tell him of my family and how I hoped to send them money once I became head chef. Then a year later he say he has a job for me in my country." Pedro spread his arms. "And here I am, no? Cooking and helping my people."

"That's wonderful." She wiped an arm across her forehead. "How do you stand the heat in here?"

"I am used to it, no?" He smiled and wandered back to the stove.

The tent wiggled. Isabella glanced at the door. Tino stood in the opening, his gaze resting on her. Proprietary popped into her head at his dark expression. He noted her watching and shuttered his eyes as he advanced.

Tino was still trying to figure out the true relationship between

Martin and Isabella. On one hand, they portrayed a parent and child relationship, and on the other, they touched like lovers. He didn't like the idea of them being lovers and found it hard to believe given the kisses he'd shared with Isabella. But he'd overheard Martin invite Isabella to stay in the tent next to his. That was pretty convenient for midnight trysts.

"I'm glad you're spending the night. I…" her voice trailed off. Her eyes, however, sought his.

"I needed time with you—" He stopped short noticing the joy emanating from Isabella.

Her lips curved into a sexy smile. Her eyes lit with excitement. He groaned inwardly at the flash of heat ripping through his veins.

"—to talk." That cooled the heat in her eyes.

"What do you want to talk about?" She bit into a banana. Her lips remained near the end of the fruit, brushing the tip seductively as she chewed.

¡Coño! She pushed his control to the limits.

"Not here." He wrenched his gaze from her tempting lips and noticed the cook listening. He leaned in closer and whispered, "I will come for you after dark. We will take a walk into the forest."

She leaned toward him and whispered. "Why the secrecy?"

Wide green eyes framed by wire rims inches from his dared him. He glanced at her mouth. Her tongue swiped once across her full lips and disappeared. His *miembro* became engorged, and he wanted her so bad his gut tightened.

"Tonight, *pichón*, I will tell you tonight." He pushed to his feet before he lost control and pulled her onto the table.

Tino walked toward the exit as fast as he could with his desire rigid in his pants. Once he exited the tent and spotted Walsh arguing with Martin, his need vanished and his instincts took over. From what he'd garnered from talking to the workers, Walsh and Martin hadn't been getting along. He wasn't sure why, but he intended to find out. He also intended to discover the identities of the men Walsh had met with in the settlement, and why Walsh then met with narcos. If Walsh was the liaison between the Guatemalan government and the dig, did he also keep the peace with drug traffickers? Or was he in with the narcos?

He'd left his pack against the tent near where the two stood arguing. Tino casually sauntered to his belongings and bent as if taking something from his pack.

"You have to pay the narcos if you don't want them storming in here and taking everything we've dug up and feeding us to the government saying we stole the artifacts." Walsh's voice didn't warble or whine like a person scared of the narcos.

"I won't pay them anything. All the money investors gave me will go into the dig and not into the hands of renegades. How many ways do I have to say it to make it clear to you? The next time you go to the settlement bring back men to stand guard at night. I'd rather use the investors' money for protection than extortion. I'll not have anyone here harmed, and I'll not give in to the narcos's threats." Martin's gaze drifted from Walsh. His brow furrowed when Tino rose and slung his pack over his shoulder.

"Do you care where I put my tent?" Tino asked, walking toward the two men as if he hadn't heard every word.

"On the far side. I'd rather you weren't in the midst of our work." Martin walked away from Walsh without another glance and straight toward Tino. "I'll show you where."

Tino fell into step beside the archeologist. The man was a couple inches taller but as long and gangly as Isabella, giving Tino nearly twenty kilos on the man.

"I didn't care for your familiarity with Dr. Mumphrey." Martin spoke low in almost a growling rumble.

"*Sí*, we became friends," he replied nonchalantly. Did he detect jealousy? Tino glanced out the corner of his eye. The man watched him intently.

Martin stopped. "Put your tent here."

He indicated a spot on the side surrounded by the jungle and farthest from the trail. A good place for the narcos to sneak in.

"This works." He couldn't contain a smile when he noticed it was also not far from the tent assigned to Isabella.

Martin glanced around and stepped closer. "I'm going to be watching you. Dr. Mumphrey happens to be special to me. I'll not have you preying on her innocence."

Tino nodded, hoping he projected a bit of confusion when he really wanted to ask the man how special she was to him. His gut sensed the man's infatuation was more than mentor or good family

88

friend. The thought soured his disposition.

Tino turned his back to the doctor and pulled his tent from his pack.

"How long have you been a guide?" Martin's question seemed fair enough.

"In Guatemala, two years. I have traveled much." Tino continued to erect his tent.

"Juan? How long have you known him?" The skepticism in the doctor's voice yanked Tino's instincts into high gear.

"A year, *señor*. We met on the river and a couple times off the river, no?" Okay, so that was a stretch but unless Martin talked to the real guide, he wouldn't learn any different until Tino finished with this assignment.

"Is this to kill predators?" The doctor pulled Tino's rifle from the pack.

"No. I am also a licensed wild cat tagger. That is the gun that puts the cats to sleep." He claimed his rifle from the doctor and slipped it into the sheath and under his sleeping bag in the tent.

"Then you're pretty good with weapons?"

He didn't know what the doctor was getting at, but he wished the man would leave and let him finish setting up his space. "*Sí.* I can shoot a jaguar from the tall branches in the copal tree."

The doctor nodded his head and stared into the trees surrounding the compound. "Would you be willing to stay on here for a couple days? Just till Marsh has time to bring in some locals to stand guard at night."

Tino kept his face impassive. The man had just given him a chance to stay close to Isabella. But would that be a mistake considering the way he couldn't get her out of his mind?

"Why do you need guards at night?" He knew the answer but wanted to see how forthright Martin would be.

"We've spotted some unsavory men around here, and I'd like to know my crew isn't in danger." The man didn't look him in the eye and quickly added, "We'll only need you a couple nights, then you can continue on."

Martin was making it plain he wasn't welcome except as a guard until he hired locals.

"I had planned to use the settlement as my base while I hunt for jaguar. I guess I could use this camp instead." Even as he said the words he wondered at the sanity of remaining close to Isabella. The more time he spent with her, the harder it would be to disappear from her life. But he found Walsh's actions unsettling, and the fact there was a narco group so close to the dig increased his curiosity about their dealings in the drugs making their way into Mexico and finally the U.S.

"I'd appreciate it and don't let anyone know the reason. I'd hate to have some of the women panic." The man's eyes shone hard and unwavering.

"That is not wise. If there is danger, your employees should know. The more people watching the better." He zipped his pack and shoved it into the tent he had erected while Martin watched. The man gave him one last, long look then wandered back to the compound.

Tino stared into the forest. Would remaining here a few days jeopardize or help his mission? From the unsavory characters he'd encountered so far, this dig could be sitting in the middle of more corruption than he'd bargained for. And how in the world was he to keep it from affecting Isabella?

Chapter Ten

At dinner, Isabella sat between Virgil and Eunice, savoring the delicious spicy stew and talking about past exploits and the artifacts found so far. The conversation around the table inspired her academic side to burst forth. She held everyone's attention, discussing her project and all she knew about the people enshrined by this tell. She glanced around the table. A trill of happiness clamored up her spine at Tino's interested expression.

She gazed into his rapt eyes and her words faltered. A nudge in her side brought her gaze level with Virgil's. His forehead creased as he glanced at Tino and back to her, his eyes narrowing.

She shrugged off his concern and turned to Eunice. "After seeing the stone this afternoon, I don't know if I'll be able to sleep thinking about all the possibilities I could uncover in the drawings."

Eunice nodded and patted her hand. "I remember once you found the drawings on those vases in Arizona, you didn't sleep for two days you were so engrossed in deciphering their meanings." The woman glanced around the tent. "That was when she came up with the thesis she is working on at the university."

Isabella caught Tino nodding and smiling.

She'd heard him say little during the meal. It was as if he didn't want anyone to know he was more learned than the front he put on. There were many layers to Tino, and she planned to peel away each one and discover the real man underneath all his subterfuge.

"If you can connect the Chol Mayas with the Hopi you will clear up another mystery about the history of the Mesoamerican people," Professor Walsh's voice boomed down the table.

She couldn't tell by his tone if he was impressed or putting her down. That was the trouble with the British; one never knew whether they were poking fun or being serious.

"I believe that by discovering connections among the ancient peoples we will uncover even more knowledge about them. My findings here will help support funding for DNA testing." She'd worked toward finding a connection since learning of her own ancestry.

"Fascinating. And what do you expect to accomplish by that?" Again, Professor Walsh's ingratiating tone seemed to mock.

She glanced at Tino and recognized the anger blazing in his eyes. Walsh's tone upset him, too.

"I hope to use the information I discover about their travels to classify the peoples and help them understand their roots. Isn't that what everyone wants? To know their roots and to find a place that brings them peace because they know it was a part of their people for generations?"

"Where are your roots?" Jaycee asked, her gaze darting to Virgil and back to her.

Isabella held the woman's gaze. "Part of this quest is to discover my roots. My great grandmother was Hopi. That's how I stumbled onto the Mayan connection. With my mother's refusal to acknowledge our ancestry, it made me even more determined to discover more about Native Americans."

Jaycee's eyes widened as well as those of several others sitting around the table.

"Isabella's work is more than a shot in the dark. It's her heritage and a subject she doesn't take lightly, which is why I've been behind her one hundred percent. She is driven to find the truth, and I know she has the capabilities to do it." Virgil smiled at her.

Her heart warmed, again, knowing he believed in her. If only her father had half Virgil's belief and her mother cared about her heritage.

But they were both too caught up in the present and future to care about the past.

"I'm going to get to work. See you all in the morning." Isabella stood. Everyone bid her good-night, including Tino. She stepped out of the tent and breathed in the cooler evening air. What she wouldn't give for a long shower, but first, she wanted to compare her drawings from the stone in the settlement with the one in the artifact tent.

The half moon shone a muted light into the clearing. This larger area was easy to navigate, but the narrow paths between tents harbored dark shadows, booby trapped with crates and digging tools.

"Ouch!" She leaned down and rubbed the shin she cracked on a crate. Reaching into her vest, she extracted her survival tin and plucked the LED flashlight from the contents. The beam was small but enough to help her navigate the darkness and find the lantern inside the artifact tent. She lit the kerosene lamp and walked through the tables and shelves of artifacts in various conditions. One wall held the pieces with minimal damage while stone and pottery shards lie scattered across tables waiting to be pieced together.

The stone of interest to her leaned against the end of a table. It appeared that once Virgil had recognized its significance, he ordered the cleaning halted. Only the top line of characters had been brushed clean. And not completely.

Retracing her steps, she found a tool caddy and returned to the stone. Isabella knelt in front of the three-foot by two-foot, flat stone about eight inches thick. The top had a corner missing and jagged edges poked into the dirt. Excitement skittered up her back and tingled down her arms. This carved storyboard would help her claim the money she desperately needed.

She selected a soft bristled brush and finished exposing the top row of glyphs. Her fingers glided over the rough sandstone, dipping into the etchings, feeling the bumps, grooves, and indentions. She sat back and pulled out her journal. The carvings on the stone in the settlement were a close replica to those on this stone. She replaced the journal and stilled her shaking hands. This was a yet undiscovered Mayan ceremony. Her heart beat with anticipation of what it would reveal.

Isabella picked up a sturdy brush and carefully swept away the years of soil encrusted on the second row of glyphs. When images started to appear, she switched to a softer bristle brush and worked to expose the intricately carved glyphs. The second row of carvings stared back at her when cooler air stirred around her.

"I thought they exaggerated about you staying up for days when working on a project."

Tino's seductive whisper wrapped around her; arousing her body and dragging her mind away from the markings.

"My mind won't rest when I'm onto something, so my body suffers." She stretched her arms above her head and glanced over her shoulder. The shadow of whisker stubble no longer darkened his face. He'd shaved. She sniffed. And cleaned up. Her body itched from sweat and mosquito repellant. She had to give off a body odor as well. Her deodorant couldn't have held out this long.

"You should take a break, refresh yourself with a shower, and then come for a walk. It will soon be time for the others to rise for the day." He held out a hand.

She'd been working that long on this one row? Isabella glanced at the stone and then at his hand. He was right. A shower would do her some good. Her hand slipped into his comfortably. He drew her to her feet and caught the lantern with his other hand.

"I already have your pack in the shower tent." He glanced over his shoulder as he led her into the moonlight.

"Didn't someone make a comment about your being in my tent?" She found his chivalry enchanting, though a bit old-fashioned.

"Everyone is asleep." They crossed to the small tent with a barrel above it at the back of the compound. "Be sure to tuck the mosquito netting around the enclosure so you do not get any bites while showering." He handed her the lantern and held the tent flap open.

She stopped and looked into his eyes. "You'll be here when I get out?"

He nodded and his gaze traveled from her eyes to her mouth.

His heated perusal escalated her temperature and raced her heart. Why did he look at her like that? Did he expect her to swoon and dive into his arms? She wanted to, but the statistics for their relationship didn't add up.

Isabella ducked into the tent. She found a hook by the shower curtain and hung the lantern. After acquainting herself with the layout, finding her backpack, and laying out her clothing and toiletries, she

94

quickly stripped and ducked through the mosquito netting and shower curtain. The water was lukewarm, captured in a large barrel, and gravity fed through a hose to the nozzle above her head. She lathered up her hair, inhaling the spicy scent of her shampoo. She didn't apply makeup or go to extremes to remove hair, but she did like wearing exotic scents.

Dried and clothed, she hurried out of the tent and bumped into Tino's back. A laugh bubbled in her throat at the way he stood guard, arms crossed and feet braced shoulder width apart.

"We will drop your pack in your tent and take that walk." His low voice rumbled near her ear as he took her by the arm.

"Why do we need to go for a walk when everyone is asleep?" she whispered back.

"Everyone may not be asleep. In the jungle, we will know if someone is getting close enough to hear."

His comment started her thoughts bounding. What didn't he want heard? Was he after all an organ trafficker? Every bone in her body said to trust him. It was her head that balked.

At her tent, he relieved her of her bag and tossed it into the tent.

"Why do we have to go in the jungle?" She crossed her arms to take a firm stand.

Tino faced her. "Are you afraid of going into the jungle in the dark?"

"No."

He grasped her hands, unfolding her arms. "Then it is me you fear." He sighed deeply and tsked. "If I had wished to rob you of your valuables or organs I would have done so before showing up at this dig with you. Come." He dropped one hand and led her past her tent, and his, straight into the jungle. The ground cover was denser on the edge of the clearing as if protecting the tell where the Mayan chambers had been hidden for so many years.

After several minutes of pushing through vines and dodging trees, he drew her to sit on a downed tree.

"Why all this cloak and dagger stuff? The people at the dig are my friends." Her hand remained clasped in Tino's. His knees pressed against hers. The heat of the contact crept up her leg and ignited a slow burn in her pelvic region. She squirmed. Why did this man affect her this way?

95

"Not everyone at the dig is your friend. Or anyone's friend." Tino squeezed her hands. "Dr. Martin has asked me to stay at the dig until he can get men in to keep watch at night."

"I don't understand. Why would Virgil need guards? Are the artifacts valuable?"

"I overheard Walsh and Dr. Martin arguing. The narcos, drug traffickers, want Dr. Martin to pay them to leave him alone. Your friend does not believe in paying extortion."

She'd never heard of this before. But then, she'd never worked a dig anywhere other than the U.S. "That sounds like Virgil." She peered through the dark, trying to see Tino's face. "What will happen?"

"The narcos could attempt to take some of the artifacts as payment. Walsh said they could turn the government against the dig and anyone who is working here."

"Will they resort to violence?" Her body shivered at the thought.

"Not at first, but who knows." His arms wrapped around her, drawing her against his strength. Mosquitoes buzzed close to her ear.

Tino released her and something drifted down over her head, flowing around her body. She ran her hands over the material. A mosquito net.

"How?"

"I figured after you showered you would not have any repellant on." He sniffed. "You smell much better than DEET."

The fact that he noticed and liked her spicy scent tickled her insides. "Thank you. You don't smell half bad yourself." A clean masculine scent had delighted her senses the minute he escorted her from the artifact tent.

"I will go to the settlement tomorrow to gather the rest of my gear. With Dr. Martin asking me to remain at the dig, I will make my base camp here." He placed a hand on either side of her face. "I want you to be careful. Do not go into the jungle and stay close to the dig."

"Are you that fearful of the narcos?" She didn't like the idea of his traveling alone if the drug traffickers were that dangerous.

He drew her up, brushing his lips against hers and sending her thoughts to much pleasanter things.

"I am only fearful for you." His words vibrated against her mouth.

He deepened the kiss, seducing her tongue, taking her breath, and dismissing anything other than the pleasure of his touch.

His lips hovered over hers. "Promise me you will stay in the compound."

His voice drifted in and out of her dazed state. She nodded and leaned closer for another kiss.

He shifted, refusing her overture. His lips hovered over hers. "Say it."

Her mouth, plump and tingling from his kisses, grieved for more. "What? Say what?"

"That you will stay in the camp while I am gone."

"I'll stay." She craved his mouth upon hers. The intensity of her need both shocked and exhilarated. But she wouldn't beg even though her body was pleading with her mind.

He chuckled and seduced her mouth, numbing her body, lighting her mind with sparks, and heating her blood.

His hands slid down her neck, thumbs pressing slighting under her jaw, directing her head to another angle. The mating of their tongues fired shock waves to her toes. Her hands kneaded the pectorals underneath his shirt. She ached to touch his skin. Sliding her fingers between the buttons, she edged her finger tips in to touch the sprinkling of hair on his chest and feel the heat of his skin.

He growled and ripped his mouth from hers, sucking and dropping kisses down her neck as his hands kneaded her sides and back.

Sensations exploded, giving way to laughter and moans of pleasure. She'd never felt so liberated.

"Ezzabella, you are more enticing than any woman I have ever held in my arms."

Tino's declaration stunned her. She pulled back, aching to remain in his arms but needing to know what he meant. "You've been in the jungle a long time. You're needy." She had to justify his declaration because to believe he meant it could leave her heartbroken.

"No. It is true. I have had many women cross my path. And you are completely different—innocent and smart. The timing is all wrong. But believe me—you are special and I promise I will keep you safe."

Safe? She opened her mouth to ask what he meant—

The fierce cry of a howler monkey pierced the air, tingling her neck hairs. Isabella gripped Tino tighter.

"We must get back to the compound before the others rise and see us coming out of the jungle." He kissed her nose. "It would be bad for your reputation."

The netting slithered up her body, taking with it the magic of the moments they kissed and allowing the threat of reality to seep in.

"You'll be careful tomorrow, I mean today, going to the settlement?" The thought of harm coming to Tino when she still had so much to learn about him chilled her body.

"I will return before dark. Do not worry." Tino grasped Isabella's hand. He had warned her, and now he had to trust she would keep herself safe. "Stay in the compound and tell no one about our talk. Panic would be a bad thing. If the others try to leave the jungle in a hurry, they could lose their lives."

She yanked on his hand.

He stopped and peered through the growing daylight at her worried face.

"Do you truly believe the danger is that real?" Her whispered words, laced with fear, stabbed at his conscience.

"There is always a threat in the jungle. That the narcos are so near doubles the danger." His arms ached to draw her close and promise to keep her safe, but he couldn't. He'd gone too far this night with their intimacy. It would be best for them both if he went to the settlement and set out through the jungle tracking the narcos he was paid to find. But that wouldn't keep the people of the dig safe.

"Come, you must sneak into your tent from the back." He tugged on the hand he still held, drawing her along the path.

"Why must I sneak in the back? I'm a grown woman and can come and go as I please. They'll see I've been working in the artifact tent."

A few more meters and they'd step into the open behind his tent. He stopped, releasing her hand. "You are right. Continue on alone and do whatever you wish."

Her eyes searched his face. "I've injured your pride, haven't I?"

She had crushed his pride, but he wouldn't let her know. He puffed his chest and raised an eyebrow. "*Mi pichón*, you have not wounded my pride. I was merely protecting you. But I have learned you do not need protecting. Take care." He waved her on even as his gut told him he wouldn't rest until she was safely back in the United States.

Isabella's full lips opened as she studied him, her head canted to one side.

His body burned to drag her against him and savor those enchanting lips again, but his mind, though low on sleep, screamed at him to get away and do his job.

Tino stepped into the tangle of foliage and made his way perpendicular to her. Minutes passed before he heard the rustle of Isabella moving toward the compound. He followed at a distance, peeking around a tree as she entered the open area. Her feet stalled, and she spun back to the forest, her eyes searching.

She squared her shoulders and marched to the opening of her tent, ducking inside.

Ten minutes later, Tino sauntered out of the forest to his tent and emptied everything but his revolver, rifle, ammunition, binoculars, and water out of his pack. He strapped the pack on and headed in search of Martin.

Dr. Martin and several others were in the mess tent. Some of the tension that pulled at his muscles and throbbed in his head subsided when he didn't see Isabella in the tent. He didn't need her looking doe-eyed at him. He'd been stupid to drag her into the jungle and kiss her. And completely out of control. He grimaced. The kissing had not been part of his plan. He had wanted to warn her. *Augustino, you can lie to Isabella and everyone else but not to yourself.*

He shrugged out of his pack and wiped a hand across his face. Kissing had crossed his mind when he'd told her he would come get her last night. It had also been on his mind as he watched her meticulously clean the stone and trace the carvings with her fingers. But it had to stop. To continue would not be good for him or her.

"Guide, I'm surprised to see you still here."

Walsh's booming voice and condescending nature grated on Tino's nerves.

"Rupert, I've asked him to stay until you follow through." Martin indicated a seat across from him.

Anger flared in Walsh's eyes and his mouth formed a tight-lipped line. The Englishman wasn't happy with the information. Why didn't he want someone not engrossed in the dig hanging around? Perhaps because they would notice his absences?

Tino took the offered spot on the bench and studied the people seated at the tables. The woman who followed Martin around like a puppy sat beside him, Walsh and two of his British helpers, along with Isabella's friend and another woman sat at an adjacent table. It was obvious by their conversations and casualness Martin hadn't told any of them about the narcos's threats. Interesting.

"I will go to the settlement today to bring back the rest of my supplies," Tino said, leaning back as the cook placed a steaming plate of scrambled eggs and fruit in front of him. "*Gracias.*"

"I would think a tracker and guide wouldn't need that many supplies. What could you possibly need that we don't have here?" Walsh narrowed his eyes, studying him.

"I do not wish to impose. I was paid only to bring Dr. Mumphrey, no? After today, I will eat my own rations." Tino dug into the eggs. The creamy texture and flavor surpassed the dried food he would be eating to stay undercover.

"That's so admirable." Walsh rolled his eyes. "I'd think one of your bloody lot would jump at the chance to siphon off others."

Tino swallowed the fury gurgling in his throat. "You, Professor Walsh, do not know the likes of me." Rage curled in his gut. How did this pompous *pendejo* deal with narcos when he believed himself so superior to others?

"Walsh, back off." Martin glared at the British professor. "Guide, you're welcome to eat in the mess tent any time you want and use the facilities. It's the least I can do." He stopped short of saying any more.

Tino glanced round the table. No one appeared offended by Walsh or surprised by Martin. Apparently, Walsh's rudeness was as normal as Martin's hospitality. He'd take great pride in knocking the British professor down a notch a two. Martin was a mystery, asking for help, but refusing to tell anyone they were in danger.

Both men required his surveillance: Walsh to lead him to the narcos, and Martin to decipher his relationship with Isabella.

Chapter Eleven

The afternoon heat and lack of sleep caught up to Isabella. Her head bobbed on her shoulders and her sight blurred as she brushed at another line of characters on the stone. Half the story stood out in stark relief above the still dirt-encrusted lower half of the tablet. The intricate carvings, many she knew, told a story of a moon and how—she couldn't decipher the name—traveled a great distance to hold the moon and discover its power.

"Take a break." Virgil's voice broke into her semi-consciousness.

"Yes. I do need one. I worked on this late last night and early this morning." Isabella set the tools aside and allowed Virgil to help her stand. She wobbled a moment, dizziness and fatigue joining forces. Virgil caught her in his arms. Arms she'd known for years; yet, they felt more foreign to her than Tino's strong, youthful arms.

Isabella shifted out of Virgil's embrace as Jaycee lugged in a bucket of cleaned artifacts. The student had wandered in and out all morning, taking note of everything Isabella did.

"Tell me what you've discovered so far." Virgil studied the stone.

Isabella squatted slowly and bounced twice to stretch the calf muscles bunching in protest. Tracing a carved indention with the pad of her finger, she said, "This is the symbol of the moon. The story on this stone is about this moon and the people who came from a great distance to hold its power." She glanced up at Virgil. "*Ch'ujuña* means moon in Cholan. I'm not sure how it all fits together. I'm going to take a nap then check my reference notes." Her gaze returned to the carvings, her mind trying to remember where she'd seen these before and what they meant. "I may need to contact the university for more information, too."

"I'm sure that guide would be willing to take you back to Saxyache to contact your school."

Jaycee's haughty intonation referring to 'that guide' dug into Isabella's skin like a thorn.

"I'm sure Tino would be more than willing. I'd enjoy his company." Isabella rose slowly to avoid another dizzy spell. "If I'm not up by dinner, wake me." She'd start sleeping during the heat of the day and work at night. Even with both flaps open on the tent there was poor ventilation. The moist, hot air pressed around her like a smothering blanket, making it hard to breathe and baking her body.

"I will. Sleep well." He leaned toward her, his lips pursed to buzz her cheek. Jaycee's loud throat clearing stopped him short.

Isabella was thankful Jaycee's jealousy stopped Virgil from kissing her. His unusual amorous attentions had become creepy. She didn't remember him always reaching for her or attempting to kiss her. His new behavior caused a nauseous roll in her midsection. She wanted to get away and think. Stepping into the bright light of afternoon, the blast of tropical light quickly darkened as a huge shadow spread over the compound. Dark gray clouds swooped in front of the sun, converging overhead for the usual afternoon rain. The reprieve from the merciless sun and the refreshing rain were welcome. She ducked into her tent as the first drops pelted the canvas. Stripped down to her tank top and panties, she lowered the mosquito netting over her bed, closed her eyes, and drifted off to the cadence of the rain.

~*~

Tino straightened his pack for the hundredth time. In his haste to return to the dig, he'd packed the bag unevenly. The weight pulling on one side annoyed him as much as his infatuation with the skinny doctor. He stopped, dropped his burden, and untied the flap. One by one he removed the items, relocating them to redistribute the weight.

The murmur of deep voices drifted through the silence of the forest. He scanned the area to make sure none of his belongings remained on the ground and hurried off the trail, hiding behind a large fern.

Walsh and two narcos in fatigues, toting AK-47 assault rifles, came into view. The coloring and features of the men labeled them ladinos. Like most narcos in Guatemala, they weren't indigenous natives. The large land owners were also seldom full natives. They had Spanish roots and more education, and while they married Maya women, they still caused problems with the Mayas. His first excursion into this region he'd been pleasantly surprised by the Maya's generosity. His ladino features gave him the appearance of their oppressors, but they'd quickly recognized he wasn't Guatemalan. His dialect had set him apart from the upper-class Guatemalan and won him respect.

Snippets of Spanish and English drifted to where he hid.

"...items will be bloody ready." Walsh's booming Brit voice was unmistakable.

"Don Miguel is expecting...."

"He'll have better..."

They continued down the trail toward the settlement.

Tino remained hidden for fifteen minutes, making sure they didn't backtrack. How did Walsh get away from the dig every day to meet with the narcos? What were the "items?" He hadn't heard drugs called items before. Merchandise or product, but never items.

He opened his pack, dug through his supplies, and extracted a small receiver from an apparatus that resembled a tracking device. Using the GPS on his watch, he pointed the antennae toward the satellite and dialed in the secure frequency.

The crackle of the radio reverberated in his ear buds.

"Konstantine. Over."

He listened, waited.

"Ginger. Why are you contacting me? Over." The familiar female voice relieved him.

"Need background on Rupert Walsh, professor of archeology, British. Virgil Martin, Ph.D in archeology, United States. Don Miguel, Guatemalan, presumably Petén. Over."

"Contact me in twenty-four. Over."

"Why so long, *mi amor*? Over."

"You aren't the only agent I'm helping. Over." Her teasing voice lightened the situation.

"Ah, *mi amor*, you have broken my heart. Over." He'd met Ginger during training. Her robust, fifty-something figure and orange box-dyed hair made her hard to forget.

"Same time tomorrow. Out." The connection ended.

In his line of work, Ginger was often the only person he talked to for weeks at a time besides drug traffickers. Over the last two years, they had become long-distance friends, if only in a business capacity.

Right now, he wanted to get back to the dig and find out where Walsh was supposed to be and what his job at the site entailed. As easily as the professor met up with the narcos, they had to have a base camp not far from the dig. Why? And most importantly, where? He didn't want to contemplate what could happen to an unsuspecting worker at the dig, should wander off and land in the middle of the narco's camp. Tonight, he'd do reconnaissance and find the exact location.

~*~

Isabella woke feeling refreshed. She dressed and stepped out of her tent as Tino turned from talking to one of the British students.

His blue eyes crinkled at the edges and a warm smile curved his lips. Lips that had kissed her with passion early this morning. His words had played in her head while she slept. Could she believe he really cared for her and wasn't toying with her inexperience in matters of men and women?

"Did you retrieve your things from the settlement?" she asked, walking toward him.

"*Sí*, I have all my belongings." He stopped in front of her, close enough to carry on an intimate conversation. "You look rested."

"I just woke from a wonderful nap. I've decided to sleep in the afternoon and work in the cool of the evening and mornings."

His lips curved into an even more devastating smile and his eyes sparked with desire.

"*Mi pichón*, are you inviting me to visit you each evening?"

The innuendo in his voice and desire in his eyes jolted her libido and snagged her virgin body like a sexual magnet. Heat scorched from her toes to the tip of her ears. She had no doubt from his searing kisses, he would be a great lover.

"We'll have to wait and see, won't we?" Flirting with him was dangerous, but she loved the freedom she found in bantering with Tino.

"I will take that as an invitation." He winked.

Her insides tumbled with elation and nerves.

"There you are."

Virgil's voice broke into her sinful fantasy involving her and Tino entwined like the vines she'd hacked at in the jungle.

"You asked me to get you up for dinner." His gaze landed on Tino. "I trust you retrieved your supplies. You're still more than welcome to eat with us." He cleared his throat. "It's the least I can do considering."

"*Gracias*, doctor, I would enjoy sampling more of your cook's food. He is an interesting fellow."

The undercurrent between the two men rippled with distrust and animosity. However, they seemed to have bonded over something mutual. She believed it was keeping the camp safe. When they each grasped one of her elbows, she realized their mutual bond—her.

Isabella grinned and enjoyed the attention. There had never been a time in her life when she'd felt wanted. Having the two men use her like a rope in a tug of war would get old after a while, but for now, she'd bask in the warmth of their attention. It would be all too fleeting. Tino would move on any day, and once she and Virgil deciphered the ceremony, he'd be back to digging up artifacts.

Mosquito netting draped the opening of the mess tent. Virgil pulled it to the side and she entered, followed by Tino. Isabella scanned the interior. Counting twenty heads, the number added up to everyone being present. Heat from the cooking and sweating bodies made the tent interior hotter than a sauna and just as moist.

Tino directed her to one of the smaller tables. Before she could sit, Pedro placed a cool glass of juice on the table.

"*Gracias*. Dinner smells delicious." She smiled at the cook.

"I have prepared roast *pecari*." He licked his lips. "It is *bueno*."

Isabella faced Tino who sat beside her. "*¿Pecari?*"

"They are kind of like domestic pigs only they are wild, smaller, and without snouts." He guzzled down the juice Pedro had placed in front of her.

"I was looking forward to drinking that." She eyed the empty glass still in Tino's hand.

"Save my seat. I will get you more." Tino rose with her glass and headed to the containers of drinks laid out on a table to one side of the cooking station.

"How much do you know about this guide?"

Virgil's comment twisted her in her chair. She'd been so engrossed in the cook and then Tino, she'd forgotten Virgil had entered the tent with them. Scanning the tables, she found Jaycee once again staring daggers.

"He tags wild cats for the government besides being a guide, and he's skilled in jungle travel." She slid her gaze from Jaycee and back to Virgil. She'd have to have a talk with Jaycee and let her know Virgil was all hers.

Virgil shook his head. "He isn't what he seems."

She stared into his weathered but still handsome face. He'd noticed Tino's dual personalities as well. "What do you mean?"

"Juan wouldn't hand over a job I gave him to just anyone. Something isn't right. And Kosta agreed to stay without my offering him money. Every person in this damn country has his hand out, government included. He's up to something. I don't want you to get messed up in whatever he's doing." Virgil straightened and smiled at Pedro as the cook placed bowls of food on the table in front of them, family style.

"I'm glad you found such a good cook, Virgil. The ranks shouldn't get unruly when their bellies are filled this well." Isabella believed in giving credit where due.

Pedro flashed a toothy smile.

"I'll probably have trouble sending them home when their tour is up." Virgil laughed.

Tino had watched the earnest conversation between Isabella and Martin while filling the cups. He returned to the table placing a glass of juice in front of Isabella and one in front of his plate. Taking a cue from Martin's last comment, he asked, "How long will you be here?"

Isabella raised the juice to her lips. "*Gracias*," slipped through her sweet lips before she took a drink.

¡Coño! He had to forget her wide, full mouth on his if he planned to accomplish his mission.

"Ahem."

Tino's gaze snapped from Isabella to the stern face of Doctor Martin.

"I could ask you the same thing. How long will you be in the area?" The doctor's question was hard edged and his stare held suspicion.

"Here the two days you requested. A week along the Usumacinta. If I do not find a trail or sign of the cats, I will move on." He shrugged as if Martin's not answering his question didn't matter and he wasn't offended by the man's questions. He would show Isabella he was the bigger man.

"How long do you think you'll be here?" Isabella asked Martin.

Tino smiled inwardly. The man would be rude not to answer his protégée.

"That depends on how much we find that gives us insight into the people who lived here and how long the Guatemalan government allows us to stay." The man smiled at Isabella and dug into his food, dropping the subject.

Isabella chewed a couple of bites, took a drink then looked at Martin. "When I've been at other digs, the workers came and went. Is that going to happen here or is everyone here for the long haul?"

Irritation flickered in the doctor's eyes before he wiped his mouth with a cloth and faced Isabella.

"Professor Walsh, Eunice, Pedro, and I are the only people who will remain until I say we are finished." Martin peered around the room. "And the few locals who are helping. They'll be here until we leave or they need to go."

Tino had a pretty good idea of who was who from the conversations he'd had with most of the workers. He scanned the tent. "Is everyone here right now?" Walsh sat at a table with a couple of the local workers. For once his British voice didn't boom across the room.

Martin searched the room and nodded. "It appears so."

Now would be a perfect time for someone to sneak in and cause havoc or steal artifacts. He wouldn't eat when the whole camp did; instead he would stand watch. This was his first encounter with archeologists. They were too trusting. Just because artifacts had remained undisturbed for hundreds of years, did not mean no one besides scientists wanted them.

The trafficking of artifacts had become a big enterprise in Central and South American countries. Another faction he dealt with in conjunction with drugs. There were park guards stationed throughout the parks to deter artifact stealing, but he'd yet to see one in this area. *Ch'ujuña* was such a new dig it hadn't made it on any of the tours. Its small size and poor funding, no doubt, led the government officials to believe little would come of it. They would pad their pockets with the proper fees and paperwork and forget to send protection from the park guards.

"Tino? Tino, I'm anxious to hear your answer, too?" Isabella nudged him with her shoulder.

He stared into her eyes. Who asked him what? "I am sorry. I dozed off with my eyes open." Tino tilted his lips into a roguish smile. "I was preoccupied last night and missed *siesta* earlier."

Isabella's cheeks deepened to a bright red. Her eyes glistened with mischief. Ahh, she is one magnificent *señorita*.

"Virgil asked you how long you've been a guide and tracker." Her right eyebrow peaked provocatively waiting for his answer.

"In Guatemala, three years. Before that I was an assistant on the Amazon." The truth was a little different, but if anyone investigated his past, it fit Tino Kosta's history.

"How did you get from the Amazon to Guatemala?" Martin asked, shoving his finished plate away.

Tino took a bite of pecarí, chewed, swallowed, and answered. "I have always wanted to see the United States, no? As a boy *mi abuela*, grandmother, spoke of her grandparents on her mother's side traveling to the United States and no one has heard from them since. I have always dreamed of finding out what happened for my *abuela*. I started working my way toward the United States and ran out of money here."

"What a wonderful gift. I can help, I have contacts—"

Tino cut off Isabella with a hand on hers. "By the time I made it into Guatemala, *mi aubela*, had left us, and I had run out of money. The only trade I know is tracking and guiding." He shrugged. Isabella's small hand turned, clasping his.

"I'm sorry to hear about your *abuela*. I would still be honored to help you find your great-great-grandparents. I'm sure the rest of your family would like to know what happened to them."

There is no one left. The words stuck in his throat. Her large caring eyes and warm smile spun his thoughts in a million directions.

He wanted to tell her the truth, but Tino Kosta had no living relatives. Augustino Konstantine died in the eyes of his country when his father fled Venezuela in '84 during the university riots. No longer able to contain his anger at what the Venezuelan government was doing to its people, his father slipped out of the country with his family to keep them alive. Tino hissed disgust out between his teeth and shoved his anger back where it belonged—in the graves with his family.

"When I've saved enough to move on, I will continue my search. I would be pleased to accept your help when I set foot in your country." He included Martin in the comment, but he had no intention of ever seeking the man. His interest only encompassed Isabella.

"I love a good puzzle. It will be fun helping you." Isabella refilled her plate with a spoonful of every food on the table. "I missed lunch." She giggled, pushed her glasses tighter on her nose, and continued eating.

Tino glanced at Martin. The man watched Isabella eat with a hunger in his eyes that had nothing to do with a platonic relationship. Jealousy smoldered in his gut and scorched up his spine, singeing the hair on the nape of his neck. The thought of the two being intimate burned his throat with rancid bile.

He peered at Isabella. She chewed her food, eyes closed, enjoying the delicious fare. He would bet his *abuela's* Bible Isabella didn't have a clue the doctor harbored lecherous thoughts. If he brought it up, she'd call him a liar. If she discovered it on her own, he would remain in her favor.

Tino pushed back from the table. The motion captured Isabella's attention. Her eyes opened and she put down her fork.

"Are you leaving?"

"I did not get a *siesta*." He didn't have to fake a yawn. "I am turning in early and will take a turn around the compound later tonight." He added the last for the benefit of the man on the other side of her. After all, he was allowed to remain at the compound by keeping an eye on things.

Isabella's eyes sparkled and she winked. She wouldn't make a good spy. Their clandestine meeting would soon be all over the camp if anyone glanced at her face at this moment.

"Good," Martin lowered his voice and glanced at the people nearby. "I don't think we have anything to worry about, but I don't want to arouse any fear if we can help it."

Isabella spun in her seat. Tino only witnessed the back of her head as she leaned closer to Martin. He couldn't watch her leaning into the man. He scanned the room and found one of the female interns staring daggers at the couple.

Witnessing the woman's obvious hatred, he decided to make sure the camp knew he and Isabella were intimate. That would possibly get Martin to leave her alone and save her from whatever vicious thoughts the intern might have in mind.

Chapter Twelve

Isabella stretched her back and unfolded her legs. She'd worked on the stone for three hours and had dislodged the worst of the centuries old dirt from the carvings. The majority of the glyphs were in excellent condition; if she only knew more about the code. That was why Virgil had called her. He hadn't the time to research the origins while running the dig and knew she couldn't leave any puzzle unsolved.

She blew out a huge, disgusted sigh and stared at the drawings. The curve and slant of the carvings was familiar. In the back of her mind she reconstructed why it was familiar.

A cool breeze rippled across her sweaty skin causing her to shudder. Would tonight bring a blessing of cooler air? Another cool puff fluttered the hair on her neck. She peered over her shoulder. A face appeared mere inches from hers, blurred in the shadow of her body. Her throat constricted, emitting a squeak.

"Shh... *Mi pichón*, I will not harm you."

Tino's soft, melodic voice hurtled her racing heart from a tempo of jarring fear to elation. His arms wrapped around her, drawing her against his hard body.

"Do you wish the same as last night? A shower and a walk in the jungle?"

"Yes. The heat and humidity are stifling tonight." She'd come close to removing her vest earlier as the heat baked her skin and the humidity trickled down her neck but remembering the reason Virgil asked Tino to remain at the dig, she kept the garment firmly buttoned.

He rose, drawing her to her feet. Tino pulled her into his arms and nibbled on her lips. She drew back, fighting the urge to succumb to his wishes. It was obvious he thought nothing of kissing her freely. She wasn't willing to acquiesce.

"Your attention is exhilarating, but I'd like to take things slower." She enjoyed his affection but refused to induce Virgil's anger and lose her chance at the money.

"Slower or do you fear someone will see us together?" He leaned back, his eyes black as the darkness behind him. A faint glow from the lantern revealed his features in sepia.

"Both. As much as I want to believe you, your infatuation with me doesn't add up. And I don't want to lose anyone's respect." The minute the words slipped out her lips, they hung in the air like a wall between them.

Tino released her and stepped back. "I see. A doctor of anthropology cannot be intimate with a lowly ladino guide."

"No. That's not how I feel, I just…" Shamutz. "I don't care if you're a guide. You show more sophistication than half of the nerdy archeologists I've encountered. And your attention has gone to my head. But you'll move on, as will I, and I can't afford to have people twice my age who are the pillars of the archeological an anthropology society have any more reasons to turn their noses up at me than they already do." She grasped his arm. "Do you understand? It's not your position. It would be my cavorting with anyone that would raise eyebrows."

He nodded curtly and picked up the lantern.

"Thank you." She stopped him with a tug on his shirt. "You have allowed me to feel pretty and flirty. For that I will be forever grateful and your friend. But I've spent the last nine years proving to people I belong in this profession, and I can't allow anything to interfere." She placed a finger on his lips. "Even your wonderful kisses."

"We will remain discreet. Your things are in the shower tent."

Tino snuffed out the lantern, and they exited the tent, stepping into the light of a half moon. Nocturnal chattering and rustling spilled into the compound from the forest around them.

"I'll only be a few minutes." Isabella ducked into the shower tent, excited to have confronted Tino with her fears and expectations of their friendship.

Tino stared at the shadow alongside Walsh's tent. The darkness undulated and grew, unlike the staid darkness around the other enclosures. He walked casually toward his tent and circled around to a position between the professor's tent and the jungle. Within minutes, the British archeologist slithered from the shadow and hurried into the jungle.

Where was the man going at this time of night? Tino glanced at the shower tent. Isabella was a nice distraction, but he must focus on his mission—to stop drug trafficking. The muted shadows of night wrapped around him as he entered the jungle. Steady rustling to his left gave away Walsh's direction of travel. Tino followed, silently sliding between the foliage and placing his feet slow and deliberate. Monkeys chattered and played overhead masking the sound of the professor's movement through the forest.

Tino strained to hear at ground level and kept a steady forward motion. Voices registered and he stopped to reconnoiter their distance and direction. Using their conversation as a beacon, Tino found Walsh and another man standing in front of a cave entrance.

Two men dressed in fatigues and cradling AK 47s stood guard at the mouth of the cave. Narcos. Was this their base camp? Tino set the coordinates on his GPS and started to his left, making a wide circle around the entrance and searching for another entry or their mode of transportation. They couldn't move large quantities of drugs without the aid of motorized vehicles.

Two hours later, tired and his legs aching with fatigue from the circles and crisscross patterns he'd trekked through the thick vegetation, he still hadn't found a means of transportation. Walsh shook hands with the man and headed back in the direction of the dig.

Frustrated, Tino wavered between following the professor and hanging out close to the cave. This was his first substantial lead on the traffickers. As much as he didn't trust Walsh, he saw more to gain by inching as close to the cave as he could to see what, if anything, the guards might divulge in their conversations.

~*~

Isabella hurried out of the shower tent, clean and refreshed. The warm, humid night air clung to her skin instantly erasing her rejuvenation. She searched the area for Tino and found only darkness and solitude. Why had he left? Had her words hurt him deeper than she thought? She crossed the compound to his tent. Without a word, she whisked aside the flap and dropped to her knees to enter.

The small space held only his sleeping gear and his backpack. No Tino. Could she find the place he took her to last night? Maybe he waited there. She left the tent and stared into the dark jungle. A shiver vibrated her skin. There wasn't a clue to the path they'd taken the night before. Sighing, she resolved to return to work. If Tino wished to see her, he'd know where to find her.

She entered the artifact tent and stopped. Darkness, murky and cloying, met her. What had Tino done with the lantern she'd used earlier? She replayed Tino's motions of extinguishing the flame as they exited the tent. She groped first to the left and then the right of the opening until her hand smacked into the still warm chimney of the lantern. One step out into the moonlight aided her relighting the lantern with matches from her vest.

Stepping back inside the tent, she scanned the interior. Something wasn't right. The dark shapes and undulating shadows of the pieces in the lantern light replayed in her mind. She took her time walking around each table and scanning the contents of each shelf. She stopped at a table and reflected on the shadow. There had been a tall object on this table before. An urn Eunice planned to photograph tomorrow—well, technically today—was missing.

Unease swirled in her stomach. Who came in here after she left? Or were they in here the whole time waiting for her to leave? The thought that someone other than the workers lurked in the shadows of the tent shoved her unease up a rung to distress. Her breathing accelerated. Her heart boomed in her chest as if she ran for her life.

Who? Why? Should she wake Virgil? Where was Tino? Her heart jerked to a stop and her blood iced. Had he stolen the urn? Did he use her for access to collectable artifacts?

Nausea replaced her distress. She should have known he was only coming on to her to get close to the artifacts. Shamutz! Thumping her forehead with her palm, she cursed her naïveté and virginal body. She stomped to the stone and sat cross-legged in front of it. So stupid! She wasn't going to wake Virgil in the middle of the night to inform him she'd brought a thief into the compound. Stupidity and anger swirled in her head and belly making her nauseous.

The stone stood solid in front of her. Tears, burning in her eyes, blurred the markings. Lantern light flickered the images. The caricatures undulated and danced in her vision, drawing her deeper into the story and freeing her mind from the constraints of academia. As she'd always known, the ancient stories carved into the stone held no lies and could be trusted. Distractions like the dishonest guide had to stop. Her career depended on it.

She pulled out her journal and compared the glyphs on the stone in the village to this one. Pushing her glasses up on her nose, she leaned closer. The thrill of discovering a clue tingled the hair on her scalp. "They were carved by the same person!" The indentions, flourishes, and small details were identical, making the stones one story. The characters she didn't know, she added to her journal and circled. She'd research those back in her tent. Crosschecking with the glossary she'd built in the back of her journal over the years, she painstakingly deciphered the glyphs she could with her research.

Excitement bubbled in her chest as she slowly made sense of the lines. She stretched her arms above her head, relieving her hunched back.

"Someone... I have to figure out this name." She fingered each carving and translated the ones she knew. "Came seeking the moon treasure... I can't decipher this character..."

A soft thud behind her ripped Isabella's attention from the stone. Was that no account Tino coming back to steal more? She slipped her journal into an inside vest pocket and stood, pivoting toward the sound.

"Dr. Mumphrey, I see you are living up to Virgil's high regard for you." Professor Walsh's voice carried to her ears out of the darkness.

"Professor. What are you doing in the artifact tent so late?" She checked her watch. "Or I should say so early?" His stealthy approach triggered her self-protection nerve. Isabella set her feet in an offensive stance and shook her tense muscles loose. She couldn't throw a kick if her body bunched in knots.

"I went to the loo and spotted the light on in here. Thought I'd better check to make sure no one left a lantern on. It would be a bloody shame to have all this charred from a fire after it survived so many centuries." He walked into the light of the lantern. Fully clothed.

Did one dress completely when using the facilities at night? She didn't. Maybe it was some kind of British prudishness. She'd ask the interns Professor Walsh had brought with him.

"If you see a light on in here in the future you can rest assured it's me. I work best in solitude and the less stifling heat of night." She moved to return to her work, believing he would take the hint.

The scent of his rancid cigar breath and tangy sweat crept into her space.

"I've been helpful with Mayan glyphs before."

"When I get stuck, I'll ask for help. Right now, I'm doing fine." She backed away from the man and the lantern light. His eyes glowed as they devoured the stone she'd been studying.

Could he know the glyphs she didn't? His brow wrinkled in a frown as he continued to study the carvings. He was stumped on some as well. Elation fluttered in her chest. She and Virgil would decipher the glyphs and be paid, not Walsh.

"Professor, doctor, have you discovered the mystery behind these carvings?"

Tino's voice started her heart pattering until she remembered the missing urn. She glanced at Professor Walsh. Annoyance and anger darkened his face.

Isabella shoved her fists on her hips and spun toward the thief in guide's clothing. She started to open her mouth, when the professor kicked over the lantern, snuffing the light.

"Oomph." A body ran into hers, heavy groping hands and rancid breath accosted her.

"Hey! Get your hands—" A wide palm slapped over her mouth. Judging his position, she brought up a knee and grimaced at the soft connection.

Walsh swore and crumpled to the ground.

"Ezzabella?" Tino's concern riveted her attention to his voice moments before his arms banded around her. He drew her away from the moaning, cursing body at her feet.

"Come with me," Tino's soft whisper warmed her ear. He grasped her hand and led her into the moonlight, across the compound, and directly into her tent. Inside, he sat, drawing her down beside him and pulled the mosquito netting over them. He leaned close, his nose nearly touching hers.

"What was the professor doing to you?" His hands skimmed up her arms and over her shoulders. His fingers probed, like a doctor inspecting injuries.

"Don't. You can stop pretending." His actions muddled her thoughts. How could she accuse him of stealing when he acted like this, like he truly cared?

"Pretending? What am I pretending?"

His hands rested on her knees—knees that butted up against his, making her very aware of his close proximity even though she couldn't see him.

"I know there's a missing urn. It was there when you took me to the shower and it was gone when you disappeared." There, she said it. Accused him of stealing. Her stomach clenched. Why did it feel so wrong?

"There is an urn missing? You are sure it was there before I came for you?"

"Yes. It was a little taller than the rest so it stood out in the shadows when I walked by with the lantern." She placed her hands over his. "You didn't take it?"

He snorted. "First you accuse me of not being good enough to be seen in daylight with you, and now you think I am a thief?" He held her head and drew her face to his. "Your words hurt me to the core, yet you are a *sirena* I cannot resist."

His rough kiss sparked intense passion. She fisted her hands in his hair and clung to him, returning the heat and tangling their tongues in the mating ritual her body craved.

"*Mi pichón*, you rattle my senses and make me weak when I should be strong." He kissed her neck and worked the buttons of her vest and long-sleeved shirt loose.

His hands heated her skin and made her blood pound. She searched for a fragment of the conversation. Why was she mad at him? Oh, yes, the missing urn. "You didn't steal the urn? Or are you just taking my mind off the missing artifact?" She wanted to give in to his seduction, but she couldn't until she knew the truth. And even knowing the truth she wasn't sure she could stop her desire or curiosity.

"I did not steal the urn." He opened her vest and shirt. "While waiting for you, I spotted the professor heading into the jungle. I followed." He kissed her neck and slid his hands up her sides under her tank top.

The wet kiss and his hot hands were new wondrous sensations. Her level head told her she'd enjoy this from any man—her heart said differently.

"Professor?" She fought the fog of desire wiping out her thoughts. "Where was he going?" She didn't want him to know how badly she wanted to touch him. But her hands had their own agenda and slid up his sides. His hot skin and firm muscle triggered more sensations. She moaned, squeezed the muscle, and wished this moment would never stop. Yet her head barged in. This must stop. She wasn't an adolescent girl exploring her sexuality in the back seat of a car. She was an adult—a virginal adult, but still an adult who needed to act with decorum.

Breathing in his male scent and exhaling, she withdrew her tingling hands and leaned back. "I think things are going too fast." She nearly choked on the words as his fingers brushed the sides of her breasts.

"There is nothing wrong with sharing kisses." He pulled her closer and captured her mouth, sucking the air from her lungs with a long, deep kiss that drugged her body and limbs but left her throbbing.

He drew back from the kiss, and she felt the cushion of her sleep pad under her back. He'd maneuvered her body to the ground. Her mind kicked into survival mode. If he could lay her down this slick, she feared his ability to make her do other things she wasn't ready or willing to do.

"No. It's time you left." The apprehension she felt vibrated in her words.

Tino's hands stopped their exploration. His breath puffed warm against her cheek. "When you stop thinking and follow your heart, you know where to find me." The tent fluttered, and she was left alone. For the first time in her life she despised her analytical mind.

Chapter Thirteen

Tino stood beside Isabella's tent. What had happened? Never had he craved a woman as he did Isabella. If her voice hadn't held fear when she asked him to leave, he would have cajoled her into more intimacy. That realization scared him.

The woman would be the death of his mission and the death of him if he didn't keep his hands to himself. She was everything that didn't usually pique his interest. But somehow, she had become everything his body craved.

Resentment wracked his body. What had the professor been doing in the tent with Isabella and why had he attacked her? He couldn't believe the man had the audacity to do so with him present. Walsh moved about the jungle like a snake. He wound around the narcos and slithered back into camp like shedding his skin to become a creature that fit into whichever environment.

Tino stalked toward the artifact tent. Would whatever Isabella did to the man incapacitate him for this long? The dark interior smelled of kerosene. The low budget dig meant no generators like the larger more popular digs. The remoteness and newness made his job easier. If there were also tourists hanging around, it would be impossible to know who was friend and who was foe. The list narrowed with each person he talked to. At the top stood Professor Walsh, then Doctor Martin; Isabella would be stricken to know this. But the man didn't feel right. It was a poor excuse to keep him at the top of the list considering he was in a way a rival for Isabella's affections, but something about the doctor set off his sensors. He was surprised that as intuitive as Isabella was, she didn't sense it as well.

He felt along the right side of the tent and found another lantern in the stack of supplies. Fuel sloshed and nose-hair-curling fumes seeped into the air when he shook it. He lit the lamp and stepped deeper into the tent. If something were missing, he wouldn't know. Eunice kept the log of artifacts found. Had the item Isabella said was missing been logged in?

Walsh had left the premises. Tino stopped at the stone that held Isabella's attention. It was absurd to feel jealous of a centuries-old rock, but he'd witnessed how reverently she ran her fingers over the carvings and noticed the glow in her eyes as she gazed at the stone. Passion drove her need for knowledge. He smiled. Passion drove everything about Isabella. One day, he hoped to share her passion, but not until he could clear his conscience and tell her the truth.

He picked up the broken lantern. Kerosene soaked the dirt. A footprint remained in the fuel-soaked ground. The logical answer was Walsh. He followed the trail out the back of the tent and to Walsh's. What had the man been up to? As badly as Tino wanted the answer, he was sure the professor would not tell the truth so to confront him would be a waste of time. Keeping an eye on the man to make sure he wasn't alone with Isabella again and catching him with the narcos when the DEA team moved in would be his best course of action.

Tino replaced the lantern in the artifact tent and started a perimeter surveillance of the compound. The professor hadn't carried anything to the cave, so who'd stolen the urn and why? How long had Isabella been away from the artifact tent? Her shower the night before lasted ten minutes at the most. When she didn't find him did she return immediately to the stone? He should go to her and ask, but he didn't trust his body. Not yet. After the sun rose and others mingled around, then he'd approach her.

A broken frond caught his attention. He used his penlight to search the ground. Multiple shoe indentions with toes pointed toward the compound proved someone had stood here watching. He stepped to the spot and stared at the camp. The center of the compound spread before him like an open window. All activity to and from the tents could be seen from this vantage point. Was the person spying one of the group or an outsider?

He'd find out tomorrow night.

~*~

Isabella slept until the first gray light of dawn lightened the interior of her tent. She stretched and her mind kicked into action. Tino had been in her tent kissing her with unrestrained passion and she'd order him to leave. The heat and good feelings his kisses had rendered from her body came back in vivid detail. Her body called her a fool, but her head still wanted things to add up and they didn't.

She sat up and tugged her tank top into place. If only the bugs weren't so bad, she could work in this and not be so hot. A couple of the other women worked in T-shirts, but they must have slathered their skin with DEET. She didn't like the idea of spending twenty-four hours a day with the chemical on her skin. Grudgingly, she shoved her arms into the long-sleeved cotton shirt and buttoned it up. Her vest lay in a pile beside her. She extracted her LED light, journal, and then her research notebook from her backpack.

The symbols she didn't know would take some detailed study to decipher. Virgil traveled everywhere with his extensive library. She'd take a peek at it after breakfast and see if he had books that would help her.

Isabella replaced the journal and light in her vest, adding the research notebook before donning the vest. Her stomach growled. Pedro would have coffee and possibly something she could munch on until breakfast was ready. She exited her tent and stretched her arms overhead, enjoying the cool, early morning air and chatter of the jungle animals waking to the new day.

Her gaze traveled to Tino's tent. Was he sleeping? Did she dare go talk to him? He never really said he didn't steal the urn. Had she allowed a thief to steal her body? For he had. His touch would forever be ingrained in her memory and on her body. She doubted there could ever be another to fill her body with such passion. Yet, did she dare allow herself to let go and enjoy his attentions? That question could plague her all day and quite possibly until he was on his way out of her life.

Tino crawled out of his tent. Her heart raced at the sight of his tousled hair and tight-fitting tank-style undershirt. The white cloth stretched taut across his chest and belly, enhancing the contours of muscle. A masterpiece. One she wished to run her hands over again.

He glanced up, and their gazes locked. Her heart flipped in her chest and her body throbbed.

"Morning, Ezzabella."

His deep, scratchy voice rippled heat along her skin.

"Morning, Tino." Her voice wobbled, and her cheeks flamed with embarrassment. He'd shown her his passion, and she'd tossed him out.

He walked toward her, drawing on a long-sleeved shirt. "You look rested."

In response to the twinkle in his eyes, she curved her lips into a welcoming smile. It appeared he wasn't upset by her need to think about his advances.

"I slept well after thinking about our...encounter."

His right eyebrow rose and he smiled. "I see. And what conclusion did you come to?"

"I-I don't want to keep pushing you away, but it's a puzzle to me that you even find me remotely interesting. Which substantiates my theory, that I'm an easy target and that's why you're making romantic overtures."

"¡Hijo jesu! There are three other women here I could seduce if all I wanted was a quick roll."

Her stomach growled loudly.

"Are you heading to the mess tent?" He changed the subject, taking her by the elbow and escorting her to the tent.

Her skin trembled at his touch. How did she pretend nonchalance when she wanted to believe his words and revel in the power his interest gave her?

He leaned close and whispered, "Your beauty, vitality, and intelligence astound me. You are the only woman I want."

Air stuck in her throat. His actions and sincerity were battering away at her resistance.

Professor Walsh emerged from his tent. His gaze landed on them. Venom oozed from his small, narrow-set eyes. They'd made an enemy of the man last night. Why he'd snuck up on her and then groped her was a mystery. The encounter was his doing, and if he didn't like the outcome—he walked tenderly this morning—it was his own fault for accosting her.

Tino took a step toward the man, but she put a hand on his arm.

"He owes you an apology." Tino's hard stare didn't waver from the man walking away.

"You and I both know he would never apologize, and he'll never tell us what he was doing. I've yet to hear him give anyone a straight answer about anything." Isabella gripped Tino's arm harder, dragging his glare from the professor. "Forget it. If you try to pound out an answer you'll only get thrown out of the compound." Walsh disappeared into the mess tent.

"What were you and the professor talking about last night before I arrived?" Tino's business tone drew her attention.

"He snuck up on me as I worked on the stone. He offered to help me decipher the glyphs. I told him I was doing fine, then you arrived and he—I still don't understand why he kicked over the lantern and then groped me." She stopped and stared into Tino's eyes. The blue irises darkened with anger. "And with you right there. It was so… bizarre."

"I agree. The desperation in his attempt was out of character for him." Tino placed his hands on her shoulders. "Do not go anywhere outside this compound alone."

She started to protest, but the determination in his eyes and the slight shake of his head stopped her.

"Someone watches the compound from the jungle. I found their hiding spot. Until I catch them, you must remain in the camp."

"Why is someone watching the compound?" She didn't like the idea, but she wasn't about to change her routine. Her faith in Tino catching the person overrode any fear.

"I think it may be your thief. He would have seen us leave the artifact tent last night and known how long we were away the night before." Tino started walking toward the mess tent. "Is the urn the first thing you've noticed missing?"

"Yes." She stopped. "But we've only been here a few days. Could they have been stealing things all along?"

"If so, you working at night is putting a cramp in their stealing. You need to take extra precautions if you continue to work after everyone else is asleep. They may get tired of waiting for you to leave." He gave a tug on her braid. "I would hate to see something happen to you."

At his soft declaration she wanted to melt into his arms. His genuine concern softened the wall she'd erected to keep him from hurting her. The more she was around him; she was beginning to believe he really cared for her.

"You two are up early." The accusation and insinuation in Virgil's voice didn't even needle.

"Did you bring your usual trunk of research books with you?" She'd change the subject and get her day mapped out.

Virgil yanked his glare from Tino and focused on her. "Yes. Do you need to use them?"

"Yes. After I eat. Did you bring any books with the Mayan code? There are some glyphs I can't decipher."

"I have two Mayan dictionaries and notes from a class I took in college." Virgil slid an arm through hers and escorted her through the mess tent flap.

Isabella glanced over her shoulder at Tino and wiggled her free hand toward him. She didn't want him to think she'd forgotten him. He waved for her to go on and didn't enter the tent. How would he spend his day?

"What has you stumped enough you have to look through my books?" Virgil released her arm and picked up two cups of coffee Pedro placed on the table they stood beside.

"Food ready in five minutes," Pedro said, smiling at her and rushing back to his sizzling pans on the over-sized camp stove.

"The Mayas believed a moon treasure was hidden here. Others from far away came to help seek the treasure. There is mention of a ceremony for the moon god." She sipped her coffee. The fresh coffee beans not only smelled heavenly, they made the best tasting coffee she'd ever had. Who would believe she found exquisite coffee in the jungle of Guatemala?

Glancing at Virgil, her contemplative thoughts dropped away.

Virgil's eyes glowed with an uncharacteristic avarice. "You've found the ceremony tablet. After you check my books, I'd like you to come down into the excavation site. There are some markings on the walls that should tie in to the tablet and help with the decoding."

"Walls? Does this mean you found a structure?" Excitement and anticipation bounced around inside her, making it hard for her to sit when Virgil pulled out a chair for her. She wanted to run to the site and forget about the books for the time being. She loved being ensconced in the areas where the ancients lived and worshiped. Their essence poured into her like water to a dry flower, filling and nourishing her. She'd tried to tell this to Virgil once; he'd merely looked at her like she'd gone crazy. Since then she'd kept the experiences to herself.

"Yes, we've opened up what looks like a worship area. It's small by comparison to other sites but is completely undisturbed due to its obscurity."

Pedro placed food in front of them, and she forgot about anything other than appeasing her hungry stomach. After two helpings, Isabella leaned back in her chair. More of the workers had straggled in while she and Virgil ate. Jaycee sat at a table where she could watch them. She really needed to set this woman straight about her and Virgil. Receiving the evil eye all the time was annoying.

Eunice entered the tent. The sight of the woman jogged Isabella's memory. Should she tell Virgil about the missing urn or wait until Tino caught the person tonight? If Eunice followed the schedule she had shared with Isabella yesterday, she'd discover the missing piece when she went to the artifact tent. Rather than throw suspicion on Tino, who she was pretty sure didn't steal the artifact and instead worked toward solving the theft, she'd let Eunice report it.

"Is your trunk of research books easy to get to?" She'd do the research and hurry to the site.

"It's alongside my bed. You can't miss it. I believe the books you want are on the right side."

Isabella stood and Pedro arrived to clear her plate and utensils. "Excellent food, Pedro. If anyone can put some meat on these bones, it just might be you."

"*Gracias, seño.* I will do my best, no?"

Virgil laughed. "If you can get her to fill out, it will indeed be a miracle, Pedro. She's been nothing but skin and bones since the day she arrived in this world."

If he had said this before Tino proved her body was worthy of a male's attention, Isabella would have been crushed. But now, she didn't care if people disapproved of her frame. She'd tried for years to change and nothing worked.

"I'll come over to the site as soon as I find what I'm looking for." Isabella left the murmuring voices and aroma of coffee and bacon. She crossed the compound in long strides and stopped outside Virgil's tent. Did the person watching them at night also watch during the day? She shivered. Was Tino keeping an eye on the spot? He disappeared a lot. From the things he'd told her, his two personas and the control he showed last night, she had a suspicion he wasn't a guide. Too many things added up to something else.

A quick scan of the compound revealed nothing out of the ordinary. She stepped into Virgil's tent. The immediate smell of his sharp aftershave, his orderly housekeeping, and the familiar trunk by his cot brought back fond memories. As a child, she'd spent hours reading books from this chest when her father visited Virgil at dig sites.

The thought of her father as always dulled her happiness. If only he had given her more than food, clothes, and money. Just a small part of him was all she asked.

She shook off the sad memories and knelt in front of the trunk, lifting the lid. Research books placed side-by-side with their bindings up lined the trunk. Isabella scanned the titles until she found the two books she wanted. Legs crossed, she sat in front of the trunk with the books on her lap and pulled out her journal and notes. The sun beating down on the tent escalated the temperature inside, causing her glasses to slide down her nose. Someday she'd have to see about contacts or laser surgery—if she planned more excursions into the jungle. Pushing her glasses up on her nose all the time was distracting and annoying.

There. She stabbed a finger at drawings like the ones on the stone. Meticulously, she read each image and compared it to the ones in her journal. Her shoulders and back ached and her head buzzed by the time she'd made sense of the glyph markings. She stuffed her journal and findings in her vest and replaced the books. Stretching out on the floor, she closed her eyes, extended her arms above her head, and breathed in a controlled relaxing rhythm to relieve her back.

She opened her eyes and rotated her head from side to side, easing the muscles in her neck. Her gaze landed on the corner of a paper sticking out from under the cot mattress. Isabella tugged on the paper. A notepad slipped out. She read the scribbles and sat up, staring at a paper on Mayan sacrifice. Virgil thought this site was one of the most sacred sites used for human sacrifice. But Mayas rarely used sacrifice in their ceremonies.

He hadn't said a word to her about sacrifice. Her mind spun images. The glyphs she couldn't decipher could speak of sacrifice. She read the paper once more, thoroughly, and replaced it under the mattress. Curiosity to see the worship hall hurried her out of Virgil's tent and over to the activity of the dig.

Isabella stopped at the threshold of the tell. She'd studied the maps and charts in the artifact tent, but nothing had prepared her for the emotions swirling in her as she descended the stone steps into the structure constructed by hands thousands of years ago. Darkness met her at the bottom of the stairs once the sunlight no longer filtered through the entry. She followed the beckoning white glow of the lanterns used by the workers.

String stretched in a grid pattern on one side of the chamber floor. Each of the British interns worked in a quadrant with a whisk broom, small trowel, and a field book held open with a pencil beside them. The local workers were clearing what looked like a passageway. She found Virgil writing in a log book as Jaycee placed fragments in a bucket to transport to the other women who cleaned and categorized.

Virgil glanced up as she approached. "There you are." He tucked the journal in his pocket and held out a hand. "I think you're going to find our discovery fascinating."

She ignored Jaycee's glare and placed her hand in Virgil's. A cold chill slid up her arm. An aftershock from the other woman's hostility. Virgil led her through an opened passage and into a near pristine altar room.

Her heart slid into her throat and beat wildly. "Virgil, it looks as if they just walked away. How did it remain so untouched by nature?"

He shook his head. "I haven't a clue, but there are glyphs on the walls. Stay as long as you like but don't forget to come out for fresh air and food." He laughed and squeezed her hand before releasing his hold.

Isabella spun slowly, taking in the structure, the carvings, and even the pottery still perched on ledges on the walls. How had this remained intact? Taking it all in, she approached the wall to the right of the door and studied the carvings and glyphs. They told the story of the king *Chächäc Ch'ujuña*—Red Moon and his family. She noted the marriages, births, and battles with other dynasties. Her heart raced reading glyphs that mentioned a visit from far away people.

She pulled out her journal and drew the glyphs, deciphering as she noted each one in her book. The lantern light wiggled and sputtered. How long had she been in here? Her fingers cramped and her eyes blurred. Reluctantly, she noted where she'd stopped and faced the altar.

The low glow of the lantern lit a portion of the wall she'd missed before. Her eyes widened at the fine detail of a carving revealing a human sacrifice. The girl's long hair hung over the altar, her face serene. A dagger protruded from her chest and blood dripped down her side. An owl sat atop the dagger handle, a smug look on its face. The king stood behind the altar, his hands raised over his head holding a bowl.

A chill chased up Isabella's back and spread from shoulder to shoulder. Fear poked holes in her curiosity.

She spun and smacked into a body. Raising her chin, she peered into Virgil's concentrated gaze. She pushed out of his arms and took a step back.

"W-what are you doing?" Her question sounded childish and scared. Vulnerability wasn't something she showed often. Not if she could help it.

"You've been in here for hours, missed lunch. This is why you stay skinny, missing meals." Virgil reached out to her, but she couldn't bring her hand to raise and fit in his.

"I was just getting ready to take a break." She walked past him, down the short corridor, and into the chamber where the workers hovered. Each one worked in the same section she'd witnessed them in when she'd arrived. Though she had patience for chasing down details in books and archives, she'd never make an archeologist. She didn't have the patience to use a toothbrush to unearth one small, possibly broken, piece of an artifact.

Isabella stepped out of the structure and rain pelted her. The deluge and large puddles on the ground proved this was more than an afternoon shower. A brief glance at her watch made her stomach rumble. She'd not only missed lunch but just about missed dinner, too.

She sprinted to the mess tent and caught a glimpse of Tino exiting the artifact tent. In her absorption of the dig glyphs she forgot about the missing urn. Had Eunice reported it missing? Virgil hadn't mentioned the urn. She stopped, her hand clutching the tent flap, and stared at Tino. Rain splatted on her head and ran down her body soaking through her vest and shirt.

Tino glanced in her direction and their gazes met. Isabella gave a tip of her head toward the mess tent and entered.

"*Seño*, you are soaked, no?" Pedro hurried forward. An inviting spicy aroma filled the humid interior.

Her stomach rumbled and the chef smiled.

"I did not see you at lunch and now it is an hour after dinner was served. How can I make you a robust woman if you miss meals?"

"She is perfect the way she is."

Tino's low sultry voice heated her skin so much she wondered steam didn't rise from her wet clothing.

"*Sí*." Pedro hurried to the table behind the cookstove.

"Where have you been hiding all day?" Tino asked, settling Isabella on a bench and taking a spot next to her. He'd made several visits to the artifact tent during the day and found the space in front of the stone empty. He didn't want to draw attention to his interest by asking someone where she worked.

"I went through some of Virgil's reference books in his tent then spent the remainder of the day down in the dig." Her eyes grew large and her face glowed. "There's a remarkably well-preserved worship hall and altar in the structure. And glyphs...the whole life span of Red Moon, a Mayan king, is written on the walls. It's fascinating."

Pedro placed heaping plates in front of both of them. The chef must have noticed their absence during mealtimes today.

"*Gracias*, Pedro." Tino liked the man and had hopes of getting him to help keep an eye on Isabella.

"I am paid to keep the people of this compound fed." Pedro winked at Isabella. "But for some I would do it even if I were not paid."

"*Gracias*, Pedro. I'm honored. Your food is delicious, even reheated." Isabella forked a mouthful between her lips.

Tino forced his body to stay relaxed, watching the rapt expression on Pedro's face. "Do you have anything to drink?" he asked, hoping to move the chef along.

"*¡Sí!*" Pedro scurried to the back of the tent.

Isabella moaned, capturing his attention. Her closed eyes and slow chewing proved her point about the food. "This is delicious. I didn't even realize how hungry I was until Virgil mentioned I'd missed lunch."

His body hummed with need watching her enjoy the food. She radiated passion like other women exuded charm or sophistication. Restraint proved useless when it came to Isabella. He captured her chin in his hand and traced his thumb back and forth across her full bottom lip. His arousal grew as her eyes slowly opened. The heat in their depths gripped him as firmly as a gaff in a fish.

"*Mi pichón*, you ignite urges in me, like no one before." He leaned into her and kissed her tantalizing lips, soft and brief. Her words about being seen cavorting with him rang in his head. He didn't want to do anything to jeopardize her career.

She placed her forehead against his. "You are slowly winning me over." Her whisper, for his ears only, jolted his system with the same impact as her sincere stare.

"I am glad. Eat." He released her chin and turned his attention to his meal. He'd known all day that if he came within arm's reach of her he would react just as he had. His plan to keep his distance after she tossed him out last night faded quickly as throughout the day his feet continually drew him to the artifact tent.

"Did Virgil say anything about the missing urn?" In all his wanderings today no one said anything about the missing urn.

"No. Did Eunice notice it was missing?" Isabella stopped with a forkful halfway to her irresistible lips.

"I never heard a thing. I saw her working with Jaycee, Paula, and Annie. Would they have noticed if the piece was missing?" He didn't like the fact no one but Isabella knew something had disappeared.

"I don't know. One of them would have cleaned it up, but as to knowing if it was with the rest of the items collected, I doubt it." She set her fork down and stared into space. "I didn't really pay that much attention to it. I'm not sure I could conclusively identify the vase."

Tino put a hand over hers. "Do not worry. There has to be an explanation. Maybe Eunice took the urn to her tent to catalog and photograph it. That could be why she has not said it is missing."

Her face brightened and she picked up her fork. "That could be. If it had intricate drawings, she may have wanted to try different angles and light to get the best picture."

He hoped that was the truth, but he'd find out for sure when he lay in wait for their jungle voyeur tonight.

Chapter Fourteen

Isabella sat in front of the stone in the artifact tent, making sure the notations she took from Virgil's books were indeed the same glyphs on the stone. Tino promised to come for her later, just like during the last couple of nights. She brushed at a glob of dry dirt and stopped. The rain had ceased, but the constant drip of water down the sides of the tent tapped a monotonous cadence. Beyond the drip another sound registered. Someone outside moved cautiously along the length of the tent. The puddles didn't slosh like that of someone who didn't care if his presence was known. The steps were a muffled splat of someone moving with stealth.

Was their thief returning? She stared at the lantern. He had to know she was in here.

Her heart raced. Adrenaline shocked her system into full awareness and defensive maneuvers. She shifted into the shadows, crouching low, and crept toward the back opening of the tent.

Once outside, she used the meager light of the moon to search for the person. Isabella pushed her glasses tighter on her nose and peered into the night. There. A shadow moved away from the artifact tent and toward the tell. Did the thief plan to steal something from the dig site?

Isabella moved into the shadows, mimicking the person, and

followed. Where was Tino when she needed him? The person peered over a shoulder before descending the steps into the dig. The furtive glance could only mean one thing, it was the thief.

She hurried to the opening, listened, and plunged into the darkness of the structure. Three strides into the passage, her toe connected with something hard and heavy. She tripped, catapulting her head first through the darkness. Her body met solid dirt seconds before her chin stabbed the hard-packed floor.

~*~

Tino set off at a run when he saw Isabella follow his suspect into the dig. He'd held his position near the thief's lookout as the man crossed the compound, but when the curious doctor followed, he knew trouble wasn't far behind.

"Ezzabella!" he called, entering the dark site. He had a vague idea of the layout after a quick reconnaissance of the area he'd made after the workers left for the day. Scurrying sounds too heavy for rodents vibrated in the darkness. "Who's here?"

The sound ceased.

Not good. He couldn't find the person in the darkness if they didn't create noise. He stood in the entry. Cautious of the need for silence, he crouched. If they swung or shot at him, they would expect a man standing.

A small beam of light flit along the passage wall and landed on the face of one of the local workers. Tino used the element of surprise and lunged, tackling the man around the legs. The force knocked the thief to the ground. Tino jumped on top of him. The light flashed in his eyes, blinding him, but he held onto the man squirming beneath him.

"Thank God!"

Isabella's heartfelt exclamation relieved the tightness in his chest. Her face was illuminated with the backlight of the small beam she held in her mouth as she dug around in her vest pockets. The sound of ripping followed.

"Here. Tie his hands with this." She held a strip of duct tape out to him.

He didn't have a clue where the tape came from, but he was happy to use it. He wrapped the thief's wrists together and stood him up.

"Are you okay? Did he hurt you?" Tino reached out to Isabella. She took his hand.

"I'm shook up. I followed him and tripped." She swung the flashlight toward the entrance. A rock sat near the right hand wall.

"We should get out of here and have a chat with our thief." Tino shoved the worker ahead of him out the entrance, using Isabella's beam of light to navigate around the rock and up the steps.

Outside, he marched the man to the mess tent. "See if you can find a lantern." He wasn't about to let the man loose.

A flame sputtered and gained in brightness. Isabella faced Tino, and his heart slammed into his throat.

"You are bleeding!" He reached out hesitantly to inspect the blood and dirt on her chin.

"I'm fine. I hit my chin when I fell." Her eyes glistened with moisture.

"Are you sure this is the only place you are injured?" He slid his gaze down the front of her. Dark patches seeped at her knees. "Your knees are bleeding." He captured a wrist and stared at the scrapes and blood on her palms. "*Mi pichón*, you are tougher than you appear." He kissed her forehead.

"*¡Caramba!* It is too early to eat, no?" Pedro emerged from the back of the cook tent in wrinkled clothes, his hair sticking out in all directions.

"Pedro, get a first aid kit and then Doctor Martin, *por favor*." Tino searched the area for something to tie up the thief who was struggling to get free.

Isabella sliced through one of the tent ropes with a small blade. He stared at her. What else did she carry in all those pockets of her vest? She held the rope out to him with a twinkle in her eyes.

"*Gracias*." He shoved the thief into a chair and tied his ankles to the chair legs. Isabella arrived with another length of rope. He tied it around the man's chest, securing him to his seat.

Pedro jogged up to them with the first aid kit. "*¡Caramba, seño!* Sit. You need attention."

"Pedro. I will tend to Ezzabella. You get Doctor Martin." Tino snatched the first aid kit from the cook and motioned for Isabella to sit. The cook was only trying to help, but he would be the one who doctored and touched the woman.

She sat, grimacing when the knees of her pants pressed against her bent joints.

"I will take care of your knees later, in the privacy of your tent," he said in a whisper for her only.

Her eyes widened and a smile curved her lips. "I like how you protect my privacy."

"This is going to sting." He applied peroxide to a gauze and wiped at the dirt on her chin.

She sucked in air and tears pooled at the corners of her eyes.

"I am sorry but it needs to be cleaned." He hated bringing her pain, but she would thank him later when her chin healed without scars from infection.

"I know. Your gentle touch helps." Her lopsided smile caught his attention. He leaned in to kiss her when he heard Martin's angry voice. "Later," he whispered and worked on one of her hands.

"What is the meaning of sending Pedro for me?" Martin stopped inside the tent. The minute his gaze landed on Isabella, he rushed forward.

"What happened?" He put a hand under her chin, raising her face to the light.

Tino wanted to slap the man's hand away, but Isabella only smiled.

"I tripped and scuffed up my chin and hands. Nothing drastic." She focused her gaze on the man squirming in the chair. "I was following this man."

Isabella stood, drawing Tino up with her. "Tino and I discovered a missing urn last night, and he then discovered a spot where someone had stood watching the compound. Tonight, this man," she pointed to the local worker in the chair, "crept by the artifact tent when he realized I wasn't leaving and slipped into the dig. I think he was going to steal something in there. Only I tripped, and then Tino showed up and captured him."

Tino watched Martin. The news didn't shock him.

The exasperated huff and glare Martin tossed at the thief showed irritation, not shock or anger.

"Raul, are you stealing for the narcos?" Martin asked the thief. "Is this how they're receiving payment?"

Isabella's hand clutched Tino's arm. He patted it. If this was an infiltration of the narcos, he had to be more careful. If his cover were blown, it would also jeopardize Isabella. They might think she was an agent, too.

Raul stared straight ahead, his lips firmly locked together. Would his punishment for talking be worse than what the government dealt for stealing national treasures?

"I see. You're not going to talk. As of right now you no longer work for me, and I want you and your things removed from this dig." Martin faced Tino. "Please escort Raul to his tent, and then out of the compound. I'll not have thieves taking the artifacts we dig up."

"What about the authorities?" Tino couldn't believe Martin was letting the man off that easy.

Martin ran a hand over his face and stared at Tino. "Do you really think he'll remain locked up anywhere long enough for the authorities to deal with him?" He shook his head. "He'd never get to the village or down the river. Whoever took him would be dead too. The narcos aren't going to let him get to authorities and give away any information."

This was true, but Tino couldn't believe Martin gave up so easily on extracting information from the man. If he pushed Martin to interrogate the man further, it would only throw suspicion on him. He shrugged. "If that is how you want to handle it. It is your business."

"You're not going to force him to tell us what he did with the items he took?" Isabella grabbed Martin's shirt sleeve. "What if he isn't the only one?" She stared at Tino.

Since meeting the woman he'd dropped the word fragile from any description of her, but right now, with her injuries and eyes beseeching him to make things right, she appeared as fragile as the orchids gracing the rain forest, and just as beautiful.

"I'll know if there are more." That was the best he could do to allay her fears until they were in private. He still didn't trust Martin and he didn't want Raul, once he was free, to tell the others how he planned to learn the truth.

She nodded.

Tino untied the man but left his hands taped. He entered the worker's tent with Raul. One empty cot had the covers thrown back. Tino nudged the man toward it and picked up items around the area, tossing them in the middle of the bedding. He tied the whole mess into a bundle and nudged Raul out. He didn't want him conversing with the few who had awakened and stared with wide eyes.

At the edge of the compound, Tino stripped the tape from the man's wrists, none to gently, and shoved his belongings in his gut. "Do not come back."

His training said to follow the man; he would meet up with the narcos. But he already knew where they hid, and he had promised Isabella he would tend to her knees. Tomorrow night he would slip into the cave and see what might lie hidden in there besides missing artifacts.

The gray light of morning hung over the top of the trees as he returned to the compound. A light shone in the cook tent revealing Pedro preparing the morning meal. Instinct told him Isabella waited in her tent. He hastened across the camp and stopped with his hand on the tent flap. The howler monkeys' roar echoed through the trees. Soon the others would be waking. Did he dare chance getting caught leaving her tent in the morning hours?

The flap moved, and Isabella's face peered out at him. Her eyes sparkled and a smile curved her lips. "I wondered when you'd show up." She held the flap back, allowing him entrance.

"I can only stay a minute. The others will be up soon. I do not want them to see me leaving—"

She pressed a finger against his lips. "Don't worry about the others. You promised to take care of my knees." She stepped back, and his gaze drifted down to take in a body-hugging tank top and denim shorts revealing her long-muscled legs. The only thing marring the sight—her bloody knees.

He swallowed a couple times to wet his dry mouth.

Isabella walked to an upside-down crate next to her bedding. She bent, retrieving items from the box. His heart raced at the sight of her shirt sliding up, exposing the lower part of her back and her denim-clad bottom thrust toward him. His control shattered at that innocent— she glanced at him over her shoulder—or not so innocent act.

"¡Carajo! You are going to be my ruin." He stepped behind her and wrapped his arms around her middle, tucking her enticing bottom against his growing length.

She slowly unbent, pressing her back to his front and leaning her head on his shoulder. "I don't want to ruin you. But your heroics and gentle touch have cracked my resolve."

Her acceptance of their attraction was as much an aphrodisiac as her body. He kissed her cheek and neck. His hand, pressed to her lower abdomen, held her bottom firmly against his groin. She fit him perfectly. His other hand snuck under her shirt and played with her pert nubs.

Isabella remained pressed against Tino's hard length. Waiting for him to return she'd decided to stop fighting and enjoy what he offered. She was a big girl and knew he would be moving on soon, so why not learn the art of loving from someone she trusted and knew would never hurt her on purpose.

His hard body, caressing hands, and moist kisses made her dizzy. Her limited experience brought on the realization she wanted intimacy with Tino. No other man up to now had drawn her attention from her academics to think only of him. She spun, sliding her arms about his neck and kissing him with the pent-up passion only Tino could unleash.

Tino returned the kiss until she had to pull back and catch her breath.

"*Mi pichón*, your body sings for me like a musical instrument." His melodic voice whispered across her cheek moments before he recaptured her lips and tangled his tongue with hers, seducing both with his kiss and his hands.

When her legs and body sagged against him, Tino gently placed her on her bedding. Her thundering heart slowed, lessening the pounding in her ears, and she realized he cleaned her knees.

Raising her head, she watched hands, that moments before turned her body into fire and lightning, now gently cleanse and rub ointment on her knees.

"I'm sorry." Since meeting this man it seemed all he did was fulfill her needs. Never once had she done a thing for him.

His dark blue eyes peered at her. "*¿Por que?* You did not fall down on purpose."

She sat up and placed a hand on his thigh. "For being so patient with me." His muscles tightened under her palm.

"You are worth the wait." He picked up her hand and tenderly kissed her scraped palm. "Your kiss just now proved it." He leaned forward, pulling her to him. His lips touched hers and she dove into the heady sensation with every molecule of her being.

The call of the howler monkey and movement around the tent

slowly registered as Tino released her. His hair stood out from her hands running through it. Isabella giggled.

Tino put a finger to her lips, but she couldn't control the giggles. Lack of sleep and the high she felt from being in this man's arms only added to the giddiness.

"*Mi pichón*, you must not bring someone to see what tickles you." The admonishment in Tino's eyes made her swallow her giggles.

"I'm sorry. The lightness I feel..." She took his hand and kissed his palm. "I've never had anyone who made me feel so wonderful or want to reciprocate the feelings."

"*Querida*." Tino's eyes brightened as he lowered his lips to hers.

The soft, tender kiss was nearly as exhilarating as the tongue tangling ones they'd shared.

"I cannot believe the *pendejos* who have hurt you so. When I meet them—"

She placed a finger on his wonderful lips. "You will never meet them."

Her stomach growled and Tino chuckled.

"Your stomach knows what it wants. I will leave and you can get dressed. I will wait for you outside." He kissed the tip of her nose and rose.

Tino stepped out of her tent.

"What the hell are you doing?"

Chapter Fifteen

Tino cursed under his breath as Martin stormed across the distance between his tent and Isabella's.

"What are you doing sneaking out of Dr. Mumphrey's tent?" Martin's eyes were wide and bulging. The vein in his forehead protruded. His anger was more than was warranted.

Before he could answer, Isabella stepped out. She'd pulled on long pants and a long-sleeved shirt. Her hair looked like she'd been thoroughly ravaged.

"What's the matter?" She stepped up beside him, and Martin's eyes narrowed before he grabbed her roughly by the arm. Isabella emitted a sharp cry of pain.

Tino grabbed the doctor's wrist, pushed his thumb on a pressure point, and forced Martin to release Isabella.

"Keep your hands off her." Tino didn't care that the tone held menace. He wouldn't allow the doctor to hurt or manhandle Isabella.

Martin jerked his arm free of Tino's grasp and glared. "Get out of this compound. You are no longer welcome here."

Tino stood his ground as he searched Isabella's face. "Did he hurt you?"

"It scared me more than hurt." She rubbed her arm not convincing him.

He faced the doctor. "I will go, but if you hurt her, I will be back and you are not going to like what I do to you."

Dr. Martin's eyes were focused on Isabella. What was his probing gaze trying to discern?

"Tino, you need breakfast before you leave." Isabella hooked her arm through his and stared at Martin. "You can't kick him out without feeding him first. He did after all catch a thief last night."

Martin nodded, but the hatred in his eyes and tick in the vein on his forehead proved the man didn't like Isabella taking his side.

Tino pivoted and headed to the mess tent with Isabella holding his arm. The grip she had on him was telling. She feared being left alone in the compound. He couldn't blame her. The rage on Martin's face when he grabbed her was possessed.

He scanned the area around the compound. Not only did he have to fear forces outside the camp harming her, he now believed she had danger inside. He stopped at the corner of the mess tent.

He had to tell her about his real reason for being here. She had to be made aware of all the dangers, especially now that he wouldn't be around to watch her. But he had to tell her before they entered the mess tent.

"There are things you need to know." He peered into her inquisitive eyes. It killed him to have to leave her alone, but he had no choice. The wrath in Martin's eyes was nothing to ignore. If he stayed the man could take out that anger on her. "But not here." He moved away from her and headed toward the jungle.

Isabella stared at Tino's retreating back. It took a second for her to realize he wanted her to follow.

She jogged after him.

He passed his tent and headed into the jungle.

She followed.

Three steps inside the trees, an arm wrapped around her middle and yanked her against a hard body she now knew well.

"What—" Hard demanding lips covered hers. His hands captured her head, allowing no escape even if she wanted it. His mouth commandeered hers. His tongue entered, tangling, seducing, making her dizzy with longing.

He finally drew back, and her legs refused to hold her. Tino twined his arms around her middle, holding her up. His hands, pressing against her lower back, sent wonderful sensations sparking through her.

"We must talk. But I wanted to make sure you know I will not leave you unprotected." His soft playful utterance started her heart racing.

"Are you worried about Virgil's anger?" She leaned back to gaze into his eyes. The desire lighting them slowly sputtered.

"Among other things. I want to tell you the truth, but I fear you are safer not knowing." His arms tightened. "Can you trust me on this?"

"My instincts are right, you aren't a guide or tracker?" She didn't like his reference to her safety, but it was reassuring to know she'd been right in her assumption.

"No, I was given the assignment to take over as your guide to get into this area undetected." He cradled her head in his hands. His eyes shone brilliant blue and peered into hers. "I cannot tell you everything, but please, do not tell anyone what I tell you. With Martin kicking me out of the camp, you are vulnerable if I do not tell you all I know."

"This all sounds so ominous. I take it you're on the legal side of the law?"

"Very much."

"Then I won't ask any more and have faith you'll tell me what I need to know."

He let out a huge sigh. "Thank you, *pichón*. I promise you will know everything when I can tell you."

"That's all I want from you Tino, the truth." Feeling bold, she tentatively pressed her lips to his. Of course, she wanted more than the truth, a whole lot more, but she'd settle for the fact she had his trust.

He deepened the kiss, devouring her mouth, and igniting her tinder dry flame of desire for him.

She twined around him like an epiphyte clinging to a tree. Closer, she wanted closer, and to touch him and kiss him everywhere at once. Knowing she might not see him again gave her a sense of how much she'd come to enjoy his presence.

"*Querida*, whoa." Tino pulled back.

The macho grin on his handsome face registered through her haze of desire.

"If I had known leaving would bring out your desire, I would have left sooner."

Isabella punched him in the chest with her palm. "I wish Virgil hadn't ordered you out of camp."

"Me either. While it helps my true mission, I do not like leaving you here alone." Tino drew her in a tight embrace. "I will sneak in at night and check on you." He kissed the top of her head. "Do the work you came for quickly. This place does not feel right."

Her throat clogged from a lump of emotion. "Come eat with me and I'll help you pack."

"No, *querida*. It is best for you if I leave now." He raised her face, kissing her with such tenderness, tears burned in her eyes and love burned in her heart.

"Come. I will take you back."

They exited the dense foliage as Virgil stalked out of the mess tent. His glower deepened when his gaze landed on the two of them.

Virgil's hand rested on a pistol in a holster on his belt. When did he start carrying a gun? She'd felt Tino's gun tucked in the back of his pants when she hugged him, but she knew he carried a gun. She'd encountered it on other occasions.

Her mentor glared at their linked hands.

"I consented to a last meal not a last grope." Virgil stared daggers at Tino, and he returned the look but didn't let go of her hand.

"Please, Virgil, he's leaving. Don't make more out of it than it is." She wouldn't allow his wrong perception to cause Tino harm.

"What do I tell your father? You came here because I asked for your expertise and in return you slept with the hired help?" Derision laced his words and suspicion stirred in his eyes. "I'll never get backing from him again. Not when he expects me to keep an eye on you and this sort of thing happens."

"I'm not sleeping with him. We're friends." She told the truth. They were close friends. His last sentence hit her. "What do you mean, backing? Is that why you've always been so nice to me? To get my father's financial backing for your excavations?"

"Don't change the subject. You want to be respected in my world; then you better not act like a slut."

His words hurt her deeper than he'd ever know. He knew her dream was to belong in his world of anthropologists and archeologists.

He'd called her a genius and advocated for her. But now she knew he only helped her to keep her father funding his digs. She couldn't shake the sense of betrayal weakening her knees and clouding her thoughts. He didn't really believe in her. All these years he'd used her innocence to get her father's money.

Tino stepped forward. "You may call me all the names you wish but do not call Ezzabella names." The two men stood nearly chest to chest, like a couple of fighting roosters. Tino's standing up for her formed a small bandage over the wounds Virgil's comments inflicted.

"Well, well, it looks like you two bloody better set a time and day for a duel." Professor Walsh walked up, his face glowing with glee over the two men standing nose to nose. "I bet my centavos on the guide. He's got youth and street smarts."

"There isn't going to be a duel or a fight." Isabella tugged on Tino's shirt sleeve. *Men.* It flattered her Tino was willing to take on the older, taller, though definitely less experienced man, but she didn't believe in violence other than to physically defend one's self.

"Go on. I'll be fine." She tugged harder and Tino stepped back from Virgil.

"You are sure?" His question went deeper than her physical being. She saw his concern reflected in his eyes.

"Yes, go." For Virgil's benefit, she added, "Look me up when you get to the states. We'll track down your great grandparents."

"I will." Tino squeezed her hand, gave her one more deep searching look, and walked away.

Even knowing she'd see him again, didn't lessen the anxiety rippling through her at the prospect of facing Virgil.

She tamped down her disappointment in the man she'd thought of as a mentor and her own stupidity to think he had championed her because of her knowledge. He'd used her as a bargaining chip for funds from her father. How stupid could she be? Not giving the man a glance, she headed to the mess tent. Her appetite had left her, but she knew a long day was ahead of her and she needed nourishment.

Isabella stepped inside the mess tent and found it empty.

Pedro arrived with fruit, tortillas, and cheese. "Where is your man?"

My man? She liked the idea, but wasn't sure their relationship was that concrete yet. "He's my friend not my man. Dr. Martin sent him

144

away." She took a cup of coffee and inhaled the rich aroma. If only life were as uncomplicated as brewing a good cup of coffee.

Her heart sat heavy in her chest. She'd been lonely most of her life. But she'd never felt as empty as she did right now, knowing she would be lucky to catch brief visits with Tino until she left. And with his line of work, who knew what could happen to him. The thought caused her to gasp. When she thought of him as a guide and jaguar tracker, while those are dangerous jobs, she believed in his skill. Knowing he went up against unlawful people changed his odds.

Pedro sat in a chair beside her. She shifted to study his face. He stared at her a long while then leaned close.

"I have been watching. You must be careful." He spoke so quiet she barely heard what he said.

"What? What do you mean?" First Tino, and now the cook, offering her warnings. What kind of trouble could she possibly find deciphering glyphs?

"I have seen others watching you." Pedro nodded his head once in affirmation.

"They're watching the camp. Looking for a chance to steal artifacts." She waved a hand and stuffed a tortilla into her mouth. She chewed and swallowed. "Besides, he was caught last night."

"They are after more than the artifacts. They want you." Pedro stood. "You must be careful."

Chapter Sixteen

Isabella finished her meal and headed to the cataloging tent to see what Eunice could tell her about the possible missing artifacts.

Eunice bent over a small table, studying fragments with the porous appearance of bone.

"What do you have there?" Isabella peered at the jagged edges and coloration of the specimens.

The older woman jumped, swaying the gray braid hanging down her back. "Isabella, you startled me, I was concentrating so hard on these objects." Eunice stepped aside after writing in a large notebook. "These are pieces of the handle of, I think, a sacrificing knife." She pointed with her pen at the largest piece. "See the carving on the larger piece? And the darker coloration near the end? It appears to be blood. These shards are pieces of bone. They would have become more brittle by now if they hadn't been fashioned into a knife and preserved." She picked up a slender pointed piece of shiny obsidian. "And this was found along with these pieces. The blade."

Isabella stared at the odd shapes of bone and the long, pointed piece of shiny, black stone in Eunice's hand. A shiver ran across her shoulder blades and down her back. The same odd sensation that had shimmied through her while she was in the sacrificing chamber. She shook it off. "Do we have the equipment here to run tests on these?"

"Only superficial testing. I'll be able to determine if it is bone and, possibly, that the dark substance is blood, but as for dating—this is such a low budget dig; all we do is clean it to identify, label the composition, put like pieces together, and categorize them. Then the artifacts are packed to ship to the *Universidad Francisco Marroquin*." Eunice shook her head. "There have been a couple artifacts I'd give my good eggs to research more."

If Eunice was willing to give up her eggs when she had waited this long for the right man to come into her life, Isabella knew the significance of the pieces.

"Why aren't we doing all the research?" This new knowledge was another puzzle in her ongoing discovery of things that didn't add up.

"Because we have to get this site excavated in two years and move out. Virgil is trying to pull out as much as he can as fast as he can and worry about the research later." Eunice picked up her camera and snapped pictures of the items.

"But if the artifacts are in a Guatemalan university how does he plan to research them?"

Eunice shrugged. "I get paid to catalogue, take photos, and not ask questions."

"Which is why I'm here. Did you mention to Virgil there was an urn missing yesterday?"

Eunice bobbed out from behind the camera, surprise widening her eyes. "What urn?"

"The one you showed me the night before that you planned to photograph." Isabella spread her hands one above the other, depicting the size. "The tall one with the ceremonial drawings."

"What makes you think it's missing?" Eunice stood with one hip cocked, the camera in her hand tipped away from her aging face.

"The other night it was sitting where you placed it when I talked to you, and then later that night, when I reentered the artifact tent, it was missing."

The older woman shook her head. "Honey, I don't doubt it wasn't there, but I took great photos of it the next morning." She placed the camera on the end of the table and motioned with her finger. "It's packed in a box over here."

Isabella watched in disbelief as Eunice opened a box and dug through the packing material to pull out the vase she thought stolen.

"I…that's the one?" If no one stole the urn, why was it missing and why was Juan sneaking into the dig?

"Are you okay? You look a little pale." Eunice placed the urn on the top of the crate and reached out to her.

"I'm fine, just confused." She ran a hand over her eyes and peered at the container. "Mind if I look it over more closely?"

"Go right ahead. I'll finish my photos of these bone fragments." Eunice returned to her camera.

Isabella reached out for the vase. Tingling at the nape of her neck made her glance around. The sensation that someone watched niggled at her mind. Her fingertips pulsed and heated when they touched the ancient urn. The lid on the container didn't budge. She shook the urn. The weight inside shifted. What was in there? They wouldn't know until someone at the Guatemalan University opened the urn. She itched to remove the lid and discover the contents. Since that was impossible without consent from Virgil, she studied the drawings on the outside.

Though many depictions of bloodletting and sacrificial ceremonies were graphic in nature, this one disturbed her more than any other. The vivid portrayal of a woman being sacrificed with gleeful onlookers haunted her and something about the scene evoked deep sorrow in her chest. She swiped at a tear trickling down her cheek and noticed a small, almost faded piece of the drawing. A moon. Crying. What did a crying moon have to do with the ceremony? She stared at the tears dropping from the moon and then back at the woman. Tears the same shape and size dropped from the woman's open eyes. The moon and woman were connected.

Excitement over her discovery surged through her body. She had to learn more about this woman and this ceremony.

"Eunice, I'd like to make notes from this urn. I'll just sit over there and do it if you don't mind?" Isabella carefully placed the urn on the floor and sat in front of it.

"What did you find?" Eunice peeked out from behind the camera.

"I'm not sure, but I think it ties in with the stone tablet and the altar chamber." Isabella pulled her journal out of her pocket and began drawing the details she believed pertinent.

~*~

Tino quickly took down his tent and relocated it one hundred yards into the forest before setting out for the cave the narcos guarded.

Halfway to the cave he stopped, moved plants, and pulled out his radio. He had stashed the equipment in the jungle to avoid it being found in his possession. His tagging transmitter could be used to communicate with DEA in a pinch, but this equipment was more secure. He checked the GPS on his watch and tipped the antenna north. With one ear pad from the headphones on an ear and one on his cheek so he could still hear if anyone approached, he listened to the crackle as he dialed in the coordinates for Ginger. She had had little to report when he stashed the radio. He hoped she had some answers for him today.

"Konstantine. Over." He waited, honing in on sounds from the earphones but still conscience of the jungle noises.

"Go ahead. Over." Ginger's voice sounded haggard.

"Working hard, *mi amor*? Over." He had to voice his thoughts. This woman had saved his butt more than once with her information.

"No more than usual." Ginger sighed. "But thanks for asking. Over."

"Have you had a chance to gather my information? Over." He hoped her investigation into the men would help him decide his next move.

"Rupert Walsh, professor of archeology, British. Known to gamble more than he can afford. Spends most of his time in the U.S. when not on digs. Though he is highly recognized in the world of archeology, it is rumored he sells artifacts to cover his gambling debts."

The man was playing both sides of the coin, no doubt, since he was tight with the narcos.

"Virgil Martin, doctor of archeology, American. One of the most revered archeologists in the world. But with the economy has found it harder and harder to get backing for his expeditions. He also dropped out of sight for a year before he started his latest dig."

Tino found that bit of information interesting. Why would he drop out of sight for a year and then come here?

"Don Miguel, Petén, Guatemala. Owner of the largest plantation in Petén. Commodities are coffee, sugar, and cattle. His name has come up in connection with Garza. He's a collector of Mayan artifacts. Over."

Sugar. There was a good possibility the man knew his estranged family still in Venezuela running the family sugar cane and rum operation. It also sounded as if he had his fingers in everything that happened on this stretch of the Usumacinta River.

"That answers my questions. Gracias. Over."

"Take care. Out."

Tino re-hid the radio and stashed his pack. Now to investigate the narcos' cave. He moved through the jungle in a direct line toward the spot where he'd watched Walsh talking with the traffickers.

The sound of voices carried to him before he had a visual of the cave entrance. Donkeys stood in a pack string outside the cave. The ten small, pack animals bulged with canvas-wrapped bundles. He inched closer to hear the conversations clearly.

"Meet Ricardo at the river at midnight. He will take the packs and head up river. Go to the settlement and wait for the next delivery." The man giving the orders wasn't Garza.

Three men with guns led the pack string and three followed. The leader and another man entered the cave. In his past trips to the cave, Tino had witnessed a small contingent of narcos. If the two who entered the cave were the only ones here, he had a chance to get inside and look around. The load that just left and the unwatched entrance led him to believe he would find little, but he needed to know the layout for future reference.

Tino crept up to the cave entrance, crouched inside the opening out of sight of anyone approaching, and listened. Muffled scrapes and low voices filtered down the dimly lit tunnel. He stood, pressing his back against the cave wall and cautiously sidestepped toward the voices and light.

He hung back in the shadows and watched the two men. They sat on folding chairs pulled up to a crate. One shuffled cards while the other placed bottles of Gallo on the makeshift table. Beyond them gaped a continuation of the cave. The area where the two played cards held only staples for daily needs. No bundled drugs or loose artifacts lay around.

He had to get past the men and into the cave. Backtracking, he found a protruding boulder barely large enough to hide his crouching body. He prayed that in the dim light and in pursuit of an intruder, they wouldn't notice him hiding behind the rock.

Tino picked up several rocks the size of his fists and tossed two toward the men, then sent one bouncing back toward the entrance and ducked behind the rock. Within seconds, the narcos ran past him toward the entrance. Tino jumped to his feet and bolted for the dimly lit area, running through the space where the men played cards, he charged into the dark passage of the cave beyond.

Once the darkness wrapped around him, he slowed his pace, extracting a small penlight from his pocket. Damp earth cooled the passage and awakened memories of the dank moldy apartment his family had lived in when they first arrived in the United States. His chest ached at the memories of his mother and father working menial jobs to support them until his father obtained his teaching credentials and they moved into a house more befitting a university professor. He and his brother then attended a private school where they could be monitored for fear their past would catch up to them.

Pushing the memories from his mind, he continued to follow the small glow of his penlight for fifteen minutes through the passageway. If he spread his arms, he'd touch both sides at once. The narrow passage opened up into a small area that held buckets of artifacts and bundles of…he rubbed his finger over the powdery substance on the bundles. Touching his tongue to his finger he cringed at the bitter taste of opium.

Half the amount of bundles that left on the donkeys stood against the wall. He flashed the light around the area and found another passage just as well traveled as the one leading him into this chamber. Tino counted the bundles, set the number in his memory, and headed into the next tunnel.

He traveled in the dark for an hour before sounds and a small spot of light filtered down the tunnel toward him. His penlight, beamed at the ground, illuminated stone steps ascending toward the light and voices.

"What do you bloody mean you can't go any farther on this corridor? The glyphs state this is the way to riches." Walsh's booming voice carried in the darkness.

Tino glanced at his watch. Underground the GPS did him little good. He had no idea which direction he'd traveled following the tunnel. Was he at the dig or somewhere else that Walsh had a hand in? The man got around.

Not wishing anyone to know about this tunnel to the narcos' drug stash until he had re-enforcements brought in to confiscate the goods, he'd sit tight and wait for the workers and Walsh to leave. His stomach rumbled. It could be a long wait.

~*~

Isabella finished copying the designs on the urn and replaced it in the crate. Eunice had long since left for lunch. Isabella's stomach growled. She'd appease the gluttonous organ now that she had the information she wanted. The woman's face on the urn haunted her thoughts as she walked to the mess tent. Small glyphs around the bottom of the urn reminded her of others she'd seen in the altar chamber.

Her feet started to turn toward the dig, but her mutinous stomach overrode her feet and she entered the mess tent. To her relief she was the only occupant. The others were evidently taking a siesta after their lunch and avoiding the heat of the midday sun.

Pedro hurried forward. "Where have you been? The others have eaten and gone back to work, no?"

"I was busy. But I'd love some juice and food." She sat close to the door, enjoying the slight breeze that blew through the mosquito netting.

Pedro hurried back to the kitchen and returned with a tall glass of juice and a plate filled with tortillas, cheese, and fruit.

"*Gracias.*" She rolled cheese in the warm tortilla and bit into the savory combination. "If you ever want to set up a restaurant in the States, give me a call. I'd vouch for your culinary prowess."

"I enjoy feeding people who take pleasure from food." He winked. "Food pleases you, no?"

"Very much." She thought of something else that pleased her very much. Where was Tino right now? Was he off looking for jaguars or more dangerous animals? Until his confession he was not a guide, though she'd suspected as much, she hadn't worried about him. Now, knowing he worked a dangerous job, she worried. Couldn't help herself. In a short time, he had become more important to her than anyone else in her life. And not just because of the wonderful way he made her body feel, but because he listened to what she had to say. Truly listened.

She finished the food and thanked Pedro. If she kept her mind busy it wouldn't have time to dwell on Tino's adventures. Rather than track Virgil down for permission to use books he'd already given her permission to use, she hurried to his tent. He'd be in the dig. He never took a siesta. She wasn't even sure he slept at night because his lantern burned at all hours. She entered his tent. It hadn't changed much since the other day when she'd used his reference books.

The book she wanted sat on top of the others. Coincidence? Or was Virgil on the cusp of figuring out what they sought? Thinking of his cruel remarks and tossing Tino out of camp, she couldn't bring herself to remain in Virgil's tent. She took the book outside and sat on the grass, opening the book on her lap.

There they were. The symbols she'd tried to figure out the other day. They represented the name of a woman. She stared across the compound, unseeing. The woman who was sacrificed. Isabella's stomach churned. The sacrifice of the virgin made the moon god cry. What about this particular woman left sorrow rather than hope? For the sacrifices were gifts to the gods to bring good weather and crops.

Sadness for this woman wrapped around her heart. Clutching the book to her chest, Isabella returned to her tent and lay down. She needed to sleep. That had to be why this information caused her so much grief. She was tired.

But sleep eluded her. Her mind spun with the drawings, the sadness, and restlessness. Finally, unable to shake the images and unease, Isabella rose, crossed the compound, and entered the dig site. Something compelled her to read the glyphs and look at the carvings in the altar chamber once more.

The workers glanced up as she entered. Virgil eyed her and then the book clutched in her arms.

"What are you doing?" he asked, stepping forward.

"I need to see the carvings on the wall in the other chamber." Without missing a step, she continued into the chamber. Virgil's footsteps echoed behind her. Isabella placed the book, open to the pages she had read, on the sacrificial altar. She stepped to her left and studied the drawings on the wall with more interest than on the day before.

The story made more sense after connecting the urn, the glyphs she didn't know, and then this artwork. It played out in her head as if she stood watching the event.

"What are you finding?" Virgil stood next to her.

153

Her skin grew cold and her heart raced with fear. *He means you harm. He brings evil.* A voice in her head warned. The voice and her reactions to Virgil were illogical, but her intelligence knew there were some things that couldn't be explained. Like her drive to learn all she could about the native people of the Americas.

The urgent voice felt more a friend than Virgil at this moment. She shook her head. "Nothing. I thought I'd found something that connected, made sense of the stone and glyphs. I-I was wrong."

His eyebrows rose and he stared at her. Doubt shimmered in his eyes. He didn't believe her. And why should he? She walked in here—the dampness of her clothes registered as her mind divorced itself from the story. She'd walked into the dig wet from rain pouring outside. Rain she hadn't even noticed until now. She'd been in a trance, induced by her knowledge that the pieces put together would give her answers.

A worker stuck his head into the chamber. "*Señor*, we leave for dinner."

Virgil waved him away and took another step toward her. Instinct moved her feet back. His eyes widened then cloaked.

"Are you coming to dinner?" The tone wasn't an invitation but more an accusation.

"No, I had a late lunch and want to remain here a while longer to see if I didn't overlook something." She didn't really want to stay here alone, but she also didn't want to be with Virgil. The whole trance-like episode, the voice, and her unease with a family friend left her unsure of anything at the moment. Least of all acting normal.

"If you tell me what you're looking for, I could help. We are in this together."

"That's the crux. I don't know what I'm looking for, but I'll know it when I see it." She offered a weak smile. "I think?"

Virgil studied her a moment longer then pivoted on his heel and left the chamber.

His departure lessened the tension in her shoulders and lightened the air. She walked over to the altar and ran her hands over the polished stone. Cold chilled her back. Her mind numbed as fear and regret entered her chest.

What did it feel like to be placed upon this stone and know that you would never see another day or embrace love?

Chapter Seventeen

Tino waited until he no longer heard Martin's voice. He climbed the stairway, easing his foot onto each stone before putting his full weight on them. A large rock blocked the top of the stairs. Light glowed from a small peephole to the side of the rock, lower than his height. Through the hole, he watched Isabella study the wall. Her expression grew sadder with each meter she walked around the room.

He grasped a stick protruding from the large stone and shoved. The rock slid sideways scraping along the floor, but moving easier than he'd expected. He stepped into the chamber.

Isabella spun toward him, her eyes wide and full of fear.

"*Mi pichón.*" Tino opened his arms, and Isabella drifted into his embrace. "I did not mean to scare you." He kissed her head and hugged her tight. This woman never had cause to fear him.

She snuggled against him, pressing her trembling body deeper into his embrace.

"You are trembling. What is wrong?" Tino tipped her face up to peer into her eyes. Dilated pupils stared past his head, trance-like. Had Martin drugged her? Anger grew like an ocean wave cresting and crashing into full rage. He hadn't trusted the man from the beginning. Isabella's father was a fool to trust his money and his daughter to the archeologist. The shaking woman in his arms couldn't know the depth of his rage. He drew in a calming breath and focused on caring for her.

He'd confront the archeologist later.

"Ezzabella, *querida*, look at me." Tipping her chin, he peered into her eyes.

Her gaze locked onto his face. The distant expression faded as her lips curved into a smile. "Where did you come from?"

She does not remember my entrance. He searched her eyes and face for evidence she was fooling with him. Truth and uncertainty peered back from behind her shiny lenses.

"What are you looking at me like that for?" Her brow wrinkled and her eyes lit with indignation.

Tino nodded toward the boulder shoved aside, revealing the pathway to the narcos' cave. "I came through that passage."

"How?" She walked to the opening and peered inside.

He grasped her shoulders, catching her attention. "I scared you when I stepped through. Do you not remember?"

She shook her head in slow motion.

Isabella stared into Tino's concerned eyes. Why didn't she remember him coming into the altar chamber? Especially when he'd moved a large rock to do so.

"Do you remember Dr. Martin in here talking to you?"

Tino's inquisition spiraled worry in her stomach. She nodded. Virgil had asked…her something. "I came into this chamber to… I found evidence that linked the stone tablet to a vase and to… It was about a sacrifice." The air grew cold. Fear quaked in her limbs and landed in her chest. "It's what Virgil brought me here to decipher." She pointed to the carving behind the altar. "This ceremony."

The sorrow connected to this ceremony was draining.

"Take me out of here," she pleaded. Something about the chamber spun images of a woman, a man, love, and sorrow in her head and infused her with confusion, fear, and heartache.

"I would like nothing more but I can only escort you to the door. If Martin sees me still hanging around there is no telling what he will do." He glanced at the dark cave. "I will have to take my chances with the narcos."

Her fear snapped from the room to Tino. "No, everyone is in the mess tent. You can sneak out this way."

"I do not want to cause you trouble." He placed a palm on her cheek.

156

"I'll go first and make sure there isn't anyone about." She kissed his palm. "Please. I don't want you running into the narcos."

Tino nodded, shoved the rock back in place, and took her by the elbow, escorting her to the dig entrance.

Isabella stepped out and inhaled the hot moist air, welcoming the heat of the evening. She couldn't fathom what she'd experienced in a scientific way, but she understood it through her study of Native American tales and her roots to them. The event she investigated had something to do with a woman, a woman who could be connected to her own past.

She shook off the thoughts and scanned the camp. All was quiet. "Come."

Tino stepped out, grasped her hand, and drew her into the closest dense jungle. Once out of plain sight, he embraced her.

"Good. You are no longer trembling." He ran a hand down her back.

She arched toward his touch like a cat asking for a favored spot to be scratched.

"What about that chamber affects you?"

"I think I'm connected to the woman who was sacrificed and made the moon god cry."

His hand stopped at the small of her back. The sensation of the pressure spun her mind to carnal thoughts.

"You believe through your Hopi roots you are connected to the Mayas?" He removed his hand and grasped her face between his hands. "*Mi pichón*, could this be why you are so centered on deciphering everything you find?"

She hadn't thought of that before. Her ancestral roots could run as far back as the Mayas if the indigenous tribes of the North American southwest had co-mingled with the Aztecs and the Mayas at some point. Even if for nothing more than trade, a marriage could have been arranged. Yes, a North American warrior could have taken a liking to a Maya maiden. Had she stumbled onto her roots?

Isabella spun out of Tino's embrace. "I can't believe I could be digging up my family history."

Memories of the voice and sadness gripped her. She had to uncover what happened after the ceremony was performed.

She clutched the front of Tino's shirt. "I have to figure out what happened after the ceremony on the chamber wall." She gazed into his eyes. Would he believe me? I have to take the chance.

"A voice warned me to beware of Virgil. And the sadness I feel…This ceremony changed things for the Mayas. I can't explain it, but it's important I discover what before I tell Virgil or anyone what I've discovered."

He gently extracted her fingers from his clothing. "I believe in your intellect and your emotions. I agree. If you feel that strongly do not tell Martin."

Holding her hands, Tino drew her body next to his. His mouth descended on hers, and she forgot everything, accepting all the wonders of his kiss.

The roar of a howler monkey jerked her back to the present. "I forgot the book." She stepped away from Tino.

"What book?" He still held her hands, keeping her from exiting.

"I had one of Virgil's books in the altar chamber. I was using it to decipher the symbols I didn't know. He can't see it. In case he figures out the symbols before I do." She took a step toward Tino but didn't dare get close enough for him to kiss her again. She needed her wits about her to translate the story on the walls of the chamber and not become absorbed in the drawings. "I need to retrieve it before someone else picks it up."

"I will go with you."

"You can't. Someone may have finished eating and see you." Even though she protested, she didn't want to return to the chamber alone. Not so soon after her last encounter.

"We will pop out of the jungle close to the entrance." He clasped her hand twining their fingers and led her back to the compound. Tino peered through the foliage before running to the cave with her in tow.

They entered the dig and her feet felt like boulders as he continued toward the altar chamber. What was it about this room that spun her to another time and place? She sensed the fear and sorrow the instant she stepped through the door.

"You are trembling again." Tino glanced at the altar and squeezed her hand. "You go back out. I will get the book."

"No. I have to get over the response my body has to this room. It's the key to discovering the past. I can feel it." Isabella swallowed the lump in her throat and walked to the altar. She stared down at the book and found it opened to a different section. Someone had been here and looked at the book. Who? And why? Only she, Virgil…and Professor Walsh would be able to decipher the drawings. She folded the page, closed the book, and spun about to run out of the room. Tino's wide chest stopped her retreat.

"Ezzabella, I will not let anything happen to you." He grasped her shoulders. "You are shaking again. Come." He slipped an arm around her shoulders and walked her out of the chamber to the dig entrance. Tino held her to his chest and peered out the opening.

"You need to eat. It will help your nerves." He put his hand out. "I will return the book to Dr. Martin's tent."

She clutched the book to her chest, inhaling the scent of pressed paper and glue. The bouquet of smells conjured memories of happy days researching in the library. "No. I want to copy some of the symbols into my journal. I'll return it later."

Peering into his caring eyes she wished Virgil hadn't banned him from the camp. "I wish you could come with me to the mess tent."

"Me too. I am not looking forward to eating my rations." He touched her nose with the tip of his finger. "Go eat. I will come see you in the artifact tent when everyone is asleep."

Isabella wasn't sure she could swallow a bite. Her stomach clenched in knots over all the strange things that had happened during the day. But she could tell by the determined set of Tino's jaw he wouldn't let her miss this meal.

She kissed his cheek. "Be careful."

"You as well," he said, kissing the hand he held and pushed her out of the dig.

She walked to the mess tent, still clutching the book. To her dismay Virgil and Jaycee were the only other occupants. She didn't want to deal with Jaycee's hostility or Virgil's scrutiny.

She stopped at the table farthest from the two, and Pedro placed a bowl of stew in front of her along with tortillas and fruit.

"*Buenas Noches.* You are the last to eat. You are lucky I saved some just for you, no?" Pedro grinned and nodded his head.

"*Gracias*, Pedro." She smiled at the cook and dug into the savory food.

The nape of her neck tingled and she glanced up.

Virgil approached the table. His gaze landed on the book beside her plate.

"Why do you still have this book?" he asked, touching the cover with his finger.

"I found similarities in this book to the glyphs on the tablet and the altar room. I wanted to compare them to the ones I found in the village." She had to give him a plausible answer without him realizing she had much of the ceremony deciphered.

"What have you found, exactly?" He stepped closer, towering over her.

"You'll know when I do. Right now it's all conjecture on my part. I'll know more once I study the charts in this book."

Virgil stared at her a moment then spun on his heel and stomped out of the tent. Isabella's shoulders sagged and relief whooshed out. She'd expected him to push harder.

Chapter Eighteen

Isabella spent the better part of the night hunched over a table in the mess tent, copying the symbols and meanings from Virgil's book into her journal. She categorized them under labels of names, places, times, and events, discovering more and more about the story not only on the tablet but also on the altar wall.

Exhaustion blurred her eyes and her hand began to cramp. She had one section in the book left to go through, but could hardly keep her eyes open. Closing the book, she slipped her journal into her vest pocket and tucked the book under her arm. She'd get some sleep then tackle the remainder of the symbols in the morning.

The air outside cooled the sweat she'd developed while concentrating inside the hot tent. A shiver tickled her skin. She smiled. After setting foot in this country, she didn't think a person could shiver here. She stared at the shower tent. Even the tepid water that collected in the tank above the shower stall would be inviting tonight.

At her tent, she tucked Virgil's book under her bedding, plucked a clean shirt and underwear off the rope holding the mosquito netting, and picked up her bag of toiletries. In the shower tent, she slung her vest over the partition between the two shower stalls, undressed, and slipped under the wonderful stream of water washing away the salty tang of sweat and vile DEET from her face, hair, and body. She lathered up her hair. Movement in her peripheral vision caught her attention. Her vest slipped over the partition and out of sight.

More concerned about her garment and its contents than her nakedness, she flung the curtain back and stepped out to catch Walsh pilfering the pockets on her vest.

"What do you think you're doing?" She crammed her fists on her naked bony hips and balanced her weight to throw a front snap kick.

Walsh froze. His gaze slowly moved up the length of her. His perusal only fanned her outrage. His beady eyes met hers. Another time and place she might have felt intimidated. Since setting foot in this country she'd learned you couldn't cower. You had to take action.

"What are you doing with my vest?"

"I was about to take a shower and this bloody thing was hanging over the partition. I took it down so it wouldn't get wet." He made a half-hearted effort to hand the vest to her. "I feel sorry for any gent wanting to ball you," he added, his gaze dropping to her breasts then her bony hips.

"I feel sorry for any female wanting to consort with the likes of you." She snatched her vest from him. "If I'm so unattractive why were you putting your hands all over me the other…" He wanted something in my vest then. "Get out of here before I scream and bring the whole camp in here to see you acting like a lecher." She stepped back into the shower stall, clutching her vest to her body. What did he want out of her vest?

Her journal.

He wanted the information she'd collected.

Isabella remained still inside the curtain, listening for his retreat. Blood pulsed in her ears, whooshing and hindering her ability to recognize if his footsteps retreated. The tent trembled as someone opened the flap. She counted to ten then stuck her head out.

Empty.

She hung her vest inside the stall and finished rinsing her hair. How far would Walsh go to get the journal? She'd have to be more cautious from now on.

Isabella dressed and walked across the compound. She should tell Tino about this latest attempt by Walsh. But she didn't know how to find him thanks to Virgil. She dropped her toiletries and dirty clothes inside her tent.

The artifact tent. Tino said he'd come to her there. Her heart accelerated walking toward the tent. If he wasn't inside, she'd wait for him.

"Tino? Hello?" She listened. Silence as heavy as the darkness of the tent closed in around her.

She began to shake. The encounter with Walsh flashed in her mind. He could have harmed her and dumped her body in the jungle and no one would have ever known what happened to her. Did he know someone was willing to pay half a million for the ceremony translation? Was he capable of murder to get it?

A waft of air blew across her wet head. She tried to peer into the darkness. Her heart hammered in her chest. Did Walsh follow her? She took a defensive stance and waited, breathing slow and easy to still her romping heart.

Something landed on her shoulder.

She spun and kicked.

"Ouch. Ezzabella, *querida*."

Isabella sucked in air and groped in the dark for Tino.

"I'm sorry, I-I…" She broke down sobbing in Tino's arms.

"*Querida*, shush, I am here. I did not mean to scare you." He whispered against her ear as his strong arms held her against his solid body.

When her tears subsided, she uncurled from his comforting embrace and wiped at her cheeks. "I'm sorry. I thought you were Walsh."

Tino cursed in Spanish. "Are you hurt?" His deep voice laced with anger sounded like an animal's growl. "I knew leaving you was not good."

"Shhh. I'm fine." She wrapped her arms around his neck and pressed her body to his.

His hands skimmed up and down her body as if he couldn't believe until he'd checked himself.

"What happened?" Tino asked, continuing to hold Isabella close. His anger was slowly receding as he held her and felt her body relaxing. If he hadn't been ready for her defensive move, he would have been on the ground at her feet rather than enjoying her in his arms.

"While I was taking a shower Walsh tried to steal my vest."

Rage rekindled in his gut. "Why? How did you stop him?" He leaned back wishing he could see her eyes, but the darkness prevented his assessing her answers.

"I saw my vest slip over the partition and stepped out of the shower and confronted him.

"Naked? You confronted a man I told you was dangerous naked?" His rage morphed into astonishment and fear. "*Mujer loca.*"

"He didn't like what he saw."

The hurt in her voice cooled his rage.

"That is his loss. But *pichón*, how did you get your vest back?"

"I confronted him and yanked it away. Now I know why he was groping me the other night. He's after my journal." The hard edge in her voice had him waiting for what else she had to say. "He's trying to learn what I know and sell the information."

Her last statement lost him. "What do you mean sell the information?" She squirmed to move from his arms. He pulled her snugger against him, "Oh no. What do you mean by that?"

"Virgil said if we deciphered this ceremony a Mayan artifact collector would pay us half a million."

His gut clenched. He'd never thought of her as money hungry. He knew her work here would help her project but he'd assumed through a paper she wrote.

"Why would you need that kind of money?"

"To fund my department. If I don't get that funding, they're shutting us down, and it will take me years to reestablish the project and get the backing to continue." The desperation in her voice made him wonder if greed would win out over what was right.

He released her and was glad for the dark. He didn't want to see her face right now. Or her to see the bleak thoughts going through his mind. Confusion muddled his gut instincts which said Isabella would do what was right, but he also had witness to the passion she had for discovering the past.

They stood in silence in the dark interior of the tent. It was foolish to jeopardize his mission for this woman but he couldn't walk away knowing this latest information.

"You should let me carry your journal. That way you will not be a target." He reached out making contact with her vest. He grabbed the garment and pulled her to him.

She slapped at his arm. "No! My life's notes are in that book. I need them to decipher the tablet, and I'll not cower to the likes of Walsh. He'd be stupid to try anything else."

"I will not allow you to put yourself in harm's way." The minute the words slipped out his lips he wanted to retract them.

"You won't allow me?" She leaned forward. Her breath puffed across his face. Any closer and he could kiss her. Not a bad idea. She made defensive maneuvers avoiding his kiss.

"I don't belong to you or anyone. No one can tell me what to do. I'm not a child. I'm a woman, and I can take care of myself. I always have and always will."

He grasped her shoulders, pulled her roughly against him, and kissed her until she relaxed in his arms. Tino pulled back only enough to speak. He loved being nose to nose with her and inhaling the air she inhaled. "*Mi pichón*, you have become very precious to me. I know you do not belong to me like property, but you have sprouted roots in my heart." He kissed her again. "When you hurt, I hurt. When you soar, I soar." He held her away, cursing the darkness, and wished he could make eye contact. "I just want you to be safe."

Isabella trailed her fingers down his cheek. The tender touch squeezed his heart. His *abuela* said he would meet a woman who would understand him and become his world. He had met her in this imp with a genius IQ, and he hoped like hell he could keep her alive long enough to show Isabella the real Tino Kosta, not the person he'd become in the last eight years.

Isabella sighed. "When you kiss me like that, I believe you. But I learned how to take care of myself a long time ago."

"Like confronting Walsh naked?" He still couldn't believe she'd been so *loco*. Rash thinking like that didn't equate with the logical woman.

"I couldn't let whoever took my vest get away with it. Like I said, it holds my life's work."

"There are times when you remind me of a child and others when you have the *cojones* of a military leader."

She snorted and laughed. "No one has ever accused me of having *cojones* before."

He smiled at the way she said *cojones*. It sounded sexier on her lips than any other time he'd heard the word. He had to steer his thoughts away from Isabella and sex. While she claimed to be a woman who could take on anyone, her heart and body were still as fragile as a teenager.

He had to make her see the dangers. "The rock I moved in the altar chamber blocks a tunnel that leads to a stash of drugs in a cave. Do not go down that tunnel and do not work in the altar room alone. There is no telling who may come through that tunnel."

"How did you find the cave?"

Should he tell her everything? She had the right to know who to trust and who not to. It could mean her safety.

"I have been following Walsh. He has met several times with narcos. Once was at the entrance to the cave."

She leaned against his chest. "I knew he was up to something. He doesn't take care of his responsibilities around here. Why on earth did Virgil hire him?"

"Walsh is known to gamble and sell artifacts to cover his debts."

Her body stiffened in his arms. He could feel her digesting the information and tabulating her thoughts.

"I bet he's behind the locals sneaking through the tunnel with artifacts. He could know the value of the items dug up." She talked to herself and slid her arms around his middle, hugging him and warming his body better than a good shot of tequilla.

"If he's giving the artifacts to the...what did you call them? Narcos? Do you think he's also dealing in drugs?" She leaned back as if trying to look into his face. "And Virgil. He needs funding. Do you think he'd stoop as low as to help the narcos to keep digging?"

He didn't like the way her thoughts had headed. If she kept playing with all the what if's she could get caught up in more trouble than he could get her out of. He'd been pondering the same thoughts and feared neither Walsh or Martin had enough authority over the narcos to keep anyone alive if things got rough.

"Pretend we know nothing." He gathered her hand, playing with her fingers. "You are going to have to continue doing whatever it is you do at the dig and forget what I have told you. I do not want something happening to you because of something I said. And while you are doing your job, I will do mine." He kissed her knuckles. "Ezzabella, promise me you will not say a word or go sleuthing about the dig."

"I promise I won't go poking into things that don't pertain to deciphering the tablet."

Her promise would have appeased him if he hadn't felt her legs brush his as she crossed them.

Chapter Nineteen

Tino walked Isabella to her tent before the howler monkeys began their morning calls. He stepped into the tent intending to give her a quick kiss. When she melted into his arms, he took the kiss to heights that even had him breathless and clinging.

"Ezzabella, you move me like no other." He'd never declared his feelings to a woman as he did with Isabella.

"No man has ever showed me passion or looked beyond my skinny body and intelligence."

"*Querida*, that was their loss and my fortune. Please, keep your brilliant mind and beautiful body out of trouble while I am gone." He kissed her once more and forced himself to leave. "Rest, so you can decipher the tablet and go home where it is safe."

"And you? Will you go home to safety?" Her green eyes peered deep into his. "Never mind. I see the answer." A tear glint in her eyes. "Be careful."

"*Mi pichón*, you have given me a reason to be careful." He peeked out her tent flap, saw no one and slipped into the jungle, heading for the narco cave.

~*~

A string of donkeys stood in front and two men guarded the entrance. Either a shipment was arriving or was getting ready to leave.

The men at the entrance straightened as the man he'd determined was the person in charge of this hideout and another man, dressed in a linen suit, walked out of the cave.

"This is an excellent place to hold shipments. You have done well, Eduardo." The well-dressed man slapped the other on the back. "Garza will be pleased."

"*Gracias*, don Miguel. But I do not understand why you are here. A journey into the jungle is not necessary."

"I have an arrangement with the American at the dig. I have come to make sure he holds up his end." Don Miguel stared toward the *Ch'ujuña* site.

Tino could only think of one American the Guatemalan spoke of, Dr. Virgil Martin. What kind of deal could there be between the two? Was Martin sending drugs to the states in the artifacts he dug up? Or did he orchestrate the passports in Isabella's box? Or was Miguel the money behind Isabella's project? Of all the possibilities this one churned his gut the most.

"Don Miguel, our cave is connected by a tunnel to the dig." The man nodded his head so vigorously Tino thought it might land at his feet.

Miguel smiled. "I know. Dr. Martin and I knew of this before the dig started. It is how I will join him to seal our deal." The man scanned the jungle again. "But first I must make sure all is set for Garza." They re-entered the cave.

Tino continued to watch until he was sure they were not returning. He made note of the men still positioned by the opening and hurried to his radio. The chatter of monkeys filled his ears as he pulled out the system and settled the earphones on one ear.

"Konstantine, over."

"Ginger, over."

"Give these coordinates to Hector and tell him to be ready to move." Tino checked the GPS on his watch and rattled the numbers off to Ginger. "Over."

"Is there a time line? Over."

He wished there were. "No. Have him as close as he can get without being noticed, and I'll radio when to move in. Over."

"Received. Over." The radio clicked. "Take care. Over."

Tino smiled. Ginger may come across as hard as nails but she had a heart.

"Will do. Out." He turned the radio off and stowed it under the tree root. The next thing was to get back to the excavation site, talk with Isabella, and get inside the dig to wait for Miguel to contact Martin.

His mind conjured up the inside of the dig as he worked his way to the compound. There wasn't a place to hide in there other than behind the altar and that would not hide him if Miguel came in through the tunnel. And how would Miguel let Martin know he was there waiting?

~*~

Tino spotted Isabella when she exited the shower tent and dropped her clothes off at her tent. She continued toward the dig entrance. He had to detain her. He moved in the shadows of the tents, drawing her attention. From her cautious approach, she didn't know it was him.

Just as she prepared her body to strike at him, Tino whispered, "Come, I need to talk to you."

He grasped her hand and led her into the jungle nearest them.

Once they'd traveled over twenty yards into the trees he stopped. "You must be careful. Better yet, you should pack and head out of here tomorrow."

He couldn't see her face due to the dark jungle and cloudy sky, but he felt her indignation.

"You know I won't leave until I've figured out what's written on the tablets and the altar wall."

He gripped her hands and drew her nose to nose with him. "*Mi pichón*, your Dr. Virgil Martin is involved with the people I am here to stop. I overheard a conversation today that does not mean good things for this dig or the people connected to it. Even you." His next words would not make her happy but he had to voice them. "Take your findings and decipher them at home where it is safe."

"I can't go yet. I have some more glyphs to copy before I can finish the translation."

He leaned, pressing his lips to hers trying to convey in the kiss his fears for her.

Tino moved out of the kiss but remained nose to nose. "Promise you will hurry and find your answers so you can leave?"

She nodded and asked, "What about you?"

He shrugged. "I need to get into the altar chamber without being seen so I can follow the tunnel to the narcos' cave and learn more."

She shook her head. "No. That's too dangerous."

He kissed her again, this time not as gentle. His tongue slid between her lips; tangling with hers, seducing her, and showing her life was worth living not throwing away.

Tino drew out of the kiss. He leaned his forehead on Isabella's. "I made a vow to my family to stop drug traffickers." His heart didn't ache as much when he thought of his family since meeting Isabella. She'd begun to fill the cracks of sorrow and guilt. He kissed her nose. "I will be very careful because I have a certain doctor I want to look up when this mission is finished."

"If anything happens to you, I'll go after the drug traffickers myself."

The venom in her words left little doubt in his mind that would be the case. "I promise nothing will happen to me." He held her head in his hands. "It is you I worry about. Do not try to find out what is going on. Just stay with people you trust and know. I will meet up with you again. I will never, nor would I want, to forget you. And when I am free of my obligation, I will come looking for you."

"Promise?"

Warm tears slipped along his hands. "I promise." He kissed her salty lips, sealing his promise and memorizing her taste, then took her hand and led her back to the compound.

"Go to your tent or the artifact tent. I am going into the dig." Tino squeezed Isabella's hand and let go.

She clutched his shirt sleeve. "Let me go in with you. If I go first and run into anyone it won't be suspicious. But for you to walk in and be seen, they'd wonder what you're doing here when Virgil asked you to leave."

"I do not know who could be in there. It could be the narcos waiting for Martin." He loosened her grip on his clothing. "I will not have you walking into a trap."

"But it's okay for you to walk into one?" She flung her hands in the air and stomped away from him. "Men!"

She gave in too easily. His feet wanted to follow her to make sure she did what he asked but, at that moment, Raul, the man Martin had thrown out of the camp, emerged from the dig. He glanced right and left, then hurried across the compound straight for Martin's tent.

Tino moved closer to the dig and waited in the shadows as Raul hurried back to the dig entrance, Martin jogging at his side. He counted to sixty and followed, creeping along the edge of the walls and listening to the movement and voices coming from ahead of him. Light glowed in the altar chamber.

"This room is exceptional, Virgil. Just as you said it would be." There was no mistaking the authority in the voice of don Miguel.

Tino stopped and knelt behind a small outcropping of a stone support in the doorway between the main chamber and the altar chamber.

"It has been kept in pristine shape by the layers of dirt and debris shielding it over the years." Awe filtered through Virgil's words. "It was last used for a virginal sacrifice to the moon."

"How fitting that we will use it in the same manner."

Don Miguel's excited tone plucked at the hairs on Tino's nape.

"I've been thinking about our agreement. There are too many people employed here to pull this off. We should wait—"

"We have a deal. You found this altar and offered me this opportunity to fund your dig. You also promised me the translations of the moon god ceremony. Unless you want to pay for your funding with your life, you will carry through with our deal." Miguel chuckled. "If this goes well, I would be more than happy to continue to fund any other endeavors you want."

"But all the workers, the specialists…"

"You will find a way to make this work. At the full moon."

The grinding of rock on rock meant Miguel and Raul had left through the tunnel. Tino shot to his feet and hurried into the area the workers cleared that morning. His dark colored clothes blended into the shadows. Martin talked to himself and scuffled around in the altar room for ten minutes before the light went out and he hurried back through the dig and out the entrance. The man, so caught up in his troubles, hadn't even glanced around as he walked out.

The full moon. That was less than a week away. They talked of the sacrifice Isabella was deciphering. He didn't like the tone of Miguel's voice. What sinister act was he up to?

Tino stopped in the altar room long enough to slowly scan a penlight over the altar wall. His occupation had enough gore, pain, and suffering; he didn't like to witness it outside the job. Yet, staring at the woman on the altar, following the path of her tears to the pool of blood on the ground, he shuddered. His gaze caught on the full moon hovering in the background, shedding tears too.

It couldn't be… Did Martin and Miguel plan to sacrifice a woman on the full moon? No, it would be… Exactly what the doctor would do for research and the madman with money would do for kicks. He had to find out who they planned to sacrifice and how to stop it without hurting his mission.

~*~

Isabella watched Virgil leave the dig site. She knew he had entered with the man they'd caught sneaking around, and she also saw Tino follow them all in. What had happened to Tino? Did they capture him?

She stayed along the edge of the compound and made her way to the tell covering the dig. This wasn't what Tino had asked her to do, but she couldn't just go to sleep and forget she saw him enter and only Virgil come back out. She slipped into the dig and pulled out her LED light. She kept the beam on her feet as she crept across the entry. Flashing the beam to the left, she noticed the workers had started clearing the room adjacent to the altar room.

She pivoted and walked into the altar chamber. The tang of burnt kerosene hung in the air along with the sharpness of tobacco. Someone other than Virgil, Raul, and Tino had been in this room. A meeting perhaps? That would explain Raul retrieving Virgil. But what were they meeting about? And where was Tino?

Her blood pumped at an accelerated pace and adrenaline flexed her muscles. The beam of her flashlight lit on the rock connecting this room with the tunnel Tino talked about. Had Tino been found and taken through that tunnel? She swallowed and stepped closer. If he was safe, he'd be furious with her. If he were hurt or a captive, he'd welcome her help. Wouldn't he?

She thought back to the day he'd snuck up on her in here. Which side had he shoved the rock to move it back in place? Isabella stood on the left side of the rock, put the flashlight between her teeth, braced her feet, and shoved on the boulder.

The grinding of rock on rock pumped her adrenaline and she pushed even harder. The boulder moved smoother than she'd imagined it would. Cool air rushed across her face and a chill crawled up her spine. She slipped through the opening, ran the beam of her light over the boulder, and found a stick wedged into a hole in the rock. She leaned her body into the stick and once again listened to the rock slide into place.

Darkness wound around her, disorienting her. No one would know what happened to her if for some reason she lost her way in this tunnel. Doubt crept into her head as the cool air fluttered her loose hair.

"I can do this!" she whispered and swept the light around her. Steps led downward. Apprehension tightened her muscles. Tino was somewhere in this tunnel. She would find him, and they'd get out undetected. She descended the short flight of steps.

The thick, musty air clogged her lungs as the damp darkness folded around her. Suffocating. She had to follow this tunnel. Fear for Tino squeezed her chest like a giant fist. Her head pounded in frustration. Her eyes ached from searching the weighty darkness beyond her small beam of light. This was the only direction Tino could have gone.

Sticky cobwebs clung to her face. Would there be cobwebs if Tino and others had come this way? She scraped the clinging fibers from her face, thinking of it as hair and the soft globs that were spiders as blobs of hair gel. If she let her mind stray to the soft-bellied arachnoids, her feet would stall.

Her palm slid along the slick, cool, dirt wall. She fought the urge to turn around and run back to the chamber. Tino needed her. Her toe struck a rock. Her breath rumbled in her lungs as loud as the howler monkey's cry. As a child, the darkness had never frightened her. But then she'd always been wrapped in familiar blankets, not creeping through a moist oppressive tunnel.

Counting her steps and keeping her light beamed to the ground in front of her feet, Isabella heard the voices before she noticed a faint glow. She doused her flashlight and crept closer. Angry male voices spoke in rapid Guatemalan. A word here and there was recognizable. Her heart stopped when Tino's voice responded and the thunk of something hard against—she cringed.

Silence.

A tear trickled down her cheek. She had to help him. Isabella

174

pressed her back against the wall and sidestepped toward the light. The voices laughed and conversed, but she didn't hear any more from Tino. The tunnel opened wider. She dropped to her knees, kept along the wall, and crawled to a spot behind a pile of pack gear.

Tino lay curled in the middle of the room. His hands and feet were tied. She choked back a gasp at the sight of blood seeping down his face and the bright gash on his temple. Fear and outrage couldn't win out. She had to keep a level head and find a solution.

Isabella scanned the chamber. Another dark tunnel veered to the left. Two men sat on the ground at the far entrance of the chamber playing cards. She either had to wait and see if they left or give them a reason to leave. The latter would get rid of them faster.

Isabella focused on the pile of gear in front of her. Rope and metal rigging rings. She pulled out her army knife and, with trembling fingers, cut loose a dozen rings, setting them carefully to the side, and picked out anything else that would make noise. Her nerves calmed as she formed a plan.

Crawling backward, placing her knees and feet slow and quiet, and sucking in any grunts, she dragged the rope back through the dark cave, until only a faint light could be seen from the chamber. She switched on her light and searched for something to anchor the rope. A section of the tunnel twenty feet from the chamber had adequate protrusions on the sides to tie the rope across the tunnel at about shin level. Urgency hummed through her body, spinning her mind and tangling her fingers as she tied the knots. She had to hurry. If more men arrived, this plan wouldn't work. And it might not work even with just the two men. There was no guarantee they would both run into the passage.

She sent up a prayer to all the deities she'd learned about and looked for a spot to secure the fishing line. A tree root, head-height, had the qualities needed. She removed the fishing line from her pocket and threaded it through the loop.

She crawled back to her spot behind the gear and, starting at one end of the fishing line, she tied the metal rings and buckles in various groupings and lengths. Careful not to clang them together, she crawled ten feet into the tunnel and set them down. Back behind the gear again, she slowly rolled the line back onto the spool until taut.

Isabella pulled out her Army knife, flipped open the blade, and stabbed it into the ground next to her, making it accessible. Inhaling deeply, she prayed her plan would work, and pulled on the fishing line.

A dull clanging and sharp pings echoed down the tunnel as the metal hit rocks. The men jumped to their feet and stared at one another. Isabella reeled in more line, causing the jingling again.

The men sprinted into the tunnel, running past her hiding spot and into the darkness. She didn't wait to hear them hit the ground. Shooting to her feet, she grabbed the knife, and hurdled over the gear, slicing through the ropes securing Tino. His head rolled loose on his shoulders, but she managed to get him to his feet.

"Come on. There's only one way we can go." Isabella draped his arm over her shoulders and supported much of his weight as they hurried to the dark tunnel. She glanced over her shoulder and spotted their footprints. Inside the tunnel she leaned Tino up against the wall. "I'll be right back."

He reached for her, but she evaded his grasp and hurried back to the chamber, unbuttoning her vest. In the middle of the chamber, she swept the ground with her vest, walking backward toward their escape route. Their shuffling exit was erased. She slipped her vest on and hurried to Tino.

"Come on," she whispered, once again slipping under his arm to give him support. She traveled another twenty feet before flipping on her light. Tino's weight gradually lightened as he started supporting himself.

"Shamutz!" A pile of dirt and rock blocked the tunnel. They couldn't go back. By now his capturers knew Tino was missing and were probably scouring the tunnels. It would only be a matter of time and they would come down this one. She trained the light all the way to the top of the pile. Isabella thought she saw a hole.

She faced Tino, shining the light on him. The sight of his bloody head twisted her stomach. "Oh, I forgot about the gash! But we need to keep going."

"I am fine. But I am not happy you did not listen to me." Tino grimaced and grasped her hand. "You were safer staying at the compound."

"When Virgil came out after you'd followed him in, I couldn't stand the idea you might have been captured. I moved the rock and followed the tunnel. And see…" She scrambled to the top of the dirt pile. "You did need help."

"Where are you going?" Tino grabbed her ankle.

"It looks like we can dig a hole and keep going."

"Let me do that." He crawled up beside her.

"If we both work at it, we can be out of here faster." She pulled her folded hat out of her vest and used it to scoop the dirt. Tino used his hands. They soon had a hole just large enough they could slither through.

"You go first," Tino motioned to the hole.

Isabella grabbed the light she'd wedged between two rocks to light their work area and held it in her mouth as she slithered through the hole. She slid down the other side of the dirt mound and studied the pile for debris to fill in the hole once Tino came through. He had to wiggle a bit more than she did, but he soon slid down beside her.

"Help me shove these rocks and sticks into the hole we made." Together they jammed the hole full then set off down the tunnel.

"We have no way of knowing where this tunnel will lead us," Tino said, glancing at his watch. He flicked the instrument with a finger. "My GPS doesn't work underground."

"I thought that was a fancy watch for a jungle guide." Isabella continued exploring the walls of the tunnel with her light. "From the dampness seeping in, I'd say we're getting close to either a river or a lake." She stopped and extracted two energy bars from her vest.

Tino took the bar and smiled. While he was angry with her for not staying in the compound, he had to admire her ingenuity and gutsiness. "Now I see why you were so adamant about your survival vest the first night I met you."

She smiled. "If you use your head it has everything a person needs to get out of trouble."

"Which reminds me. How did you get rid of the guards back there?"

"I lured them down the tunnel and tripped them." She took a bite of her bar and continued walking.

He shook his head and followed. "I have studied the maps of this area. If we are getting near a water source then we must be headed toward the Usumacinta River."

"That's the one we traveled to get here, isn't it?"

"Yes."

"But I thought there was a lake around here too?"

"It is farther north."

Tino finished the bar and wished he had something to drink. "You do not happen to have any water in that magical vest do you?"

To his surprise, she pulled out a small flask.

"Small sips. It has to last us until we can refill it." Isabella smiled brightly at him, and he couldn't resist stealing a kiss.

"*Gracias* for coming to my rescue." He kissed her again. "But now we have to get you back before anyone notices you are missing and figures out you helped me get loose." He grasped her hand and they continued. All around them the tunnel oozed water, making their progress slow and slippery.

The fluttering of wings erupted ahead of them.

"What's that?" Isabella asked in a breathless whisper.

Tino stepped past her. "Bats." He took several steps before noticing the light Isabella held wasn't continuing. Retracing his steps, he stood in front of her. "What is wrong?"

"I can't. Bats…"

Tino grasped her hand and tugged. "They will stay out of our way if we stay out of theirs."

Her trembling radiated up his arm and squeezed his heart. "We have to keep going. It is the only way out of here."

"I can't."

Chapter Twenty

Isabella didn't understand her fear of bats, but she couldn't move her petrified feet. Her ears heard only the flapping of wings. Something tugged on her hand. She jerked her hand free.

Muffled words mixed with the buzzing in her head.

Shaking—something shook her body. A light flashed in her eyes and Tino's face came into view.

"Ezzabella, *pichón*, we have to keep going. Your vest does not hold enough to keep us alive in here forever."

Tino's cajoling voice drew her gaze to his concerned face. She knew logically they must continue but making her body move seemed impossible.

"These are fruit bats. They do not harm people. They are coming in to roost for the day, which means there is an outside entrance to this tunnel." He tugged on her hand. "Come, we will soon have you back to the compound."

She wanted to follow, get out of this tunnel, and eat one of Pedro's wonderful breakfasts. Her body, however, wouldn't move. The flap of wings grew in volume. Isabella covered her ears and shut her eyes.

"I will be right beside you the whole way." Tino wrapped an arm around her shoulders and, again, urged her forward.

"I can't. The wings...I can't move." She hated her fear.

179

Something touched her hair. She batted at it with her hands and screeched.

"*Querida.*" Tino caught her hands, holding them in front of her. "It is only my shirt. I am putting it over your head so you do not have to fear a bat touching you. I will lead you through their lair." He kissed her cheek and his shirt settled around her head and shoulders.

His comforting, spicy scent filled her senses. An arm wrapped around her shoulders and they slowly moved forward. She put one foot in front of the other, her confidence building with each stride.

She sensed the motion of the bats, her heart stilled, and her breathing stopped. Tino's pace accelerated, then his arm left her shoulders.

"Tino?" She froze.

"*¡Vamos!*" His voice came from the direction of scuffling and flapping wings.

"Tino!"

"*¡Vamos!* Run to the light!" His shout scared her.

Isabella pulled the shirt from her head and in the faint light from the entrance of the cave she watched in horror as Tino flailed his arms to thwart the bats swooping at him. It took a split second for her mind to register the large ears, long snout, and sharp teeth of the vampire bat.

"Shamutz!" She yelled and smacked the bats with Tino's shirt. His tank t-shirt left too much of his skin exposed.

Her fear for Tino vanquished her own terror.

She had one goal; save Tino. Swinging his shirt, Isabella herded Tino toward the light. She kicked a bat running in a swaggering gait along the ground toward them.

She shoved Tino out of the cave, running behind him into the growing light of dawn. The bats didn't follow.

"I've never—" Isabella grasped Tino and hugged him tight. Her body shook, keeping time to her racing heart. He kissed her head and clung to her.

"We are so far from livestock I honestly thought those would be fruit bats."

"Why did they attack you?" A violent convulsion shook her body.

"They probably smelled the blood from my wound." He held her tight a moment more then drew back. "We have to get you back to the compound."

Isabella shook her head. "First we have to clean up those scratches." She pulled out her first aid kit and cleaned the gash on his head and the abrasions on his arms from warding off the bats. "Do you think they had rabies?" What would she do if Tino caught the disease clear out here in the middle of nowhere?

"Usually the bats that are near civilization are the ones that contract the disease. And they did not bite me. The scratches are from their claws. I should be fine." Tino pulled his shirt on and studied his watch.

"But what if you aren't? We have to be out of here in ten days. I read where that's the length of time it takes for your body to start showing signs." Isabella grabbed a fistful of his shirt. "You can't shrug this off. I will not let you die."

He cupped her face in one hand. "*Mi pichón*, you worry too much. I will be fine." Tino kissed her cheek and started walking.

She caught up to him. "I mean it. You could be infected and how could you carry out your mission?"

"These are only scrapes. How do you know I did not get them crawling through the hole or when the narcos discovered me?" He continued through the forest, maneuvering around large ferns and downed trees.

"Those are fresh cuts. And they are small enough that your shirt would have prevented them." Guilt seeped into her thoughts. "If you hadn't given me your shirt, the bats wouldn't have left marks." She stopped. "Shamutz. My fear could kill you!" This whole fiasco was her fault. He wouldn't be caught up in the compound and all its problems if she hadn't come to Guatemala.

She heard Tino moving steadily forward. He couldn't be left alone. She had to keep an eye on him, help him finish his mission, and get to civilization in ten days. Rushing forward, shoving the vegetation out of her way, she slammed into Tino's back.

He wrapped his arms around her. His hot breath tickled her ear. "There is a patrol ahead of us. The way they are poking at everything, they are looking for me."

Isabella turned her head, meeting his lips with hers. If he had rabies she shouldn't kiss him. His saliva mixed with hers could infect her. He hasn't been bitten. She'd take the chance. Her lips parted and she kissed him briefly, soaking in his strength and calm. "What do we do?" she whispered against his mouth.

"Take the long route. Unfortunately, that means you will not get back to the compound without their missing you." He peered into her eyes.

"If they're all out here looking for you, we can go back through the tunnels." She shook at the thought of going back through the bats.

"I am sure they are watching the tunnels." He released her and grasped her hand. "Come on. We will have to make a wide circle around them. I hope they do not find my radio gear the way they are searching."

Isabella followed Tino. He moved with stealth and stopped often, listening. Her stomach rumbled. "When will we get to the dig?" She wiped at the perspiration gathering on her forehead. The jungle canopy spared her from direct sunlight, but the heat and humidity zapped her energy.

"Tomorrow morning, if we do not encounter any more obstacles." Tino picked up the pace an hour after they'd found the men looking for him. He stopped, wiping a sleeve across his forehead.

Isabella swatted at the mosquitoes buzzing her face. As much as she hated the nasty smelling DEET, she would love to bathe in some right now. "Tomorrow? This must be some circle we're making."

"It's not that big a circle. We cannot make good time dodging the forest and the narcos." He checked his watch. "All I have to go by are the coordinates on my GPS. If I had a map, I could see the lay of the land and determine a better course."

Spider monkeys chortled in the tops of the trees.

"Why not climb up a tree and check out the terrain?" She peered up the tree she leaned against. The bark wasn't so smooth that it would be impossible to climb.

"The branches are high in the air." Tino tipped his head back gazing up the tree.

"Haven't you ever seen an electrical lineman climb a power pole?" Isabella scanned the area around them. Thick vines hanging from a nearby tree looked promising. She walked over, jumped up, and clung to the vine, dangling in air to see if it held her weight. The vine held and she didn't land on her butt. A good sign.

She dropped to the ground, pulled out her tin, and extracted the wire saw.

"You do have everything." Tino took the wire from her and sawed through the vine at the spots she indicated.

"We can't tie this together, so you'll have to hold the two ends tight." Isabella wrapped the vine around her back and the tree, showing Tino how to lean into the vine and walk up the trunk.

Her racing heart stalled when he had some problems the first ten feet, but once he synchronized his feet and the movement of the vine, he climbed steadily.

"Over that way is a bare ridge. We can make better time going along it." He worked his way back down and stopped in front of her. His skin glistened with perspiration.

"Here." She handed him the flask.

He took a sip and handed it back.

"Drink more. You expended a lot of energy and sweat climbing that tree." She pushed the flask back toward him.

"You need to drink too."

"I will. But you first. With the rain this afternoon we can refill the flask and my bag." One thing you could count on during the rainy season. Water.

He nodded, took two long gulps, and handed the flask back. Isabella sipped and capped the bottle. "Let's go."

Tino grinned and started out in the direction of the ridge. He'd marked the location on his watch. They should be there in an hour. He would keep the fact that he saw the compound to himself. The movement of more bodies than the usual crew reflected either they realized Isabella was missing or the narcos had taken over the compound. The best course of action he could take would be to get to his radio and tell Hector to move in and capture the tunnel and the narcos scouring the jungle looking for him. The problem—the narcos looking for him were between him and the radio.

"Will this ridge get us back to the compound today?" Isabella's voice reminded him he wasn't alone and had to think of her safety first.

"If we can keep a steady pace, we should arrive at the compound after dark, which will be best for sneaking you back in." He didn't want to leave her at the mercy of all the questions that would be put to her, but she was safer among the dig workers than with him dodging narcos.

"You haven't told me what you overheard last night and how they caught you."

Her comment landed as deadly as a spear in his chest. To tell her what he had overheard would put her in more danger. He'd learned enough about Isabella to know she would be more determined to decipher the carvings in the altar chamber and stop Virgil.

"I followed *don Miguel* and Raul into the tunnel. They had set a sentry twenty feet up the tunnel from the chamber where you found me. The two walked past and the sentry did not move or say a word. I did not know he was there until he thumped me on the head." Resentment at being jumped gurgled in his gut. "When I came around, two of the narcos tried persuading me to tell them who I was and why I followed them. When I did not cooperate, they punched my head with the stock of a gun."

Tino faced Isabella. "Then a guardian angel came along and lifted me from their hands."

"They would have killed you if I hadn't worried about you." She placed a hand on his arm. "You have to be more careful. I couldn't bear…" Tears glistened in her eyes.

He wrapped his arms around her, hugging her to his heart. "*Mi pichón*, I have the lives of a cat and the promise I made to you. Nothing will keep me from fulfilling that promise." Tino kissed the top of Isabella's head and breathed in her scent. "Come, we must keep moving." He grudgingly moved away from her, striding toward the ridge he'd seen. His fears for her would keep them safe. This latest encounter made him more vigilant.

The major problem was figuring out who was her friend and who was her enemy at the dig. After overhearing the discussion between Martin and Miguel, he feared the doctor couldn't be trusted. Nor could Walsh because of his dealings with the narcos. The only person he trusted at the dig was the cook, Pedro. He would slip into the cook tent after he deposited Isabella in her tent and ask the man to keep an eye on her. He had to get back to the radio and tell Hector to move on the cave.

They walked out onto the ridge. The hot tropical sun baked his bare head.

"We will keep to the edge of the trees for shade." He grasped

Isabella's hand. Here in the open they could walk side-by-side.

"A good plan."

Tino noticed Isabella's lagging steps. "Would you like to rest and eat? I see a papaya tree."

"Yes. I'm afraid no sleep and little food is catching up to me." Isabella sank to the ground at the base of a tree.

"I will be right back." Tino walked to the tree. Orange and yellow oval-shaped fruit hung in a cluster from the bottom of the fronds to within his reach. Thankful it was a wild papaya tree which was smaller and yielded smaller fruit, he plucked half a dozen papayas. The first two, he wedged into the breast pockets of his shirt. He tucked his T-shirt into his pants and dropped the fruit down inside his shirt to keep his hands free to pluck a few more.

He returned to Isabella and found her curled up asleep. She had to be exhausted. Unable to bring himself to wake her, he watched her sleep and ate a papaya. She did everything with her whole heart. He should have mentioned the conversation between the two men in the altar chamber. But she'd seek answers and that would bring her in closer contact with the two men. He couldn't chance her meeting don Miguel. He would rather she kept her passion focused on the tablet and on him. The heat of the afternoon tugged his eyelids closed and he fell asleep dreaming of Isabella's soft lips.

~*~

Isabella woke and sniffed. What was that offensive smell? And sound? Grunting and a squeal shot her to a sitting position. The noise intensified as a group of pecarí shot into the trees behind her.

"¡Carajo!" Tino sat up. A papaya with a bite out of it sat on the ground beside him.

Isabella giggled. The pecarí had sneaked up to eat the fruit beside Tino. He was so exhausted he hadn't even noticed.

"The little thieves." Tino tossed the fruit with the missing bite into the bushes.

"Is that all you had? I'm hungry." She could've cut off the nibbled side.

Tino unbuttoned his shirt and pulled his T-shirt out of his waistband. Fruit tumbled into his lap.

"You're lucky they didn't go for the hidden fruit." She crawled up beside him and kissed his cheek. "My provider." She plucked a papaya from his lap, opened her Army knife, and sliced the fruit in half.

"You can pluck my fruit any time." He joked but his eyes blazed.

"I just did." She teased and licked the juice running down her chin.

Tino growled, grabbed her behind the neck, and pulled her to him. "Two can tease, *querida*." His tongue skimmed lightly across her lips.

She parted her lips and he continued to trace the outside edges with the tip of his tongue. The light touch ignited a need for more. She tried to press her lips to his, but he avoided her, teasing with his tongue.

Frustrated she tried to pull away. His hold tightened only enough to keep her from getting away.

"Ah, ah, ah. I see you are one to tease but not enjoy being teased." He skimmed his lips across hers and pulled back when she tried to deepen the kiss.

"You're not teasing. You're torturing." Isabella thrust out her bottom lip in a pout and was rewarded when Tino drew it between his lips and rubbed his tongue across the sensitive inside.

The sensations tingled to her toes, but she remained still, knowing if she tried to take it farther, he would pull back. Her patience was rewarded. Tino deepened the kiss and his hand slid from her neck down her back, drawing her body closer to him.

Still worried he would pull away, she kept her hands lax.

"You may touch me now," he said against her lips.

She smiled. "I'm not ready."

"You are a *plaga, querida*." Tino leaned back, and she fell forward, nearly in his lap, before catching herself.

"*¿Plaga?*" It sounded like plague, but she didn't think that was what he meant.

"You are mischievous, no?" He picked up a fruit that had rolled from his lap and used her knife to cut it open.

"It takes one to know one." Isabella raised an eyebrow and took another bite from her fruit.

"True." He grinned. Juice dribbled from the corners of his mouth. "That is why we get along so well."

Isabella leaned in and licked the juice off his skin. "That's one of the reasons." She stared into his eyes.

He broke contact. "Eat. We need to keep moving."

She sat back and ate three papayas and sipped water. The flask was nearly empty. The clouds didn't appear any closer to dropping rain than earlier in the day.

A thumping sound she'd not heard in the jungle before was muffled then grew in volume. "What's that?"

"A helicopter. Slip farther into the trees." Tino grabbed her arm and they scrambled to their feet and deeper into the forest.

"Shouldn't we see who it is? It might be the park officials."

Tino shook his head and pointed through a break in the trees. The vehicle hovered over the clearing, turning this way and that. The emblem on the side looked like agricultural products.

"Don Miguel," Tino said, his face darkening and his mouth turning grim.

"You've mentioned him before. Who is he?" She didn't think she was going to like what he said.

"He is the man funding the dig. I followed him into the tunnel."

"Virgil is funding his dig with drug money?" Isabella couldn't believe the man she knew would stoop that low. "He hates drugs. He helped an assistant go through rehab." Did her father know? Was that why he had stopped funding Virgil? Stopped inviting him to family gatherings?

Tino shook his head. "I do not know if it is drug money or Miguel's money. From what I have heard Miguel is friends with the man I am trying to bring down. But I cannot say it is drug money he is using to fund the dig."

The helicopter rose and skimmed across the tops of the trees.

"They are looking for me." He peered into her eyes. "The quicker we get you away from me the better. I do not know what you will tell them at the dig about being gone, but you cannot let anyone know you were with me or helped me." Tino grabbed her upper arms. "Promise me you will not let anyone know you were with me. It could be your death if they think you know anything."

Isabella gulped, shoving the lump of fear back into her bubbling stomach. If she hadn't been through so much lately, she'd think she had an ulcer the way the acid seemed to burn in the lining.

"Promise."

She nodded. "But what do I say?"

"We must continue. We will think of something as we walk."

Tino wrapped an arm around her shoulders and drew her to the edge of the forest. "We need to stay inside the cover of the trees. That helicopter could come buzzing back by here at any time."

She nodded and snuggled deeper into the security of his arm. What could she tell Virgil and the others when she reappeared at the dig? That she'd disappeared during the time Tino was caught and freed would be looked at with high suspicion. Her fib had to be fool proof.

Chapter Twenty-One

The shimmer of moonlight reflecting through the clouds afforded little light as Isabella stepped from the trees at the edge of the compound. No one milled about. Everything looked as it had when she left. The quiet, with the faint background of night sounds, unnerved her. She had walked across this compound many nights with the same quiet, but tonight she wished for more sound to cover her entrance.

Her gaze lingered on the dig entrance. Of their own volition, her feet started that direction, but Tino's insistence she not go in the altar chamber without someone with her ate at her conscience. Her rumbling stomach broke her stride. She peered around to see if others heard.

Food, then a shower. She'd worry about telling anyone where she'd been until she was discovered and asked. Cautious steps carried her to the mess tent. She entered and, using her honed recall skills to visualize the layout of the tent, she found food and drink in the dark. Her stomach satisfied, Isabella left the mess tent and hurried into her tent, found her toiletries, and entered the shower tent.

If her luck held out, she'd get a good night's sleep before anyone found her. The water pelting her head and skin revived her lagging spirits. How could she converse with Virgil knowing the things she now did? Knowing who he allowed to fund the dig made her wonder if this don Miguel was the man who was paying for the ceremony translation. If so, she wasn't sure she wanted to give him the knowledge or take his tainted money.

Her desire to keep her department funded warred with her intuition that don Miguel was up to no-good. From what she'd deciphered so far, this ceremony was special and the outcome wasn't what the Maya's had hoped. The element she didn't know yet was what caused the ceremony to go wrong and what they'd expected from the ceremony.

Lost in her thoughts she stepped out of the shower and reached for her towel. The nail was empty. Before she dropped her gaze to the floor, her towel swung into view.

Virgil's hard stare made her take a step back.

"Looking for this?" Venom dripped from his words.

"Yes. I'd like to dry off before I put my clothes on." Isabella snatched the towel and wrapped it around her body. A quick scan of the interior of the tent registered they were alone.

"You're the only person I know who takes showers in the middle of the night. When I saw the lantern in here, I knew you were back. Where have you been?"

The barely controlled rage in Virgil's voice puzzled more than frightened. What did he care where she'd been?

Isabella dried the best she could without leaving parts of her body for his viewing and quickly donned her clothes.

"I went for a walk and became disoriented."

The skepticism wrinkling his brow and drooping the corners of his mouth set her stomach twisting.

"A walk in the jungle? You're too smart to go for a walk alone. Did you meet that guide?" He stepped forward his hands gripping her upper arms. "If I find out you were with him I'll…" He jerked her hard against this chest. "Are you still a virgin?"

Her heart banged against her ribs as fear and revulsion coursed through her body. She'd never feared this man. Thought of him as a second father and now he was treating her like a drug addict whore.

"Yes! Why do you care? The way you're treating me it's obvious all these years you've only been nice to me to suck up to my father and his money."

His face relaxed and his features softened. "Good Isabella. You've always been a good girl. I just…To think you might have thrown your career and life away by consorting with the likes of that guide. It hurt to think you'd do that after all I've done to help you."

He released her arms and backed away. "I'm sorry. I was just so worried I wasn't thinking straight." His lips curved into the doting smile of her childhood. "Forgive me?"

She swallowed and peered into his face. "I'm sorry I frightened you. I'll not wander off again." She sounded like a recalcitrant child, but all she could think of was getting away from Virgil and thinking. She'd confess to anything he wanted to get him to leave.

Isabella pulled her vest off the inside of the partition and slipped her arms through. She took two steps, and Virgil placed a hand on her arm.

"Do you forgive me?"

"Yes." She'd never choked on a word before but right now her throat felt like she vomited hot lava.

"Good." Virgil patted her arm and strolled out of the tent.

A chill slid up Isabella's back. She hurried to her tent, placed her vest under her pillow, and set the large knife beside her bed. Her encounter with Virgil had her nervous and scared. He was up to something and it had to do with her. She'd figure it out in the morning when there were people around and he couldn't bully her.

~*~

Tino waited for Isabella to enter the shower tent before he made his way to the cook's tent. He ducked through the flap and stopped. The hard, round barrel end of a gun jabbed him in the side.

"Who sneaks into my tent?" Pedro's low whisper held an edge of menace he wouldn't have attributed to the good-natured cook.

"Tino."

The gun immediately disappeared. "Has Isabella been with you? Dr. Martin has been storming around searching for her."

"*Sí*. How upset was the doctor?" Tino didn't care about the man, only Isabella's safety.

"He interrogated everyone, tore through the tents, and sent groups into the jungle looking for her. His excitement seemed *loco*." Pedro drew Tino farther into the tent and handed him a folding stool.

Interesting, the man was sitting down for a talk, but he didn't light a lantern which would project their images on the tent wall. Who exactly was this cook? Tino took the offered stool and sat.

"Ezzabella is fine. But no one can know she was with me. Her life depends on it." His gut told him this man could be trusted.

"Are you the one the narcos look for?"

He was right. The narcos had come to the dig. He had to make the call on whether or not to trust this man.

"I sense you do not trust me, no?" Pedro's hand rested on Tino's shoulder. "I know you are DEA. I am paid to keep an eye on Dr. Martin and since the arrival of Isabella, her as well."

"Who is paying you?" This new information lightened Tino's worries. He could trust Pedro to keep Isabella safe. But how did Pedro know he was DEA?

"I am not allowed to say. Where is Isabella now?"

"In the shower tent. We still need a good excuse for her being gone. She cannot say she was with me."

"No. Do not tell her I am watching her or the doctor." Pedro's hand lifted. "I only told you to ease your worries. I know you have to dodge the narcos. You can continue, and I will protect Isabella."

"It will be a relief to know I can do my job and not worry about her."

"I have seen how close you two have become. Do not hurt her. She is a good girl." The fatherly tone in Pedro's voice surprised Tino.

"I do not plan on ever hurting her."

"*Bueno. Vamos.* You have work to do, and I need sleep before I prepare the morning meal." Pedro stood.

Tino stood and held out a hand. Pedro grasped his hand in a firm shake.

"Look out for her. We have future plans." Tino ducked out the tent and into the forest. He wondered how Pedro knew the things he did, but the man had always given him the impression he was on the right side. He would listen to his gut instinct on this one. With worries about Isabella off his mind, he could concentrate on the mission. He flicked on his penlight, checked his GPS, and headed toward his radio. He would know soon if the narcos had discovered it. If they had, he'd go to plan B.

Improvise.

He worked his way through the jungle cautiously, listening for any unusual nocturnal sounds. Bumping into narcos searching for him would hinder his assignment. A large flock of macaws squawked and flew from a tree ten yards to his left. Their disturbance activated his survival mode. He had been walking on a relatively easy trail he'd used quite often. He changed course, veering to his right and quietly wove his way through a denser section of vines, ferns, and fronds. He didn't need to stay on the trail with his GPS.

His mind wandered to why Martin was upset about Isabella's disappearance. Did it have anything to do with what Martin and Miguel talked about? A virgin. His chest tightened. If they were planning some kind of re-enactment, they would need a Maya virgin. Did they plan to use Isabella to find them one? Would she stoop that far to re-enact history and get her funding?

He checked his watch. Twenty yards to the left and he'd know if his equipment had been found.

A cough resonated through the foliage. *¡Coño!* They found his pack and waited for him to come for it. His heart accelerated and his mind raced through possible actions.

Plan B.

Tino retraced his steps, putting distance between him and the narcos. He pulled out his knife and sawed at a vine. He walked back toward his equipment's hiding spot, stopping a safe distance away and used the method Isabella taught him earlier to climb the tallest tree.

He spotted movement of a man mixed with the darker shapes of the forest near the spot where he'd stashed his equipment. The dusky gray of dawn lightened the area with the glow of the emerging sun. There stood another man. And yet another. Three men were positioned too close together to take out one without the others noticing.

He had to get to the radio. They couldn't stay alert forever. He'd hang out in the tree and see if they had replacements. He shimmied farther up into the limbs and greenery of the tree, rested his back against the trunk, and watched the men.

The howler monkeys' morning tribute rolled through the canopy. New noises on the ground proved to be the arrival of three men with guns slung over their shoulders emerging from the east. They exchanged greetings with the three standing guard. Their conversation floated up to Tino in pieces. They were still searching for him. If he didn't show by the end of the day his equipment would be taken to the cave. The three new men moved into the positions around the pack and the other three left

I have to get my things.

Tino peered through the canopy to the floor of the forest. His pack and radio bag sat in the open, ready for him to snag if he could just distract the men guarding it.

A snuffling, grunting sound registered in the distance. Pecarí. He slipped down the tree and headed toward the sound. With a little luck, they just might be the diversion he needed to get his gear.

Over a dozen of the smelly creatures rummaged across the forest floor, grunting and squealing each time a smaller one would get in the way of a larger one. If he could just get them headed toward the men…

The sweet scent of ripe fruit slithered by Tino's nose. He scanned the area and spotted a papaya tree. The animals snuffled along the ground toward the fallen fruit. Moving slow and quiet to not frighten the pecarí, Tino slid his shirt off and piled the rotting fruit into his makeshift sling. He left half a dozen overripe fruit under the tree and walked toward his equipment, dropping fruit along the way. Twenty feet from the guards, he dropped the remainder of the papayas on the ground and found a spot where he could get behind the pecarí when they stopped to eat the fruit.

He didn't have to wait long. Within minutes he heard the animals moving through the forest toward him. His adrenaline rose. Tino zeroed his senses into the men he wished to distract. The guards' voices rose as they registered the animals coming their way. Tino jumped out of the brush, scaring the pecarí toward the guards. He ran behind the animals, but stayed back far enough to avoid the men seeing him.

Crashing and swearing echoed in front of him. Tino hurried to the tree and grabbed his bags, darting off in the opposite direction of the stampeding wild animals and men. He traveled steady for two hours before he stopped and checked his GPS. The archeological dig and the narcos cave measured close to the same distance from him in different directions. He pulled out the radio and dialed in Ginger.

"Ginger, over."

"Konstantine, over."

"Are you ready for Hector? Over."

"*Sí.* Send him to these coordinates. Over." He read off the coordinates to the cave he'd locked into his GPS. "I will be waiting for him. Over."

"I'll tell him. Be careful. Out."

Tino flipped the radio off. He didn't know how close Hector and his men were to the cave. He would head in that direction and hope they arrived at the same time. He shouldered his pack and moved out in a straight line for the narcos' hideout. After stealing back his belongings, he didn't doubt they would turn over every fern looking for him. He'd have to take his time and use extreme caution.

Chapter Twenty-Two

The whisper of air carrying a fragrant scent seeped into Isabella's consciousness. She fought the need for sleep as the memory of her confrontation with Virgil shred her sleepy haze. Who had entered her tent? One eye slowly opened as her hand clutched the knife by her side.

Empty.

She was the only person in her tent. The spicy scent filled the small confines. She pushed to a sitting position and noticed a cloth bag next to her pack with a note pinned to it. Had Tino left this for her?

She unfolded the note and glanced at the name on the bottom. Pedro. Opening the bag, she scanned the contents. Spicy, aromatic leaves.

Returning to the note, she read:

Isabella,

These are allspice leaves. Tell the others you heard me say I ran out of them and while wandering in the forest you ran across a tree. You picked the leaves and lost track of time. When you returned it was after dark and everyone was in bed.

Tino and I have spoken.

Pedro.

Isabella smiled. She'd known Pedro was a good person and could be trusted. He and Tino concocted this alibi. She hummed a jaunty

196

tune as she dressed and prepared to face the others. How could she concoct the story to make it plausible that she was gone all day just picking these few leaves?

Something would come to her. She hated lying, but fabricating a good story to keep herself and Tino alive was worth the small fib. She exited her tent and swallowed the lump creeping up her throat as the others filed into the mess tent. Shoulders back, spine straight, she walked to the mess tent with the small bag.

She opened the tent flap and stepped inside. Eunice ran forward.

"Isabella! Where have you been?" The woman wrapped her long arms around Isabella and squeezed. "We thought the worst had happened to you."

"I'm sorry to have worried you." She scanned the tent for Virgil. Not seeing him gave her more confidence.

Pedro emerged from the cook tent. Isabella slipped from Eunice's embrace and walked up to the cook.

"I overheard you saying you were out of these. I happened across them yesterday on a walk and set my mind to getting them for you."

Pedro opened the sack. "*Seño*, these are the leaves of the allspice tree. Now I can make my secret recipe. You are so kind to give these to me. But how did you find them?"

"I was out for a walk, trying to clear my head after so much studying on the tablet." She peered around the room at everyone. Besides Virgil and Jaycee, Professor Walsh wasn't present. Some nodded, others looked skeptical. "I saw the allspice tree and remembered hearing you say you needed some. Only I had to wait for a herd of *pecarí* to leave the area." Someone snickered. "I wasn't sure if that many of them were dangerous or not. They finally left, then while I was climbing to get the best leaves, I slipped and twisted my ankle so I had to sit awhile and wait for the pain to ease."

"How awful. Do you need me to take a look?"

Eunice's concern had guilt burning a hole in her stomach. "No, it's much better this morning. Anyway, by the time I could walk, it was growing late and I became disoriented. I heard men in the jungle, but they sounded angry so I hid, and I was right to hide, they were carrying guns." She shivered and watched some of her audience nod. "And I eventually found my way back to the camp."

"I think after that adventure it would be best if you stayed inside

197

the compound from now on." Eunice's face wore motherly concern.

"I agree. Pedro, I'm starving." She faced the cook who winked and headed to the kitchen.

Isabella took a seat next to Eunice. "Where are Virgil and Professor Walsh?"

"Your disappearance yesterday greatly disturbed Virgil. He couldn't sleep for worry. I had Jaycee take him a sedative early this morning." Eunice took a sip of coffee. "As for Mr. Pompous, I don't know where he's at. He seems to be gone more than he's here doing his job."

Pedro placed the family servings of eggs, ham, potatoes, and fruit on the table. "I will have my famous dessert just for you tonight, *seño.*"

"That would be wonderful Pedro. I look forward to tasting something I had a hand in bringing about." Isabella dug into her food. Thankfully, no one asked further questions about her disappearance. She wasn't sure she could keep the details straight if someone questioned her since she made it all up off the cuff.

After the meal she returned to her tent to gather the *Mayan Book of Codes.* If Virgil was sedated, she could go in the altar chamber and finish the translation without his knowing.

~*~

Tino made his way without problems to the cave. He hunkered down behind a fern where he could watch the entrance. Now he had to wait for a sign from Hector that his team stood ready to seize the drugs and narcos.

He pulled an energy bar from his pack and ate it. The thought of Pedro's good food turned the energy bar to sawdust in his mouth. Usually existing on these bars and water never bothered him. Having access to good cooking the last few days, it took effort to swallow the dry nourishment.

Had Isabella come up with a good story? He'd yet to hear anything other than the truth come out of her kissable lips. He must shake his worry for her and concentrate on his job. Pedro would look out for her. The cook's comments that he watched Martin, and now Isabella too, had given Tino much to ponder as he observed the narcos who guarded his pack. Why did Pedro watch Martin? At first he thought Miguel asked the cook to keep an eye on his investment. But

Isabella? Miguel would have no reason to spy on her. Who had hired Pedro and why? To see if Martin misused funds? Was it the Guatemalan government? Too many questions and not enough answers. He preferred finding the source of a problem and snuffing it out. Like this den of narcos and their goods.

Two hours passed without any sign of Hector or the narcos. He didn't like the lack of activity from the cave. Every time he had observed the entrance before, someone would wander out or in. And where was Hector? He should have been close enough to the site to have moved in by now.

Tino crept along the edge of the forest near the cave entrance. He listened, hearing only the sounds of nature behind him and silence from the mouth of the cave. Did he dare enter? Did he have a choice?

¡Coño! He had to check out the cave.

He tucked a penlight in his back pocket, his gun in his waistband, and stashed his pack and radio at the base of a frond. With his back pressed against the cave entrance, he slipped into the darkness and stood waiting for his eyes to adjust.

Attentive to the sounds in the darkness, he heard his own breathing and nothing else. Where were they? Not everyone would be out searching for him. He skimmed his feet along the floor to keep from tripping. One hand on the dirt wall, he moved deeper into the dark, cool cavern. He'd traveled enough distance he should be standing in the main chamber.

No light.

No sound.

His hackles vibrated.

Swearing under his breath at the stupidity of his next move, he pulled out the penlight and switched it on. The strong but small beam confirmed he had entered the first chamber.

No supplies. No drugs.

¡Coño! They'd cleared out as soon as he and Isabella had left. He continued deeper into the tunnel and found the area where he'd been held cleaned out too.

Tino leaned against the wall. If he'd done his job and not run away to get Isabella to safety, he would have caught them clearing out and brought Hector here sooner. He ran a hand through his hair and stared at the empty cavern. What an idiot he was to have neglected this chance.

He would contact Hector and let him know the drugs had slipped away. The thought ate at his gut like a caiman. He always stopped the shipments assigned to him. Always!

Heavy footsteps hurried toward him from the cave entrance. Tino ducked into the tunnel he and Isabella had used to escape but remained close to the entrance to listen.

"I do not care. I want that woman held until I am ready for her. I cannot believe that moron Martin let her slip away from him so easily." The Spanish words boomed in don Miguel's voice and echoed through the dark as a beam of light approached. "We had a deal and he will honor it or not only find himself with no funding but also humiliated as well."

Miguel and two men passed through the chamber. The men by his sides carried a cloth sack and rope.

What woman? The only one he could think of that got away was Isabella. It would take him too long to go through the jungle to the dig compound and warn her. By the men's steady pace through the tunnel, they were headed to the hidden door of the altar chamber. His heart squeezed as he slipped into the darkness behind them and followed.

Chapter Twenty-Three

Isabella spent the better part of the day finishing her translation of the ceremony. What she'd found drew her to the altar chamber after the workers left to eat dinner. This room and the woman depicted on the wall and urn jangled her senses and drifted her into a meditative state.

Sorrow washed over her as she read the glyphs and now realized the woman had been sacrificed to the moon god to bring about good health and prosperity. The woman was to be a virgin, but she'd fallen in love with the moon god and had already given her virginity to him. Was that the sorrow? She didn't come to the altar as a virgin and so they both wept knowing the sacrifice was for naught?

She registered the sound of stone on stone at the same moment she caught a flash of color out of the corner of her eye. Then all went dark as rough cloth cloaked her head and shoulders and hands gripped her arms tightly. She balanced on one foot and kicked out, landing a blow. A foreign curse filled the darkness. The round cords of a rope bit into her arms and bound them to her body. Isabella tried to kick out again but landed on her bottom when her other leg was knocked out from under her.

"Do not bruise her. She needs to be perfection," a male voice said in Spanish.

His comment made her struggle even more. If he wanted her

unblemished, she'd do all she could to be damaged merchandise. Hands pinched as they dug into her armpits, raising her body. Her legs were lifted and her body swayed to the awkward gait of the men carrying her.

The grinding of the boulder closing the passageway echoed in her head as the men carried her into a cooler, darker environment. The musty smell and muffled footsteps confirmed they carried her into the tunnel.

It led only one direction—to the drug traffickers.

Did the traffickers also sell people? Surely, they couldn't think someone of her scholastic aptitude could be sold as a slave?

She hung between the two men for five hundred and twenty-two steps. They stopped and her bottom hit the floor, then her back, head, and lastly her feet.

"¡Suave!" The only voice she'd heard so far other than cursing urged them to be gentle.

"You stay here and make sure she does not hurt herself. You, come with me and bring back supplies. She will remain here until I am ready for her," the voice commanded.

Isabella moved her feet, hoping the bindings from her knees to her ankles would prove to be loose. They weren't. Her hands were free, but with her arms bound to her sides, she had only the maneuverability of her wrists and fingers.

"Could you at least take the cover off my head?" she asked, inhaling dust from the cloth and sneezing.

The sound of a blade hacking through burlap held her motionless. The cloth whipped over her head. Her glasses caught on the fabric and disappeared.

"I need my glasses." Isabella strived for composure, shoving her fear to the back of her mind. The world blurred without her glasses. The man standing several feet away didn't make a move to get them. "Por favor, my glasses."

The darkness and her blurred sight made it impossible for her to see where the sack and her glasses had landed. If she could find either one, she could wiggle her way close enough to grasp her eyeglasses. Of course, how would she get them on her face? *One problem at a time*. First the glasses then she'd figure out the rest.

Another blurry object moved slowly behind the man standing

above her. Was it his companion? If so, why was he trying hard to not announce his arrival? She watched as the man behind brought something down hard on the other's head. The thud and crack turned her stomach. The man crumpled and the other blurred form surged toward her.

Her heart raced.

Her protective instincts didn't give her time to be scared. She curled her legs up tight against her body, ready to catapult her feet into the assailant's knees.

"Ezzabella, it is Tino."

The blurry form dropped to her side as his voice sprung loose tears of relief.

"Tino?" Her glasses settled on her nose, and she focused on the face of the only person she trusted. "How did you know I was here?" The ropes slipped from her upper body, and he sliced at the ones on her legs.

"I came here to capture the narcos, but they had left. Then don Miguel and two men entered the cave talking about capturing someone. I followed. I could not do anything when they grabbed you since it was three against one, so I waited until the odds were better."

He captured her head in his hands and kissed her until all her fears were dwarfed by the realization this man would move mountains for her. She returned the kiss and leaned back.

"Thank you for saving me, again. I'm beginning to feel like a damsel in distress."

His lips hovered above hers. "I prefer the scholar whose passion cannot be contained." He kissed her hard and quick. "Come, we must leave before the other returns." He rose, pulling Isabella to her feet.

"Please, don't drag me through the tunnel with the bats." Her body froze at the thought of their past encounter.

"We will go back to the dig. Come." He gripped her hand and hurried into the dark tunnel.

His warm hand in hers gave her added strength and security.

"Does don Miguel also deal in human trafficking?" She couldn't shake his comment about not damaging her.

"That activity was not on his dossier. But with someone who is friends with a drug dealer and linked to stolen artifacts, I would not doubt it." Tino's heart was finally settling after seeing the men kidnapping Isabella. He flipped off his penlight and approached the secret door. A light shone from the other side.

His heart had nearly stopped when he watched the men tie up Isabella and haul her through the tunnel. Were they after any female? He didn't think so, considering the comment Miguel had made. Why were they after Isabella? A frightening thought pulsed at the back of his mind. The sacrifice. He planned to remain by her side until he could get her safely away. Once the cook heard about the kidnapping, Pedro would help him convince Isabella to leave.

"Is someone out there?" Her warm breath whispered across his neck as her chin rested on his shoulder.

The intimacy they shared warmed his heart and slowly, inch-by-inch, cracked open the door he had slammed shut when he lost his family.

"No, the light is the one you were using before they kidnapped you." Precautions were now more important since he had no idea who to really trust, other than Isabella. He grasped the stick handle protruding from the boulder, pulled the rock, and stepped through the opening. Isabella followed.

Tino shoved the stone back. He searched the area for a rock to wedge under the entry stone and detain the men should they come this way. Securing the door, he faced Isabella and noticed tears glistening in her eyes.

"Shh, *mi pichón*. No one will harm you as long as I am around." He drew her into his arms and kissed her forehead, breathing in the exotic scent he associated with Isabella.

She sniffed. "I'm not crying because I'm scared. It's this room. Every time I step into it emotions overwhelm me. The sensation is stronger each time. I don't understand. First it was fear of Virgil, which I learned was real. Then it was a deep sorrow, and now...I can't explain it. I feel as if I've lost my lover, yet, I've yet to have one." Her glistening eyes stared into his.

His groin ached and his heart flipped. "*Querida*, I will gladly be your lover when you are ready." He kissed her with all the pent-up desire raging in his body.

Her arms wound around his neck, pressing her body the length of his. His resolve wavered at the heat and urgency of her passion. Pounding in his temples pushed away all thoughts other than loving her—here. Now.

In the back of his mind he knew this wasn't the time or place having just eluded the kidnappers, but his body and mind pulsed with the demand to make Isabella his.

He maneuvered her against the altar and worked his hands under her vest and shirts, relishing her hot, soft skin under his fingers. He seduced her with kisses as his hands worked the buttons on her vest and shirt loose. Pushing the garment down her arms and to the floor at their feet, he pulled the tank top over her head and stared at her heaving chest. His gaze traveled to her face. The rapture of her curved full lips and the heat in her eyes brought a groan from deep inside. He had never wanted a woman as he wanted this one. She would be his after tonight and no one would keep them apart.

Tino bent, taking Isabella's hardened nipple into his mouth to savor her taste. Her hands ran though his hair, holding his mouth to her as she moaned with pleasure. He captured her mouth and tangled their tongues as he unbuttoned her pants and slid a finger into her hot, hidden treasure. Her moan of appreciation caught in his mouth. He savored her shudder and couldn't hold back.

Isabella wanted Tino with an ache so sharp it nearly took her breath away. Her body craved his touch. A Chol chant circled and repeated in her head asking for his body to complete hers and reassuring her this was the time.

He slid her pants and panties down her legs, his warm hands heating her skin. His hands grasped her bare waist, lifting her to sit on the altar. The cool stone grew hot under her.

She reclined on the altar and watched him reveal a muscular body with a patch of dark hair on his chest that arrowed down to dark curls cradling his engorged passion.

"You are as magnificent as I dreamed." She held out her arms, uninhibited, and he balanced his body over the top of her on the altar.

"You will forever be mine after I make love to you." The finality of his words lit her passion even more.

She nodded and gulped at the knot of emotion clogging her throat. This man knew her like no other and he wanted her, a misfit no one else wanted.

His mouth captured hers, and she lost track of time and place. All that mattered was the completion of their communion, their commitment. The urgency that they must become one spun in her mind. After tonight, she would be whole and need no one but Tino.

The heat of the stone, mixed with Tino's passionate kisses and hot length gliding inside her, rippled flames along Isabella's skin and ignited unsurpassed pleasure. Her fingertips skimmed down his muscled back and squeezed his buttocks, marveling at the hard muscle and rhythmic movement, spurring more sensations.

Chol words stole through her lips in a chant. Her body shook, shuddered, absorbed, drawing Tino deeper, making them one and melding their hearts. He covered her mouth with his. Their breath mixed, their bodies shuddered, and white light burst in her head showering her body in electric sparks.

The light faded, the world stopped spinning, and Tino's reassuring weight pressed her to the stone. He pushed up, his biceps bulging, then descended to kiss her lips one more time, before lifting his whole body off her and sitting on the edge of the stone. "I do not know what came over me. We should not have stolen these moments." He frowned. "But it was as if my body and mind were separate."

Isabella swung her legs over the edge and sat next to him, their thighs touching, her heart expanding. "Time was held still so we could come together."

Tino stared at her. "What do you mean?"

"The gods held time for us to mate." She waved a hand at the wall carving. "As it was pre-ordained that woman would be sacrificed to bring the Mayas good health and prosperity, it was per-ordained you and I would make love on this altar."

"How do you know this?" He watched her like a doctor watched an unstable patient.

"The chant in my head while you loved me, and I've translated the tablet. The ceremony went terribly wrong because the virgin wasn't a virgin. She'd been the moon god's lover. That nullified and actually made the opposite happen. Instead of prosperity, illness came that wiped out a large number of Mayas."

Tino picked up her hand and played with her fingers. "If anyone else told me this I would believe they were crazy, but knowing you like I do I can believe." He gazed into her eyes. "This was not a very romantic place to make love the first time. But I swear I felt the Mayas give their assent."

Isabella sighed and leaned her head on his shoulder. "I agree. It was magical."

"What were you chanting?" One by one he kissed her fingers.

"I honestly don't know. My head filled with the wonder of the moment and the words just fluttered out." A delightful shiver slithered up her arm as he kissed her palm and the underside of her wrist. "Keep this up and I'll drag you back onto this stone."

"I would love to accept the offer, *querida*, but we have lingered too long as it is. The men could come looking for you."

Tino kissed her lips, long, deep, and with such sweetness, that her heart ached with love.

He drew back. "I will help you dress, wait here." He slid off the stone and quickly donned his clothing, all the while devouring her with a heated gaze. "You are such a passionate woman; I am blessed to have found you."

"I'm the lucky one." Isabella wrapped her arms around his neck when he stepped in front of her to slip her panties up her legs. She pulled him against her chest and breathed in his spicy shave lotion, musky maleness, and the evidence of their love making. Nuzzling his ear, she whispered, "You are the only man for me."

He groaned, captured her head, and drugged her with a deep passionate kiss. Dizziness buoyed her head when he pulled back and continued dressing her. Her movements were fluid but her mind saw it all in slow motion. She never wanted to leave the altar chamber. She wished her life could remain this unfettered always.

"Come. We need to find a safe place for you, and I need to radio my contact." He grabbed the lantern, slipped his hand in hers, and they walked out of the chamber.

Isabella glanced over her shoulder at the drawing fading in the waning light. She'd experienced a life-altering event this night—being loved by a man who cherished her—and something more, something that had to do with the drawing. Warmth started in her middle and spread to her extremities. The chamber no longer caused her fear or unease. It welcomed.

Tino continued through the main chamber and stopped inside the door of the dig. His hand tightened on hers and his body stiffened when she placed a hand on his arm.

"What's wrong?" she whispered. To peer past him she had to

move her body into the light illuminating the opening.

"Don Miguel just came out of Virgil's tent." Tino slid deeper into the dig.

"He came to see Virgil after kidnapping me?" Conversations spun in her head. Virgil's. Don Miguel's. Virgil asked if she was a virgin. Don Miguel wanted her unblemished.

She was the sacrifice.

Her heart raced. Did she tell Tino? Could they use her if they didn't have the ceremony translated? Her thoughts were spinning so fast it took a minute before she caught on Tino was talking.

"My guess is he is telling Martin he has you and not to cause trouble looking for you." Tino kissed her knuckles. "You will stay with me. Don Miguel had to have headed here right after capturing you for him to have made it here this quickly without using the tunnel. Once he discovers you are missing, he will come back here." Tino sidestepped to the opening and peered out. "He is gone. We will tell Pedro you are with me and ask him to listen in on conversations. We will gather my things and hide out in the jungle for a couple of days."

Isabella didn't mind being with Tino for a couple days, but she didn't like leaving the rest of the group vulnerable to Virgil. Were any of the other women virgins? "I fear Virgil may figure out the ceremony on his own if I'm hiding out in the jungle. If I remain here, I could stall—"

"You cannot stop the inevitable. If you keep stalling him, he will find another way to translate the ceremony. If you are with me you will remain safe."

"But what about—"

Tino pressed her against the wall with his body. His seductive lips covered hers in an open-mouthed kiss that fevered her body as his hands roamed up her sides under her clothing. Her body slid down the wall, resting on Tino's leg bent between hers. Her hands fisted in his shirt, both wanting to push him away and fearful he would pull away and she'd lose the heat and exhilaration of his touch.

He drew his head back, tugging on her bottom lip with his teeth. "*Mi pichón*. If you were not the target of Miguel, I would leave you here so we could both accomplish our missions."

She started to protest. His lips covered hers with a short brief kiss.

"No. Do not argue. He has plans for you, and I will not allow him to take my woman." He buzzed her lips with another quick kiss. "You are my woman now and I will protect you."

Isabella wanted to object to his chauvinistic attitude, but she couldn't argue with the fact she was now and forever his. If his acceptance of her intelligence and physique weren't enough, his making love to her had wrapped the chain around her heart and bound them together.

He drew her along the edge of the compound staying to the shadows under the trees until they sprinted for the back of the cook tent. She ran into Tino's back when he stopped abruptly inside the tent flap.

A click resounded in the dark enclosed area like a clap of thunder.

"It is Tino and Ezabella," Tino hissed in a whisper.

Chapter Twenty-Four

Tino gulped and waited what seemed as long as the presidential term of Juan Vicente Gómez for the cook to pull the pistol barrel from his gut.

"Isabella is with you?" Pedro asked in Spanish.

"Here." Isabella stepped out from behind Tino.

"*Seño*, you have been disappearing so much lately, no one knows what to expect, no?"

The gun disappeared from Tino's stomach. He let out a quiet breath of relief and clung to Isabella's hand.

"Come. Sit."

Isabella moved forward and sat on something. He reached out and found the edge of a cot. Tino sat beside her.

"Can you turn on a lantern?" Isabella asked.

"No." He and Pedro responded at the same time.

"A light would draw attention to this tent and eventually to us." Tino squeezed her hand hoping it gave her reassurance.

"I should know that. Sorry."

"Hiding is new to you, *querida*. Do not apologize." He leaned over and kissed her temple.

"Who are you hiding from now?" Pedro asked. "I heard the narcos have moved on."

Pedro's knowledge of the narcos sent Tino's senses on alert. How did the cook know something he just found out himself?

"How did you know?"

"The locals talked about it at dinner. Who are you running from?"

"Don Miguel kidnapped Ezzabella this evening. Luckily, I was snooping around in the tunnel and followed them. She is not safe here. Miguel has already been to see Dr. Martin. We do not know why, but it was after he captured Ezzabella and before he discovered her missing." Tino hated telling the cook everything, but they were running out of options and people to trust.

"I will keep an eye on Dr. Martin and don Miguel the next time he comes." Canvas and wood creaked. The cook must have sat down. "What are your plans?"

"I need to radio my contacts, and then I will take Ezzabella away from here."

Her body stiffened next to him and she released his hand.

"I can't leave without stopping Virgil." Her voice rang with authority.

"You cannot stop him or anyone if you are hurt or dead."

She sucked in air and remorse slapped him like a rain-saturated palm frond.

"*Mi pichón*, these men are desperate. You do not know what don Miguel wants with you. You said Dr. Martin must not learn the translation. Without you he may never. You will go with me, and when I am done, we will come back and confront Dr. Martin together."

"That's it? I don't have a say in my own life?" Frustration seethed in her words.

"Isabella, Tino is wise in the ways of these people. Do as he asks, and you can return." Pedro's calm fatherly timbre reminded Tino of his own father's soft-spoken words. They sunk in far better than a demand or order.

The chair creaked. "Take good care of her." Pedro's hand slapped down on Tino's shoulder and squeezed.

"I will. We will sneak back in a few days to see if you have learned anything." Tino stood, drawing Isabella up beside him.

"I will see what I can find out about don Miguel and Doctor Martin." Pedro gripped Tino's upper arm. "I have a pack of food I keep prepared." Pedro disappeared and returned, pushing the pack into

Tino's hands.

"*Gracias.*" Tino walked to the tent opening, leading Isabella behind him. He peered into the compound. Nothing moved. The usual nocturnal choruses in the canopy around the compound meant nothing out of the ordinary lurked in the jungle perimeter.

He tugged Isabella's hand, ducking into the shadow of the tent and following it to the corner. Twenty feet of open area, illuminated by a three-quarter moon, was between their sheltering shadow and the forest.

"We have to make a run for the forest," he whispered in Isabella's ear. She nodded and he took off at a run. Ten feet into the trees he stopped. Isabella stood beside him, her hand gripping his tightly.

"Now what?"

"We make our way to the cave entrance where I stashed my gear."

She pulled back, dropping his hand. "But that's where they'll be!"

"Maybe. They could still be out looking for you. We will know when we get there, but that is where we have to go." He recaptured her hand. "Come on."

"Can we at least get my pack? I mean if we're going to be in the jungle for days, I could use clean clothes, the mosquito net..."

"I thought you had everything you needed in your vest?" he joked. But retrieving her pack was a good idea. If anyone searched for Isabella and found it missing, they would be more likely to think she had either headed back to civilization or wandered into the jungle alone.

"I do, but there are other things I'd like to have with me."

"It is not a bad idea. If your pack is missing, they might not look so hard for you." Tino backtracked to the edge of the camp and moved through the trees to a point close to her tent. There shouldn't have been enough time for don Miguel to return to the dig after finding Isabella missing.

His heart raced at the thought of sending her by herself to the tent, but there was no other way to make it look as if she planned to head out alone.

He grasped her hands. "In case someone is watching, you need to go to your tent alone and get the pack. Hurry, get what you need and get back here." He pulled her into his arms and kissed her. "I will be right here if you need me."

She nodded and gently pushed out of his embrace. Watching her walk out into the open and duck into her tent where he could not see if anyone lurked plucked at his nerves and twisted his gut. Until she was safely out of Guatemala, he would not be able to rest easy.

~*~

Isabella slipped into her tent and hastily pulled down the mosquito net, wadding the gauzy material and stuffing it and her toiletries into her pack. The idea of slipping away and leaving the other women here vulnerable to Virgil's and don Miguel's scheme nagged at her mind. She'd help Tino accomplish his tasks, then she'd return and what... By then maybe she'd have formulated a plan. Until then she prayed Virgil didn't decipher the ceremony and find a stand-in for her.

She slung the pack on her back and peeked out the tent flap. Her heart stuttered to a stop. Two men, one with a bandage on his head, stalked out of the dig. They'd followed the tunnel, no doubt, looking for her.

"Psst. *Querida*, come." Tino held the back of her tent up.

Isabella spun and dived for the exit. His strong hands gripped her upper arms and pulled her from the tent. Hand-in-hand, they ran for the forest and didn't stop until she couldn't breathe any longer. She released his hand and doubled over, sucking air.

"We-can't-keep-run-ning," she pushed out between gulps.

"We walk from here. Running makes too much noise." Tino brushed a hand over her cheek and started walking.

She fell into step behind him, glad for the slower pace. The night sounds grew in volume the farther from the dig they traveled.

"How do you know we're going the right direction?" Something fluttered by her head. She ducked emitting a squeak. Bats.

"I have the coordinates of the cave in my GPS." He stopped when she didn't follow. "Why are you covering your head?"

"A bat flew by. I can't..." She couldn't what? Standing in one spot was as useless to warding off bats as walking.

Tino spun her. A zipper rasped open; he rummaged in her pack, jostling her body. The zipper rasped back and her canvas hat plopped on her head.

"Most people fear the bat feet tangling in their hair. This way if a bat touches your head, which rarely happens, you are protected."

He kissed her cheek and walked ahead of her.

213

"Is there nothing in this jungle that scares you?" She hustled to catch up with him.

"I fear coming upon a jaguar with her kits, a caiman that has gone hungry for days, don Miguel getting his hands on you again, and ants."

She stared at his wide back and thought about all the times she'd witnessed his strength and intelligence. His barely audible last word rang as loud as a shout. "Why ants?"

He glanced at her over his shoulder. "You do not think it is silly a man could fear ants?" His tone scoffed at himself.

"No. Everyone's fears have a justification."

He stopped and she caught herself seconds before smacking into his back.

"You truly do not find my being scared of ants humorous?"

She couldn't see his features in the darkness, but the awe in his tone rippled through the air between them and settled in her heart.

"Fears aren't unfounded." She placed a hand on his arm. "Some may seem so, but each person has a reason for his fears either from a real situation or one that was witnessed or dreamed. The mind is a powerful thing."

He pivoted and started walking again. To catch his soft-spoken words, she double-timed her feet to stay close enough to hear.

"When I was a boy, I witnessed the devastation a swarm of ants wreaked on a lizard. It was …" His voice faltered and his steps quickened. "It was something a small child should never see. I have had a fear of ants ever since."

"My point. One never knows what puts fear into a person." Isabella could sympathize with what Tino, as a small boy, had witnessed. She could also sympathize with his fear. This also explained the wide berth he took around an ant hill when they traveled to the dig.

"How far is it to the cave entrance?" The running had tightened the muscles in her legs and with each step they grew tighter.

"We are getting close."

She hoped he was right. "Where are we going to hide or go?"

"I figure we will head down to the settlement and see if I can learn anything about where the shipment went." Tino held up his hand and crept forward.

Isabella wasn't sure if she was to be quiet or stay put. When he started to disappear in the darkness, she moved forward. The vegetation grew sparser and tentacles of moonlight sliced between the trees. She found Tino hunched at the base of a tree. He pulled out a large backpack and a smaller one.

"My gear." He handed her the pack from Pedro. "Come on. There's a knoll not more than twenty minutes in the direction of the river. We will go there and see what my contact knows."

Isabella dug into the food pack and pulled out two bananas, while Tino shrugged on his packs. She held one out to Tino and peeled the other one.

The thought of walking another twenty minutes didn't relieve her aching legs, but she didn't utter a word, just fell in step behind Tino, relying on his knowledge to keep her safe. She ate the fruit and listened to the forest begin a new day. The howler monkeys' deep morning chorus vibrated through the canopy. Birds squawked and called. The shadows lightened and soon disappeared as the sun rose casting filtered light like a frosted twenty-watt bulb.

Her legs trembled as they began a gradual climb. This could only mean rest would soon follow. The light brightened. Isabella peered up at the snippets of blue sky and sunshine. The undergrowth began to thin.

Tino stopped. "You can rest now, *pichón*." He slipped the packs from his shoulders and opened the small one.

Finally. She was used to little sleep while working digs sites, but the added hiking was kicking her butt.

Isabella slathered mosquito repellent on her neck, face, and hands watching Tino remove a radio from his small pack.

Ticking noises grew louder as he swung the radio toward her. His forehead wrinkled in a frown before his eyes met hers.

"Do you have anything electronic in your pack?" he asked.

"No. The only thing electronic I have is my watch." She held up her wrist and the ticking sped up.

"That's odd. I use this to track the transmission devices on jaguars." He set the radio down and captured her hand. "May I?" He slipped the watch from her wrist before she could answer.

Isabella watched him pop the back off the time piece and with the tip of his knife plucked something from the workings.

"Don't ruin it. My father gave it to me when I graduated." She

215

snatched the watch away from him.

"This is very close to the type of transmitter I put in jaguars." His dark eyes stared at her. "Someone is following you everywhere you go."

Isabella stared at the small cylinder-shaped device the size of a match head and shook her head. No. Who? Why? "I don't understand. Who would care where I go? And mostly why?" Fear gripped her insides and twisted. Someone had been monitoring her movements for…how long?

Tino rubbed a hand up and down her arm. "We must think. When have you taken the watch off?"

"Every time I take a shower I put it in the pocket of my vest." She thought back to her two encounters in the shower. "Professor Walsh and Virgil both came into the shower and had an opportunity to take my watch, but I doubt they had the time to install a transmitter." She couldn't see either one needing to keep track of her, but Virgil was the most obvious. Why? Why would he need to know her whereabouts? She shivered remembering he planned to use her in a sacrifice ceremony.

Chapter Twenty-five

Tino pulled out his pliers and crushed the transmitter. Whoever monitored Isabella's travels would no longer follow her movements. Could it be Martin or Walsh? They both had motives. With Walsh's connections to the narcos, he could have told them Isabella was in the cave when Tino escaped. Or Virgil could have had her monitored to not lose her. In which case, he would have known where she was and not sent people out randomly searching for her. The whole thing didn't add up.

Isabella watched him, her eyes wide and full of worry. He pulled her into his arms and held her to his beating heart. Her only safety rested with him. It was becoming clear they had no one they could trust. His mind wandered back to his first conversation with Pedro. He'd said he was watching Isabella and Martin. Could the cook be the one monitoring Isabella? If so, why? Did he do so for the doctor?

"No one will find you now. I promise we will finish my mission and return you to the states."

She pushed out of his arms. "I can't go back until I've made sure everyone at the dig is safe."

"Ezzabella, what are you keeping from me? Learning about the sacrificial ceremony does not put anyone in danger." He peered into her eyes. She held something back. *¡Coño!* She knew.

He held her gaze, waiting. He wasn't sure what she would do if she found out he already knew her secret.

She looked away then studied her hands. "Don Miguel and Virgil plan to use me to re-enact the moon god ceremony." Her wide eyes beseeched his. "I'm afraid if I'm not there to stop them they'll use someone who doesn't have the knowledge to prevent their ill-advised deed." She grasped his hands. "I believe don Miguel thinks the prosperity talked about in the ceremony will make him rich. And Virgil—he has obsessed about the sacrificial rituals since I was old enough to know what they were. I have to stop them."

Her commitment to doing what was right added one more layer to why he had fallen for her. But he refused to allow her to try to stop the two mad men.

"*Querida*, you cannot stop them alone. We will think together and come up with a plan." If not for his mission, he would carry her to a boat, take her down the river, and place her on a plane, perhaps even travel with her all the way to her home. Then come back and confront the two men.

"You don't understand. It's Mayan history that I've studied and know. It has to be me who stops them. I can feel it." She squeezed his hands. Her eyes peered at him over glasses that slid to the tip of her nose. "I have to reveal the story. Something in the altar chamber has awakened and presses me to reveal the truth. I must."

"You cannot reveal the truth if you are dead." He didn't like the way she spoke of entities of another world.

"I won't die. You'll protect me." Her gaze lowered to the radio by his knee. "Don't you have a call to make?"

He picked up the radio and used his GPS to point the antenna in the correct direction. "This conversation is not over, just delayed." He dialed in Ginger and waited.

"Ginger. Over."

"Konstantine. Over."

"Hector sends his regards. Over."

Tino frowned. What did he mean by that? "Why? Over."

"The target was caught on the move. Over."

That was why he hadn't seen anything of Hector. They had been on the trail of the narcos.

"Good news. Over."

"Watch yourself. They know you're still there. Over."

¡Coño! Someone knew his true dual occupation. He would have to be careful. He couldn't trust anyone.

"*Mi amor*, you flatter me with your concern. Over." He could laugh it off with Ginger but not the glistening hazel eyes staring at him.

"Take care. Out." Ginger signed off.

The buzz of the lost connection roared in his ears as he gazed into Isabella's worried eyes.

She reached a hand out touching his cheek. "They know you're an agent."

"It appears that way." He turned his head and kissed her palm.

"You should leave the country."

He shook his head. "I cannot. I vowed to take down all who are involved in drug trafficking. They killed my family. I will not rest until the man responsible is in jail. Or dead."

"What if you end up dead?" She scooted closer, her knees pressing against his thighs, her body leaning into him.

"I shall be reunited with my family and will know I died avenging their deaths." Anger and vengeance burned in his chest. Yes, he could die any day, and on that day, he would be able to look his family in the eyes and tell them he had done everything in his power to avenge their deaths. To run now would only haunt him.

"Is Konstantine your real name?"

She asked so softly he wasn't sure he heard her.

"Konstantine," she repeated. "The name you used on the radio. Is that a real name or a code name?"

"My real name is Augustino Konstantine. Tino Kosta is my undercover name." He placed a soft, pleased-to-meet-you kiss on her sensual lips. He no longer had urgent business other than keeping Isabella safe, however, making love to her on this knoll wasn't a good idea even though his body responded to the thought.

"Mmmm…" She drew out of the kiss. "I like both names and it validates my first impression of your heritage."

"How is that?" He drew her back, holding her in his arms and resting his chin on her head.

"I could tell you weren't of indigenous descent. The European is strong in your features." She drew back. "Are you even Guatemalan?"

"You need to work on your dialects. Everyone in this country knows I am an outsider the minute I speak."

Her petite nose scrunched and her brow furrow. "Then Virgil has known from your first encounter you aren't Guatemalan, yet he hasn't said a thing."

"Is he good at dialects?" This was interesting. Why was it Martin failed to challenge me if he knew I was an impostor?

"Yes. He's fluent in many Central and South American languages and dialects." Isabella sat back on her feet. She stared into his eyes.

"What are you thinking?" He reached out, lacing his fingers with hers.

"This whole dig has felt awkward. First, it's so small. Virgil always has at least thirty-five people."

"He is on a reduced budget."

She shook her head. "That hasn't stopped him before. And Eunice said he's shipping all the artifacts to the university to be authenticated and stored. Before, he always did the authenticating at the dig, and then doled it out to the places that would learn the most and cherish the items."

"The Guatemalan government is tired of its Mayan heritage being looted and robbed. Perhaps it is the only way he can dig?"

Her head moved slightly. "Maybe, but then you'd think an official would be here watching over the whole process. And the presence of don Miguel..." She shivered.

The tremors ran down her arms and vibrated against his palm. "Did he hurt you?"

"No. I just feel he's not to be trusted or pure."

Tino watched her, mulling over her strange choice of word. He had expected her to say evil or vicious.

Her gaze held sadness. "I think this whole dig was a front for the reason I'm here—to recreate the moon god ceremony. I don't think don Miguel ever offered a half million for the translation of the ceremony. Virgil used my weakness—my work—to get me here and my knowledge to help them replicate the ceremony. I've never felt so stupid in my life."

"If you will no longer receive funding from this project you should get on a plane. There is no need to put yourself through any more of this. Go home and work on grants and fundraisers to keep your department." Tino kissed her knuckles. He wanted her far from here and danger.

She shook her head. "I may not get my funding, but I'll not allow them to hurt anyone with their fanatical ideas."

Knowing her as well as he did, he realized getting her away before they stopped the two mad men wasn't going to happen. "Then I suggest we go to the settlement and make a plan."

"Don't you have to go after the drug traffickers?"

"Hector took down the group I found. Now, I have to find another group and their hideout so Hector can swoop in and take that out as well. The best way is to stay at the settlement and learn what the locals know." He stood and drew her to her feet.

She leaned into him, her body pressing against his. If not for the growing heat of the sun he would have gladly pulled her tight and enjoyed a little afternoon tryst. An alarm went off in his head. They'd made love on the altar without any protection. What if Isabella became pregnant? The idea wasn't as scary as it had been in the past when a woman tried to say he'd fathered a child. The idea of a child between him and Isabella sat warm and comfortable in his heart.

"Is there a chance we could have made a baby back on the altar?" he asked in as casual a tone as he could muster given the carnal direction of his thoughts.

"Would that bother you?" Her body stiffened and drew away from him.

"No. The idea is pleasing. But I do not want you feeling pressured if it happened. While I believe a man should support his child and wife, I would not expect you to give up your passion for your work."

Her body molded back against him, and her eyelids lowered in a sultry display he hadn't thought her capable of.

"Due to my lack of body fat and crazy metabolism, my menstrual cycle only comes a few times a year, making me a poor candidate for producing children."

He wasn't sure if the information relieved him or made him a bit sad.

She tilted her head and favored him with a saucy look. "It means we'd have to work extra hard to have children so lots of practice would be necessary."

He gazed down at her face. The spark of desire mingled with a bit of shyness in her eyes heated him more thoroughly than the tropical sun. "*Querida*, you have captured me completely. I wish to love you slow and long unlike the hasty lovemaking on the altar."

At the mention of the altar her gaze drifted over his shoulder and a soft smile curved her luscious lips.

"What are you thinking?"

Isabella shook her head. "I've never felt as loved and wanted as I do in your arms." She hugged him tight. "If I never experience being loved again what you have given me will forever bring me happiness."

"Shhh, *querida*, I will always be with you in your heart and will work to be a part of your life. But there is much that must be finished first." He kissed her and moved away. They'd lingered in one spot long enough. They had to keep moving until they were safely hidden in a hut at the settlement. Tino picked up his pack and shouldered it.

"But we'll have tonight." Her softly whispered announcement and dreamy smile nearly had him dropping his pack and drawing her back into his arms. *¡Coño!* Who would have guessed such a passionate woman lived inside this intelligent slip of a doctor?

Isabella couldn't stop the pulse of excitement sparking her extremities at the knowledge they would spend the night together. She and Tino in a bed, together, all night. His eyes had darkened with desire while speaking, telling her he was just as excited. She grabbed her packs and trotted to catch up to him.

His current assignment was done, and he planned to help her thwart Virgil and don Miguel. Her heart ached that she wouldn't be going home with the money to keep her department open and her work going. But the notes in her journal on the ceremony would make a wonderful paper that might help extend her chances of getting funding.

She'd connected with the woman on the altar. It was bizarre, but she'd always been a firm believer in the supernatural. And there was no dismissing the way her skin warmed and mind hazed when she entered the altar chamber, or the fact that voices chanted and spoke to her. They spoke of Virgil's insincerity. Was it to her or to the Mayas? When don Miguel entered the chamber, the room had become frosty and pricked with fear. She'd known he was dangerous, but the reaction of the chamber had made her even more wary.

She stared at Tino's back. Would he believe her if she told him all her notions and how she came to her conclusions? He wasn't a Maya or of native descent. Could he understand the essence that still pulsed in the chamber? Her heart said he would understand and listen; her head said he was logical and would think her foolish. Her darn logical head always got in the way.

Who was monitoring her movement? Had Virgil slipped the transmitter into her watch to keep track of her? And Walsh, would he go to such measures to get his hands on her journal thinking he could get paid from don Miguel?

She was the person who could help them with the ceremony. She had the translation and she was the sacrificial victim. A shiver raced up her back. If she couldn't be found would they stop the re-creation of the ceremony? The zeal in don Miguel's eyes and the desperation in Virgil's made her think they would continue whether they had the ritual right or not. And that could mean catastrophe not only for the victim but the Maya future.

Isabella kept Tino in sight as they moved through the jungle, but her mind flipped through her notes page by page, trying to discern any clue she might have missed. She'd untangled one line of glyphs she had misinterpreted by the time they stepped from the trees and a wide river flowed in front of them.

Tino pointed to an area up the bank harboring three boats. She recognized the craft they'd used to get to the dig. Our transportation to the settlement and a night without worry, just the two of us.

She followed Tino. He turned the boat upright and dumped his packs into the hull. Footsteps pounded the ground behind her. She spun in time to watch the blur of two men run by her and tackle Tino.

Isabella dropped her pack, put her weight on her back leg, and kicked out at one of the assailants. The vibration up her leg proved she had executed a well-placed kick. The man yelled and came at her, limping.

"Don't harm the woman!" Don Miguel's voice boomed around her like an enhanced megaphone moments before large hands grasped her wrists and pulled them behind her back.

She struck out with another kick but was jerked back and missed her mark. A furtive glance at Tino squeezed her chest. He'd been subdued and tied. His eyes though dull with pain, sparked with anger.

"Let the woman go. You have no need—" The man next to Tino slammed a gun butt into his head and shoved him into the boat, pushing the boat out into the river.

"No!" Fear and rage flared. She struggled to get free of the man's hold. All her frustration pumped into the foot she slammed down on her assailant's instep. His hands loosened, and she lunged forward, racing for the river and the boat drifting in the current. Something caught her behind her knees and she toppled forward.

"Tie her hands and feet and bring her, quickly."

Don Miguel's voice grated on her nerves. She wished the man all kinds of torture for what he did to Tino.

"Let me go. I'm of no use to you." She struggled, giving the men trying to tie her fits. Don Miguel didn't want her hurt so she could retaliate without fear.

"The moon is nearly full. You will be my guest at a ceremony in two nights." He snapped his fingers, and the men picked her up, carrying her like a log on their shoulders.

She wiggled, trying to toss them off balance.

"Dr. Mumphrey, I suggest you remain still or I will allow my men to carry you in a less modest way." Don Miguel plucked at one of her vest buttons. "I am sure the mosquitoes would enjoy your sweet blood from your more delicate places."

She shivered at the thought of being carried naked and having the mosquitoes feast on her body. Not to mention, if she were disrobed, she would lose sight of her vest.

Isabella's thoughts flew to Tino. Could he get loose from the rope before the current carried him miles downriver? Even if he managed to free himself, he had no idea where they were taking her. She cursed at having not been more vigilant. Even though the threat of the narcos was gone, they'd known don Miguel remained in the area.

Her body swayed to the gait of the men. They stopped, placing her on the ground, and don Miguel held a canteen of water to her lips. She refused to drink. Not knowing if the water was purified, she refused to risk stomach complications.

"You will be dehydrated if you do not drink." Don Miguel offered the canteen once again after he'd slurped on the opening.

"I'll take my chances." The jungle grew gloomier and the birds' songs and squawks became more subdued. They continued on as the humid air grew heavier, signaling the afternoon rain would soon descend. Perhaps that would slow them down. At least she might get some clean water to drink.

Her shoulders ached from her arms being bound behind her back. She smiled, noticing the man carrying her legs hobbled from her kick. His injury kept them at a slow pace.

They struggled up an incline as the rain poured from the sky. The thick canopy of the trees stopped the direct onslaught, still enough water poured to nearly drown her since her face pointed to the sky. She welcomed the rain and that don Miguel barked a command to find shelter.

She had to find a way to mark her trail. Tino would get loose, and he'd find her. But would he arrive before the full moon?

Chapter Twenty-Six

Tino struggled to pull his knife from his boot sheath. The rocking of the boat grew rougher, rolling him back and forth in the hull. The violent ride meant the craft had drifted into the stronger center current, carrying him away from Isabella faster. He had to get loose, start the motor, and get upriver. Isabella needed him.

His fingers brushed the bone handle of his knife. Relief and frustration pounded in his temples as his fingers touched, then missed, capturing the handle. Calm, I have to remain calm. He drew in a long breath and let it out slowly. Rolling with the sway of the boat, he reached again, matching his movements with that of the mahogany underneath him.

Finally, his fingers wrapped around the knobby, bone handle. He drew it out of his boot and, with agonizing slowness, reversed the direction of the blade to cut the rope binding his arms to his body. His restricted movements gradually sliced deep enough through the rope he could flex his arms and spring free. Tino scrambled over his pack to the opposite end of the boat and pulled the starter cord. The motor roared to life. He shoved it to full throttle. Don Miguel and his *ratas* had a good head start, but he'd find Isabella and rescue her.

Tino's mind raced with the revved motor. He had until the full moon tomorrow night. That was when Isabella would be in danger. Even knowing he had thirty-six hours, didn't lessen the urgency. He didn't trust Miguel.

The boat landing came into view. All the boats were still there. His clenched jaw relaxed only enough to lessen the pounding in his head. He'd feared they would use a boat and travel upriver. Isabella's abductors couldn't be too far ahead if they traveled by land. The humidity clung to him as heavy and forlorn as his mood. Shouldering his pack, he set out toward the dig. Pedro had promised to keep an eye on Miguel; perhaps he knew something that would help find Isabella. The afternoon rains started when he was twenty feet into the trees.

Tino slogged on, the rain pelting his head and strengthening his resolve. Slick mud caused him to shorten his gait and take more care in traversing the rainwater rushing down the trail. A month ago, he would have hiked out of here and claimed his next assignment. But his life had changed since meeting the passionate doctor. Isabella needed him. No one had needed him since his family's deaths and his *abuela* passed. Isabella made him realize how empty his life had become.

He needed her.

And, right now, he was the only person who knew the danger she was in.

He would find her and get her safely home. Lightness entered his chest then faded. His name was still connected with the sugar plantation and a father, who in the eyes of Chavez, was a traitor. He knew how much Isabella wanted to belong—to have an extended family. He couldn't give her that. To go back to Venezuela, he would bring harm to his relatives. They would be foolish to receive him as family or Isabella as a *musiú*, foreigner. The family plantation had made great progress in staying family owned—for him to return... He shook his head. His father told him there was no going back. He understood. But would Isabella, when he was finally able to tell her his history? And would she understand his need to seek revenge?

The rain lessened as he neared the dig compound. He stood inside the trees watching the activity. If Miguel and his *ratas* were in the compound, he needed to use caution and have surprise on his side to get Isabella away from them.

Tino watched the area for half an hour. All the activities resembled what he'd witnessed while staying at the compound. People began entering the mess tent for dinner. He remained hidden and watched while all the dig inhabitants, including Walsh and Martin, went inside. Everyone conducted business as usual. Didn't they notice or care that Isabella was gone? What did Martin tell the others about her disappearance? Her pack was gone. Did he say she'd gone back home? He had little time to consider what others thought.

Isabella was alone with Miguel.

He remained in the trees and worked his way to the dig entrance. The tunnel would be the fastest way to find out if they held her captive in the cave again. Tino dug his penlight out of his pack and jogged the open distance to the dig. Inside, he switched on his light and headed straight into the altar chamber and the hidden passage door.

Three steps into the altar chamber, a breeze whispered across his damp face and neck giving him chills. He ignored the pulse in his temples. Worry and urgency caused the pounding. Pressing his shoulder against the boulder, he moved the rock and entered, closing the portal behind him.

Darkness filled the void in front of him. The chill of the altar room still clung to his skin. Tino shook like a dog ridding its fur of water and aimed the beam of light at the cave floor. They had to have hidden Isabella here. If not, it would take him days, perhaps weeks, to scour the jungle searching for her. A voice in his head hummed there wasn't that much time.

He descended the rock steps and walked as quickly as he could without making noise. The tunnel stretched longer than he remembered. His fears and worries increased with each step, accelerating his breathing and heart. Finally, he found the chamber with the tunnel leading to the bats. The dirt in front of the opening remained undisturbed. He flashed his light down the bat tunnel, honing in on the ground. There were no fresh footprints.

Tino squared his pack and proceeded toward the next chamber and entrance to the tunnel. He couldn't allow his mind to think about not finding Isabella here. Where else could Miguel have taken her? Determination propelled him forward. Fear of being discovered slowed his pace, and he switched off his light. Caution and stealth transformed his movements into that of the jaguar he tracked and tagged. From following and watching, he had learned how to approach prey. Stilling his breathing and moving with slow fluid movements, he slipped his body around the edge of the chamber.

Darkness stole his vision. His guts squeezed.

No sounds other than his heart beating in his ears.

No scent other than dirt and musty air.

Empty.

He flicked on the penlight. Desperation flooded him. Fear chilled his insides. He hadn't felt this lost and helpless since the phone call about his family's deaths.

Where could Miguel have taken her? His holdings? He lived on the far side of Petén. How did he get here?

The helicopter.

Tino went into active mode. He jogged to the opening of the cave and dropped his pack to the ground, pulling out his radio. Ginger would find out where don Miguel lived and get information about the layout and if he'd returned with a woman.

~*~

Tears burned in Isabella's eyes and stung her nose. Tino would never find her now that she'd been whisked away in a helicopter. Her heart ached knowing his search would not find her. Don Miguel goaded her with cryptic words, but she refused to carry on a conversation with the man. They'd dumped her, hands still bound, into the back of the helicopter and don Miguel himself flew the aircraft, sans his two goons.

They barely gained altitude before her stomach bounced into her throat at their descent. The machine bumped and the thump of the rotors gradually slowed and stopped. The conveyance shifted as don Miguel climbed down and grasped her by the ankles, dragging her to the opening. Moonlight lit an area littered with tree stumps. He held her by her bound wrists and shoved her forward toward a line of trees.

"Where are you taking me?" she asked, wiping her perspiring face on her shoulder and willing her stomach to not erupt.

"Some place where I can keep an eye on you until everything is set."

She stepped from the trees and gazed at the familiar surroundings. The settlement, where she'd photographed and drawn the glyphs on the broken tablet, slept under the glowing moon. She caught a glimpse of the old man's hut. Could he help her?

Don Miguel navigated her into the largest adobe structure on the outskirts of the settlement. She stepped inside the building and trepidation crept from her toes and tingled her hair follicles. Opulence shouted this man spent quite a bit of time here. The villagers would owe him, making them less likely to help her. A seating arrangement graced half the room nearest the door. Two young men sprang to their feet. Both gazed the length of her, their lips curled in a leer. Panic and acidic bile rose in her throat when her gaze discovered a large bed against the far wall.

"*¡Déjenos!*" Don Miguel ordered the two men.

Their haughty stances drooped as they shot her one last leering glance and disappeared out the door.

Her panic eased. She could deal with one easier than three. Even if he was the most vile.

Don Miguel cut the rope at her wrists and motioned for her to sit on the sofa. The rich fabric and soft cushion of the furniture was heaven after spending the last week sitting on hard chairs and sleeping on a pad on the ground. She leaned into the comfort and couldn't restrain the sigh.

He smiled and poured red wine into a glass, handing it to her. "You cannot refuse this. I guarantee it comes from the finest winery in your country." He held up the bottle, label out, for her to read.

The rain water had quenched her thirst at the time, but the heat and fear had once again parched her throat. She peered at the wine. Did she dare drink alcohol? She was accustomed to wine. But could one glass muddle her brain enough to hinder an escape?

"I'd prefer something else on an empty and altitude challenged stomach." As if to corroborate her comment, her stomach chose that moment to gurgle loudly.

"Fruit and tortillas are the best I can offer at this time of night." Don Miguel moved to a cupboard and extracted a bowl of papayas and bananas and a dish covered with a cloth. He set them on the table next to the sofa and returned to the cupboard.

Isabella raised the cloth and found tortillas. She took one, rolled it up, and bit off the end. Her high metabolism kept her on a continual search for food. She had two energy bars in her vest pocket, but she didn't want to draw attention to all the items on her person. They could come in handy planning her escape.

Don Miguel returned with a cup of white liquid. "Coconut milk."

She took a small sip, tasting for any off flavors. Sweetness tickled her tongue, and she drank.

He watched her eat without saying another word. The staring and silence frazzled her nerves. Should she come out and tell him she knew what he was up to? No, by feigning ignorance she had the upper hand. She finished the milk and set the glass alongside the empty plate and half full bowl of fruit. She'd eaten the easy to peel bananas leaving the papayas.

The smug smirk and raised eyebrow of the man said he wanted her to ask questions. Holding her tongue was torture, but she wouldn't give in. By refusing to talk it gave her more time to form a plan in her head. Isabella plumped a pillow covered in finely woven fabric of the colors she'd witnessed in this village on her last visit. She reclined on the sofa, closing her eyes.

The man growled and stomped to the opposite side of the room.

She gulped a snicker down and continued evaluating what she knew. They were upriver from the dig. She'd have to use a boat to get to the landing and then hike in. Would Tino look for her at the dig first? If not, she could stay with Pedro until he did arrive. But how did she discover if they were continuing with the ceremony?

Rustling sounds near the bed meant don Miguel planned to turn in for the night. He didn't tie her up. Did he think she wouldn't try to get away, believing she didn't know where she was? A cough resounded outside the door. The two he'd sent away stood guard. That was how he knew she wasn't going anywhere.

She opened her eyes and shifted to her side. The lantern was off. She peered around the dark interior of the mud hut, searching for another way out. Nothing. Not even a window. She'd noticed when they walked to the building it resembled the others on the outside—a bit weathered and slightly larger. Don Miguel didn't want the building to draw any attention.

The only escape was through the door and the two men. She could use the excuse that nature called and sneak away when she used the bushes. Yeah, a smile tipped her lips. She had to do it before the sun came up. The moon's illumination was nearly as bright as the sun, but she could use the shadows of buildings to hide her escape. Not tonight. She needed time to scope out everything and form a plan.

A shiver slithered up her spine. The full moon was tomorrow night. That didn't give her much time to plan or get away.

~*~

Tino stared into the dark cave, waiting for Ginger to report back.

She'd promised to make his questions top priority. How long would it take for someone to check out don Miguel's whereabouts? He couldn't sit at the mouth of the cave indefinitely. Another group of drug traffickers could find out about the cave and plan to use it, or Miguel and his *ratas* could come back.

He had to sit tight. The tunnel was the quickest way to the dig, and he couldn't risk carrying the open radio through the jungle. To go deeper within the cave would cut off reception.

Where was Isabella? Was she safe? Could she stall Miguel until he caught up to them?

"*¡Coño!*" Tino kicked the wall to the cave entrance. Waiting would drive him crazy. He picked up his gear and walked twenty feet into the jungle at the side of the entrance and set up his tent. The activity helped loosen his constricted muscles but didn't ease his mind. He shoved all his equipment into the tent and sat down to eat dried meat and nuts.

The radio crackled. He dove into the tent and plopped his earphones on.

"Konstantine. Over."

"No sign of Miguel at the plantation. Sources say he left three days ago in his helicopter. Over."

The news was good. He was still in the area, presumably.

"*Gracias*, Ginger. Over."

"Konstantine?"

He held his breath. Ginger never slipped protocol. "*¿Si?*"

"Doctor Isabella Mumphrey has a high priority status. Over."

His gut clenched. Why would the government put a high priority status on an anthropologist?

"Can you elaborate? Over."

"Classified. Out."

¡Coño! That put a whole different light on the possibilities for her abduction. And if she was a government agent why hadn't she told him when he poured out the truth to her? He flipped the radio off, uprooted his tent, and shoved all but his gun, knife, and some food under a flourishing fern.

Pedro had some explaining to do. The cook and Isabella acted like strangers, but were they? His mind ran through all his conversations with Isabella and her reactions to the people around her as he stalked through the tunnel toward the dig. She was good at playing the innocent. He'd fallen for it. Fell for her. *¡Coño!* He'd given more of himself to her than he had given anyone in years. Had dreams of giving her more. But who was she really?

He ran through the now familiar tunnel.

At the boulder that hid the tunnel from the altar chamber he stopped and stared back into the darkness. He didn't remember covering this much distance. His thoughts had ricocheted off his brain and bounced around like sparks, emitting emotions of frustration, confusion, and loss. His tightly reined emotions wanted to explode.

He loved a woman he didn't really know. Ha! Love. He seldom used the word or even thought of himself ever loving another, yet he had fallen hopelessly for this woman, and he had no idea if her responses to him were genuine or faked to…To what? Why would an agent be assigned to watch him? He'd never done anything to cause his superiors to think he was anything but ethical.

He ascended the steps, pressed his shoulder against the rock, and slid the portal open. Cold air wrapped around him the minute he stepped into the chamber. Why was this chamber always colder than the tunnel? He stared at the drawing on the wall and wondered what about it had captured Isabella's attention? Could the drawing be the real reason she came here? If so, why? And what did he have to do with it? Clearly, she'd attached herself to him for a reason.

The images blurred as he stared. Voices whispered in his head. One had the same sweet voice as Isabella. *"You can save me."*

"How?" His own raspy reply broke the spell. He hurried out of the chamber.

At the dig entrance, he peered around the compound. Everyone had retired for the night. He ran across the open area to the back of the cook tent. Pedro held answers; he was sure of it.

Tino didn't bother making his presence known. He slipped through the flap quietly, stopping to peer into the darkness. His gaze landed on the bed and he stepped forward with caution. He reached down to grasp the man's arm and came up with only a blanket.

Where was the cook at this hour of the night?

Chapter Twenty-Seven

Isabella stretched and groaned. The sofa, while softer than the floor, lacked the space for stretching out. Her lower back ached from remaining curled up all night. And nature called.

She sprang alert. This was her chance to escape. With less than eighteen hours before the ceremony, she needed to get away. Daylight wasn't optimal but she had to try. She rolled to a sitting position and glanced at the bed.

Empty.

Last night's used dishes had been replaced with full plates and a full glass of coconut milk. A pitcher of water along with a colorful, woven towel stood at the end of the table. All of her needs were thought of, except...

She stood and walked to the door. Her hand pressed against the solid wood and the door swung open. Don Miguel stepped inside. He peered over her shoulder and shook his head.

"Where are you going? I have provided all you need."

"An outhouse would be ideal," she quipped.

"The brass pot in the corner is your outhouse, *señorita*. I will give you thirty minutes to finish your morning duties." He stepped back and closed the door.

Shamutz! He didn't plan to let her out of the hut. How could she escape with two-foot adobe walls and guards at the door? Using the facilities and washing up, she thought of digging out, but there was nowhere to hide the evidence, and no time. The door held her only escape. She'd have to listen and discern when the guards grew less vigilant and figure out a way to get by them.

She plopped onto the sofa and ate her breakfast. She needed her strength for her escape.

Don Miguel entered. His gaze traveled about the room and landed on her. "I see you have made yourself at home. That is good." He sat in a chair and watched her. "For one so brilliant you have hardly asked any questions."

Ahh, her not asking annoyed him. Good. She shrugged.

"Since you are unwilling to ask, I will tell you what you need to know." He leaned back in his chair. His large hands rested on the chair arms, but his tufted knuckles gripped the ends, whitening the joints. "Your Dr. Martin has discovered a ceremonial sacrificial altar. I, as a great collector of all things Mayan, am drawn to the ceremonies of bloodletting and sacrifice. Specifically, human sacrifice. As a true scholar of Mayan history, you know that did not happen often. Bloodletting did, and Dr. Martin helped me experience that last year. Now he will help me experience another Mayan ceremony." His eyes closed, and his lips curved into a self-satisfied smile. He shifted his weight in his chair and absentmindedly adjusted his trousers.

He is aroused by the idea of sacrificing!

Isabella shuddered. His aura of evil hadn't been mistaken.

"Together, we are going to reproduce the moon god's sacrifice tonight. We wish you to be present." His eyes opened. Dark dilated pupils peered at her.

She'd witnessed this kind of zeal before, in Virgil's eyes when he'd uncovered some relic of historic importance.

"If you wanted me to attend, all you had to do was ask." Her sarcastic remark hid the chill of fear creeping up her spine.

His laughter boomed through the small hut. "*Señorita*, you are as charming as Dr. Martin said, and just as innocent." He stood. "Make yourself at home. I have matters to attend." He walked to the door and pivoted. "Do not think of leaving this hut; my boys will not allow you." He disappeared and the heavy wood door thunked shut.

Isabella paced from the door to the bed. How can I stop this? He has to know why Virgil brought me here. Yet he acts as if I've no idea about the ceremony. She pulled out her journal and read the translation. Every aspect of the ceremony was in the book. Did Virgil know this and plan to use the notes? That wouldn't be like him. He'd have the whole ceremony mapped out and rechecked before he preformed it. *What am I missing?*

On a pass by the bed, she noticed papers hanging out of a folder. Isabella plopped on the bed and picked up the folder. The familiar handwriting on the pages squeezed her chest and she gasped.

"No!"

This was the reason the ceremony would continue without her notes. She stared at the same information she'd discovered. It detailed the sacrifice to the moon god. The obsidian knife, height of the full moon, the chant.

They had everything they needed to recreate the ceremony. And she was the virgin. Shudders rippled up and down her body as the images of the drawing on the chamber wall flashed in her mind.

A cool breeze fluttered her neck hairs. Knowledge filled her mind and she knew.

This was the real reason Virgil lured her here to decipher the tablet. She was as intimate with the ceremony as the first moon god sacrifice victim.

Her body chilled, icy shards pierced her chest. When had they begun to concoct this? When she was in grad school? Before? How stupid she'd been to believe the great archeologist, Dr. Virgil Martin, supported her thesis. Supported her. She'd only been a pawn, first, to elicit financial support from her father and, when that dried up, to acquire financial support from don Miguel.

And all to resurrect a ceremony the two greedy men thought would bring them wealth. That was the one thing Virgil had wrong. The prosperity the ceremony brought would not be monetary.

Could she convince don Miguel the ceremony wouldn't bring him wealth? No, she'd witnessed his exhilaration just thinking of the sacrifice. He was out for the thrill as much as the money.

Anger shot Isabella to her feet, melting her icy center and lighting a fire of action. *How dare he!* She paced, anger fueling her motions. How many times had he called her naïve? So many she'd quit listening. He'd never thought of her as a colleague. She'd show him. She'd stop him.

How?

She choked back a sob. Only Tino knew don Miguel had her. She had to have faith that Tino had cut himself loose by now and searched for her.

Her chest constricted, squeezing her heart. He had no way of knowing she was in the settlement or that don Miguel and Virgil had everything they needed. She couldn't count on Tino. As much as she loved him, this would play out just like her life so far—she had to do it alone.

~*~

Tino fought sleep, waiting for Pedro to return. Where could the man be? Was he missing too? The light in the mess tent flickered and glowed. Tino shoved to his feet and moved through the cook's quarters into the cook tent behind the mess tent.

Pedro bent in front of the stove lighting the gas. Tino stalked behind him quietly, slipping an arm around the man's throat, and jabbing his gun into the cook's side.

"Where's Ezzabella?" he demanded, ignoring the man's talon grip on his forearm.

"I have been looking for you to ask you the same." His choked voice loosened Tino's arm.

He spun the man around and stared into his watery eyes. "You are looking for me?"

"*Sí*. You and Isabella keep company and I have los—I have not been able to find her. I am worried." Genuine concern shone in the man's eyes and his voice wobbled with emotion.

"Have you seen don Miguel?"

The cook's back snapped straight and his eyes hardened. "Not since his earlier visit. *¿Por que?*"

"He has Ezzabella. They knocked me out, tied me up, and sent me downriver. I believe he took her somewhere in a helicopter." Tino couldn't squelch the rage boiling at the thought of the man and his *ratas* harming Isabella.

"I heard a helicopter fly over the compound last evening. It was headed toward the settlement." Pedro picked up dough and rolled tortillas. "I overheard Dr. Martin tell everyone there would be a movie in the mess tent tonight." He stared at Tino. "Why are they having a movie tonight? And when did the movie and player arrive?"

Tino knew it was a rhetorical question, for he didn't have an answer. He watched the cook roll out a tortilla. "What do you know about Ezzabella?"

Pedro returned his stare. "She studies people and came here at the request of Doctor Martin. *¿Por que?*"

His fluid movements continued, but his face had grown taut. If the man did know something about Isabella, he wouldn't tell. Tino shrugged and moved to the back of the tent.

"I am going to find her. And when I find her, if I discover she has been harmed, I will kill everyone responsible." Tino left the cook tent the way he entered and stomped into the jungle. He was tired of chasing after don Miguel. He and the doctor had plans for tonight if Martin wanted everyone in the mess tent where he knew they were detained.

Tino stared at the cave. Martin and Miguel planned to sacrifice a virgin on the full moon. His heart banged against his constricting chest. Tonight would be the full moon.

They would perform the ritual in the chamber on the altar. Indecision weighed heavy against his better judgment. He wanted to save Isabella from Miguel, but he would waste time and possibly miss stopping the sacrifice if he went running all over the jungle when he knew they would all be in the chamber tonight.

A large lump of dread settled in his stomach as he decided to return to his gear and try to sleep. He knew where he'd meet up with Isabella. And it would be before anyone harmed her. He wasn't good at waiting but this was one time when more than his life depended on it.

Chapter Twenty-Eight

Isabella shoved the papers back where she'd found them. After reading through Virgil's notes and set up for the ritual, she had to go through with the ceremony. She knew the ceremonial chant, each step leading up to the sacrifice, and she knew the way to stop the men.

Her mind wandered to the glyphs she'd painstakingly deciphered. All the pieces fit together with the knowledge Virgil had discovered. She knew the reason the woman and the moon god cried. Her heart ached for them. Two lovers sworn to secrecy because of a commitment that couldn't be broken. Yet one that started the decline of the Mayas. The ritual had done the opposite of making the Maya prosper because the virgin had not been a virgin.

What would happen if tonight she couldn't stop the two mad men from sacrificing her? She was no longer a virgin either. What kind of power or riches did they hope to possess with this ritual?

She sank onto the sofa and plucked a banana from the bowl of fruit. Tonight. She had a little over twelve hours to figure out how to thwart Virgil and don Miguel.

The door opened and two women entered carrying a beautiful, tightly woven, white cloth. They smiled and held it up to her as if measuring for a garment. Her mind swept the pages of books she'd read on Mayan rituals. They were making a *huipil*. With only the

239

women in the room, she whispered her concerns for her safety and asked them to sew two pockets to the inside of the dress. They nodded and their faces became sober as she told them she was being kept against her will. Their fear and dislike of the man shone in their faces and whispered words.

~*~

That afternoon, Isabella held up the finely woven garment. Its pristine white color shouted purity. Guilt swamped her. She wasn't pure and didn't deserve to wear such a fine garment.

Don Miguel cleared his throat. "Put this on. I shall return for you in half an hour." He placed another glass of coconut milk on the table along with a dry looking biscuit. His hand waved up and down. "And no undergarments."

"I don't think that's—"

He cut her off. "You shall dress just as in ancient times. Only the garment and sandals."

Isabella scowled and nodded. She understood his need to make it correct but hated leaving her vest. Once the man left, she sat down and ran her hands over the dress. The finely woven cloth slid through her fingers like the finest cashmere. Her fingers encountered the two small pockets, and she smiled, mentally thanking the women. She extracted her journal and a thin blade from her vest and slid them into the pockets.

Her stomach rumbled. She ignored the biscuit and unwrapped one of her energy bars. She drank half the glass of milk before a bitter aftertaste registered on her tongue.

Isabella took off her vest, shirt, and tank, dropping the garment over her head. She stood to step out of her pants. The room swirled and everything became hazy. She plopped onto the sofa, closed her eyes, and the dark world behind her eyelids moved. The milk and energy bar swirled in her stomach. She opened her eyes to the spinning room basked in an ethereal glow. Bending to untie her boots caused her to swoon. Her rubbery arms dangled to the floor as she remained bent in half, staring at shoelaces.

He drugged me.

It took great effort to raise her arm and swipe the glass off the table. She didn't want to take a chance of drinking any more.

She leaned back on the sofa, fighting to remember what she was to do next. Euphoria washed over her, and she sat on the soft cloud and smiled. She closed her eyes and watched beautiful colors swirl and spin.

"Why are you not dressed?" A harsh male voice invaded her tranquil thoughts.

Her mind jerked from her serenity when rough hands yanked on her feet. She opened her eyes and watched a large man toss her boots to the side then remove her pants and underwear. Unease rippled down her back and shot a small injection of fear into her hypnotic state.

Isabella worked to gain control of her thoughts. He'd laced her coconut milk with a hallucinogenic drug. She should've been more careful. She'd read about the drugging in Virgil's notes but hadn't expected it until they arrived at the dig. The victim is given a drug to make her malleable and obedient. She'd have to play the part so he wouldn't give her any more. Her racing heart and the ethereal glow of the surroundings worried her. She couldn't be incapacitated during the ceremony. She'd battle the drug's effects and hope it wore off soon since she hadn't drunk the full amount.

Don Miguel held her feet and massaged them before slipping the sandals on. She didn't like his taking liberties with her body. She forced her mind to work, but her limbs remained rubbery and of little use.

"Dr. Martin was right. You are a fine specimen of virginal qualities. A youthful body and innocent personality." He ran a hand up her leg.

Her mind saw her striking out with a kick; her body remained listless as his hand moved up her leg. Filthy. The man had his filthy hands on her. Revulsion lodged in her throat.

She opened her mouth to tell him what she thought. Only a pitiful sound escaped her numb tongue and lips. Damn the man for keeping her mind alive and her body dead.

He grinned. The creep enjoyed her disgust and despair at his groping hands. His eyes sparked with the knowledge.

Don't let him go any higher. The thought of his hand touching where only Tino had touched repulsed her.

He released her leg and tugged on her braid. "Your hair needs to be free." He pulled off the band on the end and ran his fingers through her braid, unleashing her straight hair to fall around her shoulders.

"That is better."

Don Miguel slipped her glasses from her face. She tried to object but nothing intelligent formed. Her world, already revolving, now grew out of focus as well with the disappearance of her eyewear.

One of the doormen walked in. "The boat is ready."

Don Miguel grasped her hands and stood her on her feet. Her legs wobbled. He slid an arm under her armpit and braced her back against his arm as he half-carried, half-led, her out the door.

The heat of the late afternoon warmed her cold extremities, but they still wouldn't work, no matter how hard she tried. The villagers formed an alley for them to walk through. They chanted and tossed colors in their path. From the sweet scent, she deduced they threw orchids.

Isabella tried to draw the blurred faces into focus. According to Virgil's plan, these people thought they were replicating an ancient marriage ceremony. If they knew the truth would they help? Her body couldn't even shudder. She'd never experienced hate for another human being, but this man had given her a first. She hated him. And hoped Tino caught the man and took him to jail.

At the boat, don Miguel picked her up in his arms and stepped into the hull. He sat still cradling her in his arms as the other two shoved off the landing and jumped in.

She wanted to tell the man to put her down but, again, her tongue and lips refused to work. How would she stop them from plunging the obsidian knife into her chest if she couldn't speak?

Refreshing air floated over Isabella as the boat puttered down the river. If only she could raise a hand to brush the hair out of her face. She still rested in don Miguel's lap. He didn't treat her like a virgin. His hands wandered up and down her sides, over her breasts, and even cupping her butt when he shifted her. The other men chuckled as his hands roamed. She wanted to slap him and smack the other men's faces.

She hated this handling. It made her feel violated, and she feared he would discover her pockets and the journal. Her ability to speak had to come back. Otherwise, she wouldn't be able to stop the ceremony to save not only her life but also the truth of the Mayan history.

She tried one more time to utter a protest to his groping. "Get your hands off me." The words came out as a pitiful gurgle. He laughed and squeezed her butt. Anger sparked hot. Damn the man!

The boat motor sputtered and the wind stopped rushing by her. The two younger men stepped around her and don Miguel. Water splashed, the boat lunged, and don Miguel rose with her still in his arms.

"What's wrong with her?" Virgil's worried tone brought a moment of hope to her situation.

"She drank that stuff you gave me." Don Miguel set her feet on the ground.

Her legs had gained strength, but she didn't want them to know, and purposely swayed into him.

"You weren't supposed to give it to her until we were in the altar chamber." Virgil grabbed her other arm. "Where are her glasses?"

Don Miguel patted his breast pocket. Good, she knew where to get them when she could move her arms.

"I have the workers in the mess tent watching a movie," Virgil said as they linked arms and carried her up the trail to the dig.

Don Miguel's men walked one in front and one in back. Did they know what the two older men planned? From their actions, she had a feeling they'd enjoy watching. The thought quaked her insides.

Too soon they stepped into the compound. The sun was setting, making way for the inevitable full moon. If she could stop time as the ancients had for she and Tino in the altar chamber, now would be the perfect moment.

"Tell your men to stand guard at the entrance. We don't want any unwanted guests."

Virgil's orders and calm presence rippled a shiver up her spine. How could she have once thought of this man as a surrogate father? His actions equaled a criminal with no heart.

Don Miguel ordered his men to stay at the entrance. He and Virgil hauled her into the dig, through the main chamber, and into the altar chamber. Smoke and a sensual earthy scent veiled the room. Without any pretense the men walked straight to the altar.

Isabella steeled herself for the onslaught of emotion that usually settled over her in the chamber, but none came.

Virgil put both hands under her arms and held her against the cold stone of the altar.

"Go in the other room and put on your ceremonial garments.

They're set out," Virgil said to don Miguel. The other man sauntered out of the room.

"Isabella," Virgil lifted her chin and stared into her eyes, "I regret the loss of your intelligence to the archeology and anthropology circles, but that same intelligence has come too close too many times to discovering the fraud that I am and I can't have that happen. I'm too old to start over."

Isabella tried to think back over the years and what she would know that could prove him a fraud. But trying to think only increased her confusion.

Virgil studied her and smiled. "And you're the perfect sacrifice for this ceremony. You studied the ceremony, have empathy for the Mayas, and you're a virgin."

She peered into his eyes and tried to shake her head. She had to make him know she wasn't a virgin. This ceremony wouldn't bring about what they wished. If they went through with the atrocity it would only bring about bad things just as the ceremony did thousands of years before.

Not to mention, she wasn't ready to leave this earth. She'd finally found a person who loved her unconditionally.

His eyes softened. "Don Miguel has offered me something I can't refuse. Even over the wrath of your father and the loss of a great mind." He kissed her forehead and placed her on the altar. "Your purity is unsurpassed and will give us power and prosperity."

Virgil reclined her on the altar with care. Anger and frustration burned in hot tears behind her eyes. His hands fluttered her dress, and she worried he might discover her hidden treasures. He fanned her hair around her head.

"I wish you could be by my side witnessing this miracle, but then I wouldn't have the perfect sacrifice or be able to take care of a thorn in my side." He picked up a small bowl, dipped his fingers into it and dotted the liquid around her face, down her neck, and between her breasts, chanting in Chol.

Her mind rushed in a thousand different directions as she tried to remember the sequence of the ceremony. But all she could think about was Virgil, the man she'd looked up to for so long, planned to watch as don Miguel cut into her with an obsidian knife and took out her heart, a heart they believed to be pure.

Don Miguel returned. He wore a white loincloth, sandals like hers, a cape of bright colors, and a headdress of colorful tropical bird feathers. "Are you getting dressed?" he asked Virgil.

"I'm just about done. Do you remember your part?" Virgil dotted oil the length of her arms on the tender undersides, pouring a small pool in the palms of her hands. He folded her fingers around the oil and chanted. His voice faded and his hands disappeared from her vision.

She tried to move her head to follow the sounds, but her body wouldn't respond.

"Here are your words." Virgil said. "Read and memorize them but don't say them. They can't be spoken out loud until the right moment." Virgil's steps faded. She could hear don Miguel pacing to her right. She couldn't see what either one was doing.

Where was Tino? If ever she needed someone it was now, and she wished it to be the one person she could depend on.

Virgil returned. He and don Miguel stood near her head. They put their hands on her shoulders and Virgil chanted about her pureness, their journey to greatness, and the moon god. The chant ended, their hands raised, and her arms tingled. Her numbness was wearing off.

Chapter Twenty-Nine

Tino peered through the small hole by the hidden door. It had taken all his control to remain in the tunnel and watch the two men drag Isabella into the chamber. If her eyes hadn't blinked, he would have sworn she was dead. Her limp body worried him, but he'd glimpsed the light of intelligence in her eyes. They may have made her unable to move, but her mind still fired. He wished he knew the sequence of the ceremony. Moving the rock would alert the men to his approach and with Isabella incapacitated barging in now could put her in danger. He would have to wait for a moment when the two men were at a disadvantage.

The men were crazy, and he didn't want this to be a suicide mission with he and Isabella the bodies that were found. Miguel didn't bother him. He was a rich man paying for this new experience. He'd be easy to subdue. Martin did bother him. The doctor's zeal and calmness reflected what he had witnessed and studied about killers. Martin had reverently kissed Isabella's head and told her sacrificing her was worth everything.

Words of a madman.

Martin returned dressed in a colorful robe and wearing a headdress similar to Miguel's. The two men spoke quietly on the far side of the altar near Isabella's head. He wished he could hear the conversation.

They parted and Miguel stepped up onto a raised rock beside the altar. He lifted his loincloth. Tino watched in disbelief as Martin chanted and handed Miguel a bowl of white papers. Miguel placed the bowl on another raised stone between his legs. Martin continued chanting as he held up, and then offered, a stingray spine to Miguel.

Miguel took the object, pinched the skin on his *miembro,* and pushed the object through his foreskin. The man's member surged a moment before he pulled out the stingray spine and inserted a small rope through the holes. Blood saturated the rope and dripped into the bowl, staining the white paper red.

Miguel swayed, his eyes glazing over.

Martin placed a hand on Miguel's shoulder. Miguel pulled the rope out of his *miembro* and dropped it into the bowl. Martin picked up the bowl of bloody paper and distributed small pieces among the bowls placed around Isabella on the altar.

The paper was lit and Martin placed a crown of flowers on Isabella's head. The beautiful flowers and Isabella's serene repose were a stark contrast to the obscene actions of the men.

Tino's temples throbbed. When should he make a move? He didn't like the unattached way Martin treated her. His adrenaline surged and his heart raced.

Do something Isabella.

Stop him.

Miguel swayed on his pedestal. Martin steadied him and held a black shiny blade to the ceiling and chanted. He placed the knife in Miguel's hands and waved his arms over Isabella. He opened her dress exposing her chest and stepped back.

Rage and fear catapulted Tino. He grabbed the wooden handle on the boulder and shoved with all his strength. He had to save Isabella.

The sight of don Miguel's trance and the shiny obsidian blade in his hands surged adrenaline through Isabella. She tried to sit up, knocking the burning offerings to the floor. Her body still didn't respond completely.

"No Virgil—not work." Frustration at her unintelligible words also hampered her movement. She swallowed and tried to work her tongue. The sound of rock scraping rock registered. Help had arrived.

Virgil clutched her wrists and held her to the table. "Now!" he shouted.

Fear sliced through her as don Miguel raised the knife above her body. Warm flickering light from the oil pots glistened on the shiny black blade clutched in his hands. She willed her arms to work to wrench free of Virgil's grip.

A blur hit don Miguel and he disappeared from her sight.

Cursing and flesh hitting flesh resonated from the floor.

Virgil's eyes peered into hers. Now her vision cleared as she stared into the eyes of evil. The evil she'd caught only glimpses of since arriving at the dig shone like a beacon. He dove to the ground.

She had to help Tino. But her body was only slowly responding. She managed to wrap her fingers around the small oil pot by her hip.

Virgil appeared before her, the obsidian knife clutched in his hands.

"I'm not a virgin!" The garbled words only intensified her anger. She flung the hot oil into Virgil's face.

"Aahhhh!" He stumbled backward.

She swung her legs over the altar and spotted don Miguel and Tino struggling near the doorway. Grasping another pot of hot oil, she forced her legs to move in a stiff zombie fashion. She had to help Tino. He was the only person in her life to truly care about her and her career. Her heart squeezed with fear as don Miguel slammed a fist into Tino's side. The two danced a clumsy dance, don Miguel trying to get away and Tino hanging on, inflicting punches and jabs to the man's body and face.

Isabella tossed the hot oil on don Miguel's back. He roared with pain and fell to the ground wiggling like a salted snail.

"Ezzabella!"

Tino's warning came too late.

She felt hot breath and an arm band around her from behind. She shouldn't have underestimated Virgil's zealousness.

"She has to die." The loud roaring voice in her ear made her cringe.

"You haven't committed murder yet, Martin. Let her go, and you won't die." Tino stared straight at her and Virgil, but Isabella's eyes were on Tino's gun laying on the floor an arm's reach from her feet.

How could Tino stop Virgil? His arm was wrapped around her middle tight; to try and slump down wouldn't help. And even if she did, what could Tino do?

The obsidian knife wasn't as sharp as a present-day metal blade. She'd take the chance of a scrape or two. She mouthed, "Keep him talking", to Tino and slowly relaxed, flexing each muscle to see what coordination she'd have.

"Why are you doing this? Surely, you could write a world-renowned paper on the ceremony and retain your status and perhaps more funding." Tino took a step forward.

"Stay back!" Virgil moved back a step, putting them farther from the weapon.

"Don't move", she mouthed to Tino and flashed her gaze to the gun and back to him.

"Okay, I'll stay back, but you have to let her go. You have done nothing wrong so far." Tino planted his feet firmly in place. He didn't know what Isabella had planned but he would follow her lead even though he wasn't happy having Miguel at his back and Virgil holding a black knife on Isabella.

"I'll kill you, too, if you interfere." Virgil's voice held such conviction goose bumps rose on Tino's arms.

"You cannot continue with the ceremony, it will accomplish nothing." Tino started to move his foot forward out of instinct, but the widening of Isabella's eyes stalled the movement.

"I can gain all the things I haven't been able to attain. Prosperity, the funding and accolades I've only acquired by using others. And immortality. I'll go down in the books as the first and only archeologist to discover and carry out one of the most controversial sacrifices."

"It was controversial because it went wrong."

Martin's eyes narrowed. "How do you know it went wrong?"

"Ezzabella told me. The virgin they sacrificed wasn't a virgin and it caused the beginning of the downfall of the Mayas."

Stumbling and cursing behind him caught his attention. Tino spun around to catch the backside of Miguel hurrying out of the dig.

Grunts, a growl, and scrambling spun him back around. Isabella sat on the floor his gun in her hands. Martin shook his head and raised the knife charging at her.

Tino's chest constricted as he shouted, "No!" and his ears rang from the explosion of his gun.

Virgil fell across Isabella.

Paty Jager

Tino lunged for the two, pulling the doctor off Isabella, flinging him to the side and gently prying the gun from her hands.

"I had to…"

"Shhh, do not look. You are safe. I have you." Tino held her tight. If he'd lost her, he would never have been able to shake the pain or the curse of losing those he loved.

Chapter Thirty

Isabella snuggled into Tino's strong arms. She'd shot a man. Not just any man, her mentor and a man she'd thought cared about her. The revelations she'd uncovered on this trip had her unsure of everyone except the man holding her tight and whispering sweet endearments in her ear.

Voices erupted in the small confines. She tipped her head and peered into the only set of eyes she cared to see. Her glasses were slipped onto her nose, and she reveled in the warmth and love in Tino's eyes. Tears burned, and she buried her head in his shoulder. The cleansing tears washed away the fear and frustration of her past two days.

Tino's arms remained wrapped around her. She smiled as his heartbeat slowed under her ear. Sounds of scuffling and numerous male voices in both Spanish and English captured her attention. She opened one eye and watched Pedro and several other men remove Virgil. Who were all these people?

"Is there a chance I can talk to my daughter?"

Isabella froze. What was her father doing here? The only time he ever came to her was on her birthdays and then they never met at her apartment; they always met some place he and her mother suggested. Believing she still hallucinated but curious that her father's voice sounded so clear, she slowly unburied her face from Tino's shoulder.

She stared at her father's wide shoulders and authoritative stance, but she'd never seen him in camouflage. She shook her head and stared again, this time at the square chin and blue searching eyes that definitely belonged to her father. "Daddy?" She wiped her nose on Tino's shirt and continued to stare.

Her father?

In Guatemala?

What was he doing here? And at this moment?

Isabella started to push away from Tino, still unbelieving. He held her in place. She peered into his eyes but his gaze watched his hands, pulling her ripped dress together. Leave it to Tino to make her presentable.

"*Gracias*." She kissed his cheek and shifted to stand in front of her father. "What are you doing here, Daddy?

Her question pulled his assessing gaze from Tino to her and his eyes softened, reminding her of the last time she'd received a visit from him.

His gaze slid down her front. "Is that your blood?"

His question was warranted given Virgil's blood had spattered on her dress, but the casualness of the question hurt. It was as unemotional as all their contact.

"No, it's from Virgil. I shot him." She could hide her feelings as well as him. Her insides quivered like jelly replaying the squeezing of the trigger and Virgil's blood seeping from his chest as his surprised eyes stared at her.

Tino rubbed a hand up and down her back in a comforting reassurance of his presence.

"What are you doing here?" she asked again.

"When your tracking device stopped working and Pedro told me you were in trouble, I dropped everything and headed here. It looks like I didn't have to worry. You and your friend seem to have things under control."

"You're the one who had the tracking device in my watch?" Isabella backed into Tino. His arms immediately wrapped around her waist. Confusion spun in her mind, mixing with anger. Why would he track her, how—?

She slapped a hand on her forehead. "That's what you did every year on my birthday. You installed a new tracking device. Why?" She wasn't sure if the anger bubbling inside was from his tracking her or his secrecy about it.

Daddy scanned the chamber. The men had cleared Virgil from the room. Only Pedro stood inside the door. Her father glanced at the cook and he nodded. How did he know Pedro?

Her father reached out a hand. "There's a lot your mother and I have kept from you. After what Pedro has told me, I think it's time you knew." His gaze rose above her head. "Both of you."

Isabella pushed deeper into Tino's arms. Her father's serious tone disturbed her as his child and frustrated her as a grown woman. She needed Tino's restraint to keep her anger in check. High emotions only further confused issues.

"This chamber is secure," Pedro said, stepping out of the room.

Her head hurt. What did Pedro mean the chamber was secure? Why was he acting so much like…Tino?

"I know you've been through a lot, but we need to talk. Now. Before others ask you questions." Her father motioned to the altar. "Can you manage to sit there? I don't see anywhere else and you look like you need to."

The memories, both good and bad, of the altar made her hesitant. Not minutes before, a madman had tried to drive an obsidian blade through her chest on this very slab. She couldn't stop the trembling or the way her knees buckled.

"I am with you," Tino whispered in her ear. "If you wish to leave this place, I will take you."

She shook her head. "No." She placed a hand on the prickly stubble of his cheek. "This place also has good memories. I'll focus on those."

His eyes lit and he placed a chaste kiss on her cheek. Her father cleared his throat, and Tino grasped her waist, placing her on the altar.

"Did you happen to bring a medical doctor in with you?" Tino asked, hoisting his backside up on the altar next to her and wrapping an arm around her shoulders.

"Are you wondering about that bullet in Dr. Martin or don Miguel? Who by the way is in custody," her father added.

Isabella studied Tino's profile. How did he feel about her shooting a man? The firm set of his jaw and the dark scowl said it all—He knew it had been her or Virgil.

"No. I could care less what happens to either of them. If Ezzabella had not shot him, I would have killed him. I want a doctor for Ezzabella. They drugged her. I want to make sure there are no after affects."

Isabella put a hand on Tino's thigh. His concerned gaze searched her face. "I'm fine."

Her father stepped in front of her. He winked and did a cursory examination, lifting her eyelids and feeling her pulse.

"Daddy's a doctor," she said as he tapped on her tendons checking her reflexes. "Among, it appears, other things." Isabella scowled at her father. What had he and her mother been keeping from her? Why was he dressed like some military operative, and why did he have her tracked? Frustration at her stupidity mocked her. She, a genius, hadn't figured out he'd planted a tracking device in her watch every year.

"What did they give you?" he asked, continuing his examination and ignoring her jab.

"It was odorless but had a faint bitter aftertaste. Given the area and the Mayan ceremony, I'd say it was L-Dopa with a paralyzing drug of some kind mixed in. Don Miguel gave me coconut milk to drink before, and I didn't consider he'd tampered with the second glass. Once I'd realized, I didn't drink any more but it was enough…"

She shuddered and Tino pulled her into an embrace.

"Shh, *querida*. I will not let them touch you again. I promise."

She wasn't usually a crier but after all that had happened today, she couldn't keep the tears in check. "I should have known Virgil was luring me down here. No collector of artifacts would pay half a million to learn about a ceremony." The shame of having been duped would have consumed her if not for her anger at the man. "But if I'd left when I discovered the truth, they could have used some unsuspecting woman and there would have been a murder and perhaps even more unhappiness inflicted on the Maya."

The papers! She grabbed her father's hands. "Daddy, we have to make sure all the papers at don Miguel's hut in the settlement are burned along with any notes in Virgil's tent. They discovered a ceremony that could devastate the Mayan population."

Her father nodded and held up a small device. "Vincent, did you hear that? Keep Dr. Martin and Miguel isolated and go through their belongings. Gather everything and put it in a guarded spot. My daughter will decide what's dangerous and what's of archeological importance."

Daddy wanted her to go through the papers and share the important details with him. He believed in her and respected her knowledge. How many times had she wanted to show him a report or paper and he was never around? And now, when she came close to dying, he was here. Would her birthdays and death be the only times she saw him? After all these years why did she care? She'd learned long ago she wasn't her parents' first priority.

Strong warm arms squeezed her.

Tino put her first. She gazed into his eyes and squirmed as the slab under them warmed, heating a part of her that ignited from the inside at the love and caring in his eyes.

"Konstantine. I've been told you're a man who thinks on his feet and knows the jungle."

How did her father know Tino's real name? Her father's gaze flicked to her waist where her hands rested on Tino's.

"I am a good jaguar tracker." Tino squeezed her hand. "Do a little guide work on the side. That is how I met your daughter and happened into this mess."

Her father's crooked grin and sparkling eyes said he knew the whole truth.

"Yes. The Guatemalan government is pleased with your ability to track jaguars and other jungle predators."

Isabella was tired of waiting for her father to tell her why he was here. She also wanted time alone with Tino to remind herself of what she'd nearly lost. The heat of the altar reminded her of their love making. A primal beat had begun the minute Tino had placed her on the altar, and she wanted to tame the urge even her father's stare couldn't dampen.

"Why don't you tell me what exactly you do since it appears you were gone a lot on more than medical missionary trips?" She stared into her father's eyes and waited. "And why did you have to keep track of me?"

He cleared his throat and shuffled his feet. "Your mother has your genius. She's worked for the Worldwide Intelligence Agency since graduating college. She's their best kept secret. When it became evident you were following in her intellectual footsteps, we worried it would lead people to speculating about your genetics. So we opted to keep a low profile in your life."

"All those years...you denied me contact with you because I could blow mom's cover? I would rather have stayed with you and hidden my intellect, if I'd been given the chance." She shook her head and felt even sadder. The truth she'd always tried to deny slammed into her solar plexus. Her parents had put their jobs over her.

"Does Virgil know your true identities?"

He shook his head. "No. He just saw us the way we portrayed ourselves. A doctor with a philanthropic wife. If he lives, he can never know the truth. No one can." His gaze shifted to Tino. "I'm telling you because Pedro says he sees a future between you and my daughter. And I know you can keep secrets."

"I don't understand," Tino broke in. "All the intelligence organizations in the world could have traced her back to you if they tried. Why so much secrecy?"

"No, they can't." Her father peered into her eyes.

The sadness she saw melted the metal bars she'd erected around her heart toward her parents. Her voice choked. "Why not?"

"Our real names aren't Mumphrey, and all our records are official from the time of your birth. There's no connection to who we really are in any paper trail."

"But people have seen us together. Virgil, others."

"Our paper trail is ambiguous. Our bureaucratic associates think we're your godparents."

Tino held her closer. "That still makes her a target."

Her father nodded. "And that's why I have a tracker on her. Up until this latest escapade where she slipped out without our knowledge, we've pulled strings to keep her in the United States. When Pedro told us of her whereabouts, I wasn't worried knowing he'd keep an eye on you. But when he discovered this dig was for a reason other than extracting artifacts, he contacted me." Daddy peered at Tino. "We've been monitoring Virgil since his disappearance last year. Which, now appears to be his discovery of this ceremony and his collusion with don Miguel."

Isabella stared at her father. All these secrets and unemotional clandestine meetings had her heart shriveling and her mind calculating.

Frustration and dread fueled her next question. "Are you really my parents? Do we, mom and I, have Hopi ancestors?"

Tino eased away as her father gathered her in his arms. "Yes, Isabella, I'm your father and your mother has wished a million times over she could have been there for you when you struggled so with your intellect and maturity. But we had to think of your safety, not our selfish needs."

She shoved out of her father's arms. "What about my needs? Do you know how many times I had to listen to people talk about their parents and families and I didn't have a clue what that was like? To wish I had a mother I could talk to, a father to be proud of me?" She shot out of his embrace and paced the room. Tino slid off the altar and stood in her path. His eyes said much more than his words ever could. He understood her emptiness. He'd had a family and lost it. He also understood her need to want one.

Her father put his hand to his ear and nodded. "They have the items from Miguel's hut in Virgil's tent." He motioned for them to leave the chamber.

Tino stepped forward taking her hand. "We will be there in a moment."

At first she didn't think her father was going to allow them to stay behind, but he nodded his head and exited.

She folded into Tino's arms and savored the kiss he placed on her lips.

"You know we can sneak out the tunnel and spend some time just the two of us."

His words hummed across her skin. The idea tantalizing.

"He'd only hunt us down. Let's take care of the papers, then disappear." She pressed against his body and drew in his strength.

His hands slid down her sides and cupped her butt, drawing her pelvis snug against his desire. Her head tipped back, and he dropped kisses down her neck and across the tops of her breasts.

"*Querida*, I've never been as scared as I was watching those madmen prepare to drive that knife into you. I had the strength of ten men to save you, but you were strong and saved us both." His knee dipped between her legs and he lifted her, rubbing the ache that grew with his touch.

"I wish to be unvirgined, again, right here," she said, laughing at her improper use of language and thoughts.

"Isabella!" Pedro's voice called from the outer chamber.

She sobered and slid off Tino's leg. "Do you think my father bugged me again already?"

"I'll be glad to check you for any bugs." Tino's eyebrows rose in mock sincerity, and she broke into a fit of giggles.

"We better take care of business so we can get rid of my father."

Tino straightened her clothing, and they left the altar chamber hand in hand. She didn't want to leave Tino's side—ever. But he still had demons to conquer, and she had to speculate on all she'd learned today about her family.

Chapter Thirty-One

The Hotel Casa Amelia lived up to Isabella's memories of hospitality and coziness. Of course, sharing a room with Tino and spending the last two nights and most of the days wrapped in one another's arms and making love had a lot to do with her newfound affection for the establishment. That and realizing life was too short not to spend every moment you could with the person you loved.

"I still can't believe Virgil actually planned to kill me because he believed I would discover he was a fraud in the archeological world."

"He also wanted don Miguel to continue funding his digs and the prestige of writing a paper on the sacrifice for the moon god," Tino added, sliding a hand down her side.

She shuddered and burrowed deeper into Tino's embrace. "The scary part is he hadn't uncovered the truth behind the tragic sacrifice."

"The whole dig was doomed with Miguel's involvement and Walsh stealing artifacts and using you to bring in passports for the narcos." Tino kissed her head. "The only good to come of the whole mess is you."

"Do you still plan to visit me in the States? We can look for your relatives." She'd never felt as content as she did at this moment reclining against Tino's chest, his arms wrapped around her naked body.

Tino frowned. "There is no one to look for in the States."

Isabella pushed up and peered into his sad eyes. "You know the truth about my family. Tell me about your real family."

He drew in a long breath, kissed her forehead, and began, "*Mi papá* did not care for the way *El Presidente Carlos Andrés Pérez* ran the country and treated the people. *Papá* was a professor at the university and helped to organize riots. Because of his strong voice against our president, we had to leave the country and the rest of our family behind. My parents, my younger brother, and I arrived in the United States with only the clothes on our backs. My father worked as a janitor until he could become certified to teach again. Our extended family remains in Venezuela. I cannot go back, and I have no family left in the United States."

Isabella hugged his neck. "What happened?"

"My family would meet family members in Brazil since we are not welcome in our own country. My uncle would meet my father once a year and give him his share of the family's sugar plantation income. One year, I did not travel with them." He squeezed his eyes shut.

Isabella kissed his tense jaw and waited.

"On their last return flight, they were shot down over a drug dealer's air strip in southern Guatemala. Paolo Garza."

Isabella's heart ached for Tino. Her life, while lonely, was a romp compared to all the loss in his life. "Is that why you work for the DEA? To avenge your family?"

He nodded. His blue eyes darkened. "I learned Garza had ordered all planes traveling over his air strips shot down. There are others besides my family who have been hurt by this man. I have vowed to either place Paolo Garza behind bars or see him dead." His tight jaw and clenched hands proved his determination on this would not be swayed.

Peering into his eyes, she realized they couldn't have a future until he'd exorcised his demons.

"I understand." She wrapped her arms around his neck and kissed his cheek. "So you have proper credentials to enter the U.S. to see me?" She raised an eyebrow and pushed her bare breasts against his hard chest, now savoring even more every contact she had with him. His mission in life could take him from her at any moment, and she planned to take advantage of all their time together.

"*Querida*, you could not keep me away." He tipped her face to gaze into his eyes.

"You won't have to worry about meeting my father." She tried to edge her words with humor but it still hurt, knowing her past had been out of her control. Her father was in the WIA as well as her mother. That much he'd told her. She'd guessed the medical missions he went on were only covers for other assignments.

"I do not agree with how your parents handled your childhood, but you have to accept it and move on." Tino smoothed a finger across the wrinkle on her forehead.

"I'm not sure how to deal with them now. Or if I even want to." Her father had told her to contact them just as before. Nothing had changed, not even with her being an adult and knowing the truth. That hurt more than anything. She was now privy to their deepest secret yet they still weren't letting her into their lives.

Tino spread his hands over her abdomen. "You are certain you did not become pregnant from our lovemaking on the altar?"

She smiled to dispel the worry in his blue eyes. Once all the tension and worry for her safety was concluded, he'd taken on the worry of her being pregnant. "I told you, it would take great effort to get me pregnant. Now if you hadn't been using a condom the last few days…" She kissed his cheek. "Don't worry, if it did happen you would be the first and only person I told."

"If that day came, I would marry you."

His eyes didn't lie and, knowing his honor, she knew that was the truth. But she wouldn't marry him or start a family with him until he switched occupations. She'd never wish her childhood on her own children.

"Since I'm heading back to the university tomorrow, let's enjoy our time together." She rolled on top of Tino, slipping her arms around his neck. She didn't want to think about the months that would separate them or the fact that until he caught Garza, he'd never be completely hers.

Tino returned Isabella's ardor. He didn't like her changing the subject when he mentioned marriage. The new information about her family only muddied her previous evaluation of her life. He understood her need to collect her thoughts and emotions. But he wouldn't take no for an answer when he was ready to ask her to marry him.

He ran his hands down her body, drawing her closer, and inserting himself deep. She moaned and moved in a sensual rhythm that brushed her nipples across his skin, seated her deeper, and ignited the flames of passion only this woman had ever touched.

Her sweet breath mixed with his, her legs wound around his, and he climaxed at the same moment her body quivered in his arms. They were meant to be together.

Insistent beeping pierced his hazy thoughts. *My cell phone.*

Tino kissed Isabella soundly, rolled her to the mattress and reached for his phone on the table by the bed. He glanced at the caller ID. His heart had started to slow from the lovemaking, now it accelerated.

He flipped his phone open. "*¿Sí?*"

"Garza is on the move."

"I'll be there in the morning." He snapped the phone shut and stood. "*Querida*, I have to leave. Garza is moving." He quickly dressed and shoved his belongings into his pack.

"You'll be careful?"

Her softly spoken words jolted him more than an electrical shock. He sat on the edge of the bed, pushed her beautiful, long, brown hair out of her face. He held her delicate face full of intelligence in his hands. "I will be very careful. More now than before. I no longer have only blind revenge in my heart. I also hold love for you." He kissed her eyelids, nose, and full lips.

Drawing back, he waited for her lashes to flutter up and he could see into her eyes. "Once I put Garza in jail, I will no longer chase drug traffickers and we can be together. I promise."

A tear sparkled in the corner of her eye. "I'm counting on you to keep that promise."

He pulled her into his arms. "It is a promise I intend to keep." He kissed her, pouring his reverence and love into the union. He didn't want to leave her loving arms, but he had another promise to fulfill. The one he had made to himself—avenging his family.

Tino slipped out of Isabella's arms and quietly exited the room. She drew in a deep breath, stilled her quivering heart, and reached for her phone. Her finger shook dialing the number she memorized at the age of six.

"Hello?"

"Daddy, I'm coming to visit. I want to become an agent."

~*~*~

About the book & Author

Thank you for reading *Secrets of a Mayan Moon*. It was a wonderful brain stretch for me to write a character with a high IQ and one who was a cross between Indiana Jones and MacGyver. If you enjoy this book, please leave a review. It is the best way to repay an author. To continue on adventures with Isabella and Tino, look for book 2, *Secrets of an Aztec Temple* and book 3, *Secrets of Hopi Blue Star*.

I also have several mystery series. You can find out about them at my website: https://www.patyjager.net

Paty Jager is an award-winning author of 48 novels, 8 novellas, and numerous anthologies of murder mystery and western romance. All her work has Western or Native American elements in them along with hints of humor and engaging characters. Paty and her husband raise alfalfa hay in rural eastern Oregon. Riding horses and battling rattlesnakes, she not only writes the western lifestyle, she lives it.

You can catch up with her at:

Website: http://www.patyjager.net
Blog: https://writingintothesunset.net/
FB Page: https://www.facebook.com/PatyJagerAuthor/
Amazon: https://www.amazon.com/Paty-Jager/e/B002I7M0VK
Pinterest: https://www.pinterest.com/patyjag/
Twitter: https://twitter.com/patyjag
Goodreads:
http://www.goodreads.com/author/show/1005334.Paty_Jager
Newsletter: Mystery: https://bit.ly/2IhmWcm
Newsletter: Western: https://bit.ly/2JVGe4j
Bookbub: https://www.bookbub.com/authors/paty-jager

Windtree
Press

Thank you for purchasing this Windtree Press publication. For
other books of the heart, please visit our website
at www.windtreepress.com.

For questions or more information contact us
at info@windtreepress.com.

Windtree Press
www.windtreepress.com

Hillsboro, OR

Lightning Source UK Ltd.
Milton Keynes UK
UKHW020651081120
373029UK00009B/91